Unusual Produce

Two picnic tables stood on their sides at the end of the road, blocking my view. I took one of the worn ruts and suddenly the scene behind the tables became clear; unrealistically and frighteningly clear. Two police cars and an official-looking van, complete with a logo that read Crime Scene Unit, flanked a gathering of market vendors and something on the ground that looked like a large dead body. But it couldn't be a body—this was a farmers' market. Dead bodies didn't just show up at farmers' markets, did they?

Farm Fresh Murder

PAIGE SHELTON

BERKLEY PRIME CRIME, NEW YORK

THE BERKLEY PUBLISHING GROUP
Published by the Penguin Group
Penguin Group (USA) Inc.
375 Hudson Street, New York, New York 10014, USA
Penguin Group (Canada), 90 Eglinton Avenue East, Suite 700, Toronto, Ontario M4P 2Y3, Canada
(a division of Pearson Penguin Canada Inc.)
Penguin Books Ltd., 80 Strand, London WC2R 0RL, England
Penguin Group Ireland, 25 St. Stephen's Green, Dublin 2, Ireland (a division of Penguin Books Ltd.)
Penguin Group (Australia), 250 Camberwell Road, Camberwell, Victoria 3124, Australia
(a division of Pearson Australia Group Pty. Ltd.)
Penguin Books India Pvt. Ltd., 11 Community Centre, Panchsheel Park, New Delhi—110 017, India
Penguin Group (NZ), 67 Apollo Drive, Rosedale, North Shore 0632, New Zealand
(a division of Pearson New Zealand Ltd.)
Penguin Books (South Africa) (Pty.) Ltd., 24 Sturdee Avenue, Rosebank, Johannesburg 2196, South Africa

Penguin Books Ltd., Registered Offices: 80 Strand, London WC2R 0RL, England

FARM FRESH MURDER

A Berkley Prime Crime Book / published by arrangement with the author

PRINTING HISTORY
Berkley Prime Crime mass-market edition / April 2010

Cover illustration by Dan Craig.
Interior text design by Kristin del Rosario.

For information, address: The Berkley Publishing Group,
a division of Penguin Group (USA) Inc.,
375 Hudson Street, New York, New York 10014.

ISBN: 978-0-425-23387-0

BERKLEY® PRIME CRIME
Berkley Prime Crime Books are published by The Berkley Publishing Group,
a division of Penguin Group (USA) Inc.,
375 Hudson Street, New York, New York 10014.

PRINTED IN THE UNITED STATES OF AMERICA

10 9 8 7 6 5 4 3 2 1

For my agent, Jessica Faust.
Thank you for everything.

Acknowledgments

Thanks to:

Berkley editor extraordinaire Michelle Vega and all the staff at The Berkley Publishing Group who made this come together. You make dreams come true.

All the market managers and vendors who took the time to patiently answer my questions. Any mistakes I've made are mine only.

Patricia Snyder and Amy Snyder Hackbart for their Mmmm-Amazing Lemon Meringue Pie recipe. Delicious!

Kelly Hindley, the first person ever to buy something I wrote. I've been hoping for an opportunity such as this to thank you.

Marilyn, Julie, and Lloyd Peterson; Stacy, Dan, Jonathan, Michael, and Connor Bredbeck; Pat, Eric, and Megan Baschnagel; and the best buddy ever, Heidi Baschnagel. The weekend full of farmers' market shopping, recipes, good food, memories, and friendship is something I will cherish forever.

My numerous Blanchard and Ferrell in-laws, particularly my mother-in-law, Barbara Ferrell. Your encouragement has meant so much.

My cousin, Lisa Light, who is more like a sister than a cousin; my parents, Chuck and Beverly Shelton; my husband, Charlie Ferrell; and the most "epic-ly awesome" person I know, my son, Tyler Ferrell. I love you all so much and can't thank you enough for your support, guidance, words of wisdom, and ability to make me laugh until I can't breathe.

And to everyone who grows or creates farmers' market products. Your hard work and creativity are inspiring.

One

"What?" I yelled into my cell phone.

Again, Allison murmured something on the other end.

"Hang on a second, Sis, I can't hear a word." I stuck the phone (still flipped open) into my overalls pocket, pulled off my face mask and a jam-splattered plastic glove, and turned down my version of morning coffee—today it was Springsteen. The jars I'd been boiling were nicely sterilized by now, so with a turn of a dial, I flipped off one burner. The blackberry jam would be okay to boil a minute or two without supervision. I left that burner on High and made my way out of the barn/kitchen—talking without my face mask around my preserves didn't fall in line with my idea of sterile.

I stepped surely over the polished wood-planked floor of the barn, pushed open the large door, and was greeted by both my short-legged retriever, Hobbit, and bright daylight. The sun was up? What time was it? Was I late again?

I didn't have a watch, but the time was shown in large block numbers on my phone. It was just after seven in the morning, almost a full hour later than I had planned on leaving.

"Damn," I muttered to myself as I petted my happy-to-see-me-emerge-from-the-barn dog. "Hey, Allison," I said into the phone. "Are you wondering where I am?" The destination that I was late for was Bailey's Farmers' Market, the best market, in my opinion, in South Carolina and the place that Allison managed with near perfection.

"Oh—I'm so glad you're there! Thank God!" Her voice was unusually shaky.

"Allison?"

"Becca, you have to get here. Quickly."

"Why, what's up?"

"Just get here. Now," she emphasized before disconnecting the call.

Concern tightened my chest. Allison was the queen of the cool cucumbers. She rarely allowed her voice to waver with uncertainty, let alone the fear I thought I'd heard.

I tried to call her back, but she didn't answer. I tried again; she still didn't answer. Suddenly, a thousand different pictures of horror formed in my mind. Was she hurt? How badly? Was someone else hurt? Her three-year-old son, Mathis?

With a small tug of regret about the loss of the blackberry jam I'd been boiling, I made sure all of the stove's burners were turned off. Then, with Hobbit at my heels, I ran across the side yard of my small farm and through the open back door of my house. Everything would have to wait until I found out what was wrong with Allison. My strawberry plants needed their September dousing, and my pumpkins needed attention and water of their own, but those would have to be this evening's tasks.

I grabbed my backpack and truck keys off the messy dining room table and ran out the front door.

"Hey, girl, watch the place for me. I gotta run. I'll be home as soon as I can," I said to Hobbit. To acknowledge that she understood every word, she tapped one of her overly long paws on my thigh and then went to her mat on the shaded front porch. I'd fed and watered her first thing, so she'd be all right. "Good girl."

I locked nothing, checked nothing else, but jumped in my twenty-year-old bright orange truck that fortunately started with the first turn of the key, and took off up the dirt driveway and onto the old state highway.

Bailey's was only about fifteen minutes away from my farm when I wasn't in a hurry. Today, I pushed the truck to its top speed of sixty-three miles per hour and was silently grateful that my neighbor, Ted Masters, wasn't tooling down the road in one of his John Deeres.

According to the time feature on my phone, I pulled into the middle road of Bailey's eight minutes after I'd spoken to Allison. The metallic roof-covered market was set up in a U shape, and the vendors drove down this inside road to deliver their products. It snaked off here and jutted off there, the worn paths from truck and van tires marking the ways to the backs of the stalls set up with tables, product displays, and temporary walls usually made of canvas tarps. Allison's office was in a small brick building that sat next to the entrance to the market in the middle of the south arm of the U. As I passed the back of the office, I looked for some sign of Allison but didn't see her.

Right now, two picnic tables/walls stood on their sides at the curve of the U, blocking my view. I took one of the worn ruts, and suddenly the scene behind the tables became clear; unrealistically and frighteningly clear. Two police cars and an official-looking van, complete with a logo that read Crime Scene Unit, flanked a gathering of market vendors and something on the ground that looked like a large dead body. But it couldn't have been a body—this was a farmers' market. Dead bodies didn't just show up at farmers' markets, did they?

I stopped about fifty feet from the group and threw the gearshift handle into Park as I looked for Allison and tried to process the unlikely scene. The old-timer vendors, the ones who'd been selling at markets for years, the ones who were always ready to sell at 6:00 A.M., were standing together, shock and fear blanching their faces.

"Holy crap," I said, wanting to run to them and see what was going on at the same time my legs froze in place.

I couldn't figure out who was missing from the standing group. I couldn't see clearly who was on the ground, and I couldn't handle the process of elimination in my mind. I focused—okay, my close friend Linda was there, I could see her berry-stained fingers from where I sat; Barry, who sold the most amazing corn, chewed at his bottom lip; Brenton, the master of homemade dog biscuits, kept lifting and then replacing his well-worn Yankees cap.

I was still taking roll in my mind when one of the officers began to shoo the crowd backward as he pulled out a roll of yellow tape that would soon mark the perimeter of the crime scene.

"Allison," I said to myself, as she came into view. She was just as frightened as the rest of them, but doing her best to keep in control.

Though she and I were fraternal twins, she got the tall, dark, and mysterious looks of our father, and I got the small, blond, and pale looks of our mother. But at the moment, I would have said her skin tone was as green as an avocado's innards. She was on her phone, attempting to keep her eyes away from the body.

Though I had absolutely no desire to see death, Allison needed me, so I forced myself to step out of my surreal-view-of-a-tragedy-from-a-distance moment and unfroze my legs. As I walked forward, one of the police officers glanced in my direction, a stonelike, suspicious look on her face. I involuntarily quirked a nervous smile at her. She looked away.

"Becca," Allison said as she closed her phone and met me on the edge of the gathering. "Thank God you're here. When you were late and this"—she waved toward the crowd—"happened, I got worried about you. Oh, Becca!" She sounded as though she were speaking the words accidentally, almost as though the sound was following her mouth's movement, like one of those old foreign films with English dubbed in.

"Sorry, Sis, sorry." I touched her arm to reassure her that I was indeed there and that I was fine. "What happened?"

She took a deep breath and made herself stand taller. She put her hand over mine. "Okay, it's been a rough morning. There's been a terrible accident—or something. Matt Simonsen was killed, Becca."

"Matt who?" I asked.

"Simonsen."

I didn't know anyone named Matt Simonsen, and I felt terrible about both the fact that someone had been killed and that I didn't know who that someone was. I thought I was good at getting to know the other vendors. These people had been my life for some time, and I was friends with many of them, but the name Matt Simonsen didn't ring any bells.

"He just started working here last week," Allison continued. "He grows"—she cleared her throat—"*grew* and sold peaches and peach products."

"This is just terrible," I muttered as I gathered enough courage to really look at the body. He was on his back, next to an old van. He was a large man, only slightly heavy but very tall. I tried not to swoon as I looked at his bloody and violently disfigured head. The entire body was in a pool of its own blood, and Mr. Simonsen's jeans and T-shirt were soaking it up from the ground. Oddly, a bouquet of flowers had been placed on his chest. The flowers' beauty seemed pristine and out of place on the still body. "What happened?"

"As far as I've been able to figure out, none of us heard a thing. The police questioned me quickly, but didn't tell me anything except that they might want to talk to me again. I've tried to listen to what's going on. Everyone who's here got here early and unloaded without any problem. But when Abner arrived this morning, he found the body."

"Abner?"

"Yes, he and Matt were the only ones who would have unloaded from this area. Because Matt's van was hiding his body, the rest of us might have gone the whole day and not found him."

I looked up and through the crowd, finally spotting Abner as he spoke to a police officer. Abner was almost five feet of old, bald, and cranky. He'd been working at farmers' markets and roadside stands longer than any of us. He grew amazing wildflowers at some place that he kept deeply undercover. With quick hands and honed skill, he could create special and unique bouquets before customers had even pulled out their money.

From where I stood, Abner looked a mess. He was talking to the officer, but his eyes were glazed and unfocused. He kept putting his hands in his overalls' pockets and taking them back out to wipe a red handkerchief over his bald head.

"Oh, Allison," I said as something occurred to me. "The flowers on Mr. Simonsen, are those Abner's?"

She nodded. "I think so. I heard Abner say as much, but he also said he didn't put them there."

"Oh, ick! No wonder he looks so freaked-out."

"I think we all look a bit freaked-out, but there's more to it."

"What?"

"Apparently, two days ago Abner and Mr. Simonsen had a very vocal argument. I didn't know anything about it until today, when Betsy told me that she heard part of it—though she wouldn't give me any details. Apparently there were other witnesses, too, and . . ."

"And?"

"Well, Abner said—according to Betsy—that he was going to kill Mr. Simonsen if he didn't leave Bailey's."

"Oh no . . . do you think . . . ?"

"I don't know what to think."

I looked at Abner again. There was no way he could have killed anyone; he was difficult to get along with, but he wasn't homicidal. Actually, I'd never seen him get truly angry, but I had seen him be very ornery. And he'd been a friend to me when I'd needed a friend, when I'd needed guidance from someone who knew what the heck he was doing. He'd taken me under his wing; told me some of the finer points of good product display and excellent customer service. I'd worked at farmers' markets for almost seven years, but it was Abner's help and friendship that taught me that having a successful business went far beyond living on a farm or having the ability to speak to the soil and coax it to bring forth products that customers sought out. He'd been the one to tell me that it would be my passion for my products that would make me successful.

And now he was talking to a police officer about a bouquet of his lovely flowers that he himself had found on a dead man; a man he'd apparently threatened.

"Allison, what can we do?"

"I don't know, Becca. I have absolutely no idea."

Two

The police and crime scene people were very slow about their business. They shut the whole market down for about three hours so they could gather evidence. During this time I helped Allison with phone calls to vendors who hadn't yet shown up. We told them not to come in and that the police would be contacting them—no one was thrilled about this, but they understood. We explained the situation so many times that the dead body became surreal to me; a story, but not an actual event.

Then those of us who were already there helped the police put up their own tent to use for more interviews. After the crime scene people took a bunch of pictures and removed Mr. Simonsen's body, the police posted an interview schedule and allowed the market to open again.

Abner wasn't arrested, so I tried, in vain, to corner him and see how he was holding up, but there was too much chaos for anything more than fleeting glances at each other.

I hoped my eyes told him that I was there if he needed me, and his glances told me that I shouldn't worry and he was fine. I didn't believe his eyes in the least.

Somehow, I was first on the list of interviews.

The first thing I noticed when I entered the tent was that it was hot and stuffy. I figured this was on purpose, to "sweat" out the murderer. The officer who asked the questions had somehow mastered looking cool and collected in stifling air and while wearing a long-sleeved, well-pressed uniform.

Officer Brion was able to ask his questions without showing one drop of perspiration or allowing one hair to fall out of its slicked-back style.

The interview went something like this:

"Ms. Robins, where were you this morning between 5:00 A.M. and 6:00 A.M.?"

"At my farm, about fifteen minutes that way." I pointed and then wiped my hand over the drip of sweat falling from my right temple.

"Was anyone there with you?"

"Just my dog, Hobbit."

"Can you prove you were there?"

"No, I don't think I can."

"Is that blood on your overalls and arm?"

"Oh. No, that's blackberry jam—that's what I make and sell—jams and preserves." I wiped my left temple and noticed that his temples were still dry.

"Did you know Mr. Matt Simonsen?"

"No, I didn't."

"Are you sure? You worked at the same place."

"Working at a farmers' market isn't necessarily like working at the same place. Most of us work alone, and sometimes we can go weeks without having the time to socialize. My sister, Allison Reynolds, told me he just started here last week. I hadn't met him yet."

"Do you know Abner Justen?"

"Very well."

"Did he speak to you about Mr. Simonsen?"

"No."

"Ms. Robins"—the officer leaned forward, and I tried not to look scared—"do you know where Mr. Justen lives?"

"Um, well, actually, I don't."

"Do you know where some of the other vendors live?"

"Yes, some, but . . ."

"But what?"

The next words that were going to come out of my mouth were about Abner's secretive ways regarding where he lived. Even with me, his good friend, he had always been paranoid about revealing the location. But I didn't think anyone knew where he lived. I decided not to give more to the police officer than he asked.

"Nothing," I said.

Officer Brion gave me a look that stopped just short of a sneer.

After I was given his card with instructions to call him if anything else occurred to me, I was dismissed. I failed miserably at walking out of the tent with anything resembling an innocent gait.

I wanted either to talk to Abner or to go home, but I was thrown into work instead. The other vendors who were interviewed needed some fill-in help, and Allison volunteered me.

I started with Linda's fruits and pies. As Linda walked away from her stall, she told me to eat whatever I wanted. She wore clothes that reminded me of Laura Ingalls Wilder, which seemed to make her products taste even better. Like me, she was in her mid-thirties and worked her farm by herself. Unlike me, she hadn't gone through two husbands to get to that point, but we were as close to good friends as two single, working women whose idea of a good party was an extra-early dinner, an early movie, and an early bedtime could be.

Since the murder and the questioning had done nothing to diminish my appetite for Linda's raspberries and her razzleberry pie, I did indeed indulge in the sweet treats in between helping curious and concerned customers. In addition to baking her goodies, Linda also grew most of her own berries, some of which I purchased for my jams and preserves. She had the same talent for growing raspberries and blackberries as I had for growing strawberries. Every once in a while we traded berries—I made a killer razzleberry jam, and her strawberry pie brought some of her most loyal customers.

"Miss—I heard there'd been a murder here this morning. That can't be true. Is that true?" one elderly lady said.

"There's nothing to worry about." That wasn't true, but I didn't know what else to say. "What can I get for you? Some berries or some pie?"

As the day wore on, the curiosity became more demanding, and once the news made it to the media outlets, the normally medium-sized Tuesday crowd began to dwindle to a sparse few who were either still very curious or hadn't turned on their radios or televisions that day.

As I worked the Barry Good Corn stall, Allison found me and took a moment to gather her wits. She sat hidden behind an enormous table piled with end-of-the-season ears of corn.

"How're you doing?" I asked.

"I can't seem to process everything yet, but I think I'm exhausted."

"Do the police suspect anyone—other than Abner?"

"No, I don't think so. He refused to tell them his address. I went to look it up on his application form—which is over ten years old, by the way—but the address he gave is his sister's house in town. That's the same one that's on his driver's license."

"The police should know how to figure out where he lives."

"I'm sure they will. Why is he so weird about it?"

"His flowers are amazing, right?"

"The most amazing."

"He's afraid someone will figure out how he does it. He grows some flowers that shouldn't even be able to take hold in South Carolina. He grows other flowers out of season. His favorite flower is this very thorny one—he prides himself that he can grow it and that he can place it in a bouquet so that the thorns never even graze a customer's fingers. He's very good at what he does and he's very protective of how he does it."

"He is. He adores you like a daughter. You know that, don't you?"

"Yeah, he's a good friend."

"Well, if he's a murderer, I don't want to put you in the line of fire, but would you check on him before you leave—that is, if they don't arrest him? I'm worried. Abner's not super old, but he's old enough that I'm concerned about the stress this is causing him."

"He's also very feisty, and I'd be happy to check on him. I was planning on doing it earlier, but I haven't had the chance."

On cue, the young parents of a very upset baby started

working through the corn table and asking me questions. I knew just enough about corn to peel some of the husk back to demonstrate its fresh ripeness. I was very proud of myself when I sold them twenty ears. By the time I finished the sale, Allison had left and Barry Drake had come back to his stall.

Barry was another of the old-timers who had been in the market business for a long time. He and I had never been the best of friends but we'd gotten along all right. I was always amazed at how agile he was. He was a very large man who never seemed to quite get his walk up to speed. But he knew his corn.

"Well, darlin', thank you for covering for me," he said, his breathing labored from the walk.

"You're welcome. How'd the interview go?"

He said something like, "Ah, ptewy."

"That much fun?"

"Well, if you're askin' do they think I killed that Simonsen man, I don't think so. I was here, but plenty of people saw me and I never had any blood on me. Don't know if Abner could have reached high enough to hit that tall man over the head, so I couldn't give them much information about that, either." He huffed a laugh.

"Did you know Matt Simonsen?"

"Yes, and I'll tell you—only you—this," he said as he looked around for spies. "Didn't like the man one bit. I can understand why he got under Abner's skin."

"You knew him less than a couple weeks and you knew you didn't like him?"

"Naw, I met him a while ago. Can't remember the exactlys, but it wasn't at this market—didn't tell the police that, of course."

"Of course," I said, in a tone not pleasing to Barry.

"Anyhoo, he was more of a curmudgeon than Abner and lit'l ol' me combined." Barry laughed.

I smiled. "Hey, Barry, do you know what Abner argued with Simonsen about?"

"Nope. I didn't hear the battle, but some people did. Some people are saying that Abner really threatened to kill him, for what reason I don't know. And Abner taking on Simonsen? The size difference in itself makes it pretty unlikely."

"Hmm." Barry was right; Abner was significantly smaller.

"Yeah, hmm. Go ask Abner about it yourself."

"You don't need me here anymore?" I said as I looked at the emptiness all around. The hum and drone of voices and activity were much quieter than normal, giving the air a creepy leftover feeling.

"I appreciate your help, Becca, but off with you. I can handle it from here."

I was anxious to get to Abner's stall. I really wanted to talk to him, but my short conversation with Barry made me think that others might know something about what happened, too. I hurried along, wondering just how much *I* didn't know. I wished I could sit in on the police interviews. But since Officer Brion probably wouldn't allow such an intrusion, I'd have to ask a few questions of my own.

Farmers' market vendors are their own bosses, usually working alone or maybe with one other person. They're an independent, hardy crowd, most of them working the land. Some, like me, create other products from our crops, and still others are of a more artistic bent, creating products that have nothing to do with fruits and vegetables. I was continually fascinated by how hard most of the vendors worked. And though you could pick the hours you wanted to have your stall open, most of us were at the market from very early in the morning until we either ran out of product for the day or had to attend to it back at our homes or farms.

Jeanine Baker was one of the smallest and strongest women I'd ever known. I'm only about five-foot-three, but I tower over Jeanine. And until I'd tried some of her farm-produced eggs, I didn't realize there were eggs that actually tasted better and fresher than the grocery store variety.

"Hey, Jeanine," I said to her bent head.

She looked up quickly, and I thought I heard her gasp.

"Oh, sorry," I continued. "I didn't mean to scare you."

"No, you didn't." Jeanine was somewhere between the ages of fifty and ninety; no one knew for sure. Her short, dark hair always looked like it needed to be brushed, and her wrinkled face had probably never seen one ounce of makeup. She didn't make a habit of being friendly, but she wasn't rude. I'd always suspected that she was old enough to have gotten over the need to have everyone like her all the time. "I just have the heebie-jeebies, you know?"

"Yeah, I know. Rough day."

"Poor man."

"Mr. Simonsen?"

"Yes, who did you think I meant?"

"Sorry, yes, you're right." I'd actually wondered if she'd meant Abner. I thought my friendship with him might be prejudicing me, and I realized I probably needed to get a grip.

Jeanine sighed. "You don't suppose . . ."

"What?"

"Well, I guess we'll all have to be extra careful now. Do you think some of those big corporations are banding together to get rid of all the farmers' markets?"

"Oh, no, Jeanine, we're fine." My mind hadn't even gone where Jeanine's had. I hadn't felt one ounce of concern over there potentially being a mass murderer on the loose, ridding the world of farmers' markets, one vendor at a time. Maybe she had a point, but I didn't think so.

"I hope you're right." Jeanine rubbed at her knuckles.

I got lucky because one of the few customers who had stuck around was in dire need of some eggs, so I was able to slip away without seeming rude.

The tragedy that had hit us today was beyond what anyone could have ever predicted, and of course at the center of the tragedy was Mr. Simonsen.

Until we knew what happened to him, all of our businesses could suffer. Allison's job as the market's manager could be in jeopardy, too. I didn't like thinking about myself at such a moment, but I couldn't help it. I really wanted to know what had happened to poor Mr. Simonsen. I wanted to make sure that whatever it was, it wasn't going to happen to any of the rest of us, Allison included.

I needed to talk to Abner. Right away. I continued toward his stall without stopping to talk to anyone else. I smiled and waved at Stella, whose bakery items normally got my full attention. She waved back, her lovely smile only making her very round figure more appropriate. Jack the Wine Man, who not only grew his own grapes, but probably crushed them with his own feet, was busy loading his truck, giving up on any real business for the day. I sniffed deeply as I passed Herb's Herbs. Herb (really) and his business and life partner, Don, grew perfect herbs, their oregano being some of the best ever. The Herb Boys both worked their stall, but today Don was fast asleep in a folding chair with some sort of puzzle book on his lap. He didn't look like he'd tip over anytime soon, so I didn't disturb him.

I was stopped short when I got to Abner's stall and found it empty. There wasn't a flower or leftover leaf in sight. Had he been arrested? Had he just gone home? Fear for him—where he'd gone and why he'd left—tingled in my throat. In keeping with his secretive ways, he claimed to not have a phone of any kind, but if he did, Allison would surely know the number. I pulled out my cell.

"Come on, answer," I muttered. Allison didn't answer, though. And I had no idea where to begin to look for her.

As I closed the phone, one of the new vendors stopped next to me. Distracted, I nodded quickly at him but didn't say anything. His name was Ian Cartwright, and he'd been working at the market for a few weeks, though we hadn't had much opportunity to speak. He was young, in his mid-twenties, and created lawn and garden artwork. When I first heard the description of what he was bringing to the market, I laughed to myself, thinking we'd be seeing miniature gnomes or some such thing. But his artwork was actually made of copper and steel and was quite beautiful. He didn't create anything stationary; every piece spun with the wind, some of the items seemingly changing shape as they moved. His work had already become a popular item. And he'd become a popular item himself. Ian had long, black hair that he pulled back into a ponytail, which highlighted his dark eyes and tanned skin. He was exotic and mysterious. This deadly artistic combination was sure to gain the interest of lots of female customers. Allison had told me that it was already working well for him.

"He went home," Ian said.

"Well, at least he wasn't arrested," I said without thinking.

Ian laughed. "No, not yet."

"How was he?"

"Not good. Pretty shaken up. Actually, he asked me to let you know that he'd left. Sorry, I couldn't find you."

"Oh." Abner had asked Ian to talk to me? That was odd. Why hadn't Abner talked to Allison or found me himself? "That's okay. I wish I hadn't missed him."

"Yeah. I'm going to see him tonight. I'll let him know you stopped by."

"Wait. You know where he lives?"

"Sure. Oh, I don't think I was supposed to admit that, was I?"

How did this kid know where Abner lived and I didn't? I felt an unreasonable stab of jealousy and betrayal. Why was Ian considered a better friend than me? I swallowed.

"Don't suppose I could go with you?" I asked, not concerned about sounding either bold or rude.

Ian thought about it a moment. As he rubbed at his chin, I noticed the peace sign tattoo on the back of his right hand.

"Well, Abner will be mad at me, but I think he needs his friends right now, so sure, why not?"

I looked at Ian and wondered about the sort of wisdom a person in his mid-twenties had. I suspected that everything he'd just said had been on purpose. He was right about Abner needing friends, and he had planned on saying just the right words to get me to ask to go with him.

"Thanks." I tried to even out my voice. I didn't want Ian to know about the childish jealousy, but a quirk at the corner of his mouth, followed by a forced glance away from my eyes, told me I hadn't hidden a thing.

"You're welcome," he said.

We made arrangements for him to pick me up early that evening, and parted ways. I searched for and tried to call Allison again, to no avail. When she had a moment, she'd call me back. The police and crime scene people were gone, and those vendors who'd stuck around no longer needed any extra help. I felt like I could go home.

As I threw my truck into gear, I wished silently that a day like today would never happen again.

And I wished even harder that Abner wouldn't turn out to be the one responsible.

Three

The blackberry jam was a complete loss. There were worse things, of course, but I didn't like to waste anything. I threw away the unusable product and then cleaned up the mess.

I'd inherited the farm, complete with barn, from my aunt Ruth and uncle Stanley right after I'd finished college. The barn had been totally renovated and turned into a kitchen that any professional baker or chef would envy. Along with the shelving and pots and pans made of heavy-duty steel and copper, there was an oversized six-burner stove, a three-basin sink, a large worktable, a refrigerator, and two large freezers that the Abominable Snowman would be proud to keep his ice cream in.

My uncle, who'd had more money than anyone had known, had planned on making his own jams and preserves as a retirement project. When he and my aunt died in a car accident ten years ago, their will had surprised the entire family. Not having any children of their own, they had made their twin nieces the recipients of their lifetimes of hard work and savings. Allison received enough money to pay off her house and have college tuition covered for one or two future children, and I was given the farm.

I'd never shown any interest in farming, but my aunt and uncle had known something about me that I hadn't figured out at the time. Though it was an option to sell the land and have a nice full bank account, I'd chosen to keep it instead and see what would come of it. And from there, my passion grew. I loved my farm, I loved my job.

As I moved some more blackberries from the freezer to the refrigerator to thaw, a bark from outside announced that someone was coming down the driveway.

"Coming, Hobbit. Just a minute." I switched off the lights and left the barn, glad to be out in fresh air that actually had a tinge of coolness to it. Fall was almost here.

Ian's truck was probably about the same age as mine, but his was blue and he had a magnetic sign on the driver's door that read Yardworks.

I didn't know him at all. On the way home I'd become concerned that I probably shouldn't be going anywhere with a stranger who worked at the same place a murder had occurred. But when Allison finally called me back and I told her my plans, she seemed to think Ian was okay. She was just as curious as I was to find out where Abner lived, though, so I wondered if any potential concern was diluted by the upcoming discovery.

Ian waved as he made his way down the driveway. Hobbit stood beside me and growled. She'd stop when I told her he was okay, but I wasn't quite ready to do that yet.

"Hey," he said as he got out of his truck. He looked like he'd showered, and I was suddenly aware that I hadn't.

Frankly, I hadn't even thought about it, but I should have—if not to be polite to Ian, at least for Abner.

"Hey," I said.

"Awesome place," he said as he joined us in the side yard between the barn and the house. He didn't act at all afraid of my short-legged, pretend-ferocious guard dog.

"Thanks."

Hobbit growled.

"Hey, buddy," Ian said as he reached down without hesitation and rubbed her neck with both hands. She quit growling and would have purred if she knew how.

"What's his name?

"Her name is Hobbit."

"Oh, I get that. Look at those long feet. Hey, Hobbit, hey, girl."

So he'd either read Tolkien or seen the movies.

Hobbit was appropriately impressed. She might have left with him if he'd added a bacon treat to the mix.

"Hey, Ian, could you give me about fifteen minutes? I had to finish some work that I started this morning, and I need a quick shower."

"Absolutely. I'll be just fine with the dog."

Common courtesy made me want to tell him to make himself at home, but I didn't really want a stranger in my house. I said, "I'll be out quickly."

"Sure. Thanks."

Neither Ian nor Hobbit seemed to care much that I left them. I hurried through the shower, put on my nicest slacks (jeans) and another T-shirt, and found Ian and my dog in the back. Ian was looking over the pumpkin patch and rows of trimmed-back strawberry plants as Hobbit sat beside him.

"First Abner, now my dog," I muttered as I walked out the back door and onto the patio.

"What was that?" Ian asked.

"Oh, nothing." I joined them.

"I knew about the berry preserves and jams, but I hadn't heard about the pumpkins."

"Yeah, my main products are the berry things—no fruit that needs peeling. I buy some fruit from other vendors for the preserves. Strawberries are my spring crop, and my winter specialty is pumpkin preserves—really good stuff, by the way, but much more labor-intensive to make. I love growing pumpkins and I tend to overdo it, so I give a few away. I wish I could move quickly enough to use them all—have I mentioned how good pumpkin preserves are? But the pumpkins are only good for so long."

"Well, if you need help, let me know." Ian cleared his throat. Just as much as I didn't know him, he didn't know me. His offer was sincere, but a bit premature in our potential friendship. He felt the weird vibe, too.

"Those strawberry plants look great, but . . ." he continued.

"What?"

"I hate to give advice"—I was sure he meant that he hated to give advice to people older than him—"because we all raise our stuff our own way, but they need a good dousing of water. The buds for next year's fruit are beginning to form."

"Yeah, I know. I was going to do that today, too. It was a very strange day, and nothing happened quite like I'd planned."

"I get what you mean."

"I take Wednesdays off, so I'll water them tomorrow morning."

"That should work." There was something more he wanted to say.

"What?" I prodded.

"You don't have an automatic irrigation system?"

I laughed. "Nope. I do everything by hand. I'm a very organic gardener—including, I suppose, in the ways of irrigation."

"Well, you make a great jam," Ian said.

"Thank you." I didn't know he'd tried any of my product, but I didn't point that out. "So, you have some land?"

"Nope. Someday. Right now I live above a garage in Monson—I use the garage as my studio—but I grew up on a farm, and someday I'll own and work one. It's what I was meant to do."

Allison had confirmed that Ian was in his mid-twenties, but he seemed older and wiser. His confident knowledge of what he was "meant to do" was something that I didn't think I'd ever passionately felt. I loved what I did, but I wasn't sure it was a calling so much as an insightful gift from my aunt and uncle.

"I imagine you will."

"Should we get to Abner's?" he asked, seeming to purposefully ignore my curious tone.

"Well, only if Hobbit can bear to let you go." My dog, lovey-eyed and smitten, clearly thought she'd found a new best friend.

"She can come with us."

"Um, well . . ."

"I'd love to have her along. Don't get to have any animals in my garage. I'm getting my dog fix."

"Okay, then. She loves to go for rides. Let's go."

Our party of three left my farm—this time with the

house doors locked—and headed in the other direction on the state highway, away from Monson and Bailey's.

"So, Ian," I said as I leaned slightly forward and around my dog, "you and Abner are pretty good friends?"

"Sort of. He helped me set up my stall."

"Do you know him outside of Bailey's?"

"No."

"But you and he must have really hit it off."

"Well, I wasn't so sure. He gave me some good pointers, but I didn't think he liked me all that much. He's a nice man, but very cranky."

"True. So, how do you know where he lives?" I got to the matter at hand.

"Oh, that—yes, he vowed me to secrecy. He bought one of my sculptures. I had to go out to his place to set it up. He wanted to set it up himself, but he knew it would be too much for him. I'm surprised he didn't have me sign something vowing to keep the place a secret. He did make it clear that I wasn't to tell anyone, though."

"But you're okay showing me."

Ian smiled. "Well, it's no secret that he's very fond of you—like a daughter. He needs a friend right now."

"You don't think he killed Matt Simonsen?"

"I don't know him all that well, but no, I don't think that Abner could kill anyone. He could probably irritate them to self-mutilation, but he wouldn't hurt the proverbial fly."

"No, I don't think so, either."

"He'll be mad at me for bringing you along, but he'll get over it."

"We'll see," I said quietly. I wanted to see Abner, make sure he was able to deal with whatever he was dealing with, but I didn't want him to hold it against me that I'd seen his home. I understood the need to keep things close to the vest, to keep secrets. Not everybody needed to know every little thing. My curiosity was, however, much stronger than my desire to humor his elusiveness.

"So, where're you from?" I said, changing the subject and filling the space with small talk.

"I'm from Iowa."

"No kidding?" His answer truly caught me off guard.

He laughed. "That's a pretty typical reaction. Even some guys from Iowa grow their hair long and get a tattoo or two."

"Oh, I didn't mean . . . two?"

"Uh-huh. Maybe I'll show them all to you sometime," he said with such an over-the-board flirtatious tone that I laughed, too.

"How did you get to South Carolina?"

"After college, I wasn't quite ready to go back to Iowa, so I literally threw a dart at a map I hung on the wall. I was hoping for a year in New York City, but my aim was off. I knew that eventually I'd want to have some land—some sort of farm—so I figured I was meant to get that going sooner than I thought. I came out here about a year ago."

"Where did you go to college?"

"University of Missouri—I studied math and art."

"You're a very good artist. What's 7 times 8?"

"I believe that's 56."

"Outstanding at math, too."

"Thank you. How about you? Are you from here?"

"Yep, born and raised. Allison, the market manager, and I are twins."

"I heard."

"Our parents are real-estate-mogul hippie types—they live in an RV, but own a bunch of rental properties. About a hundred years ago I went to the University of South Carolina, liberal arts, but before I could go further than my undergrad, I inherited my farm from my aunt and uncle. When that happened, my whole perspective changed. I suddenly wanted to grow things and create something with the soil. Putting my hands in dirt became more important than putting them around more textbooks."

"Well, first of all, you're not that old, so stop that. Second, I understand exactly what you mean. See, you're an artist, too."

"No, I make berry jams and preserves."

"And pumpkin."

"Only for a limited time."

Suddenly, Ian took a sharp left and turned onto a dirt road that would have been very easy to drive by without noticing. I braced both myself and Hobbit. She was sitting in the middle of the truck's bench seat with a smile on her face. The turn and the bumpy ride left us all unstable.

"Are you sure this is the way?" I asked.

"Yep. The road smooths in just a second. Hang on." Ian turned again, to the right this time, and the ride became less bumpy and darker under a canopy of tall trees.

We continued on for about half a mile, then suddenly the trees stopped and a wide but shallow valley opened up before us.

"Here we are," Ian said.

There was a huge building on the property. It was an über-sized greenhouse, and it seemed to stretch on for a good couple of acres. To the front of, and a good distance from, the big building was a small, somewhat boring white house with a wide front porch. Next to the house was a large copper yard sculpture that moved in the light breeze. The sculpture was about ten feet tall and looked like a giant flower. The petals moved—somehow seemed to get small and then large—with intermittent wind, making the sculpture look as if it was continually blooming and then closing. It was breathtaking and went beyond art to a feat of structural engineering.

Ian maneuvered his truck toward the house.

"That sculpture is gorgeous. And that greenhouse—no wonder . . ." I said.

"Thanks. Abner wouldn't let me see inside the greenhouse," Ian said absently as we got closer.

"It looks like the front door of the house is wide-open," I said as I followed the direction of his glance.

"Yep. And there's something on the porch," he said, a catch in his voice. There was a large stain at the threshold of the front door. It was red and shiny.

"Oh, crap, Ian, you don't suppose that's blood?" I unhooked the seat belt and reached for the door handle before the truck came to a complete stop.

"Hang on, wait here a second. Let me check it out." He reached over and grabbed hold of my arm.

The sun was low on the horizon, and the entire property was patterned with fingerlike shadows and yellow, leftover light. Fear for Abner had already marched through my gut and was making its way to my toes, so when the front door slammed shut with the noise of a rifle shot, I should have been forgiven for my scream of terror.

Four

In the next half instant, when I realized that the sound hadn't been a shot from a sniper hiding behind the greenhouse, but a gust of wind shutting the door, I yanked my arm from Ian's grasp and threw myself out of his truck—unconsciously closing the door before Hobbit could escape. I had no idea how Ian made it to the porch first, but there he was, holding me back again.

"Becca, hang on. I know you're worried about Abner, but this could be dangerous or it could be evidence. Let's slow down."

On one level his voice of reason was highly irritating, but on another level I knew he was right and we probably needed to be smart. Actually, we probably should have stayed in the truck and called the police, but that wasn't an option I could accept. Abner could be hurt or in trouble—I couldn't just wait for someone else.

"Got it," I finally said.

I didn't realize that he'd been holding both of my arms, but as he loosened his grasp, I could still feel the pressure.

"Sorry—I hope I didn't hurt you," he said.

"No, you're right, we need to be careful."

Ian nodded and turned away from my surely frantic eyes. *Where was Abner?*

"Okay, this doesn't look like blood," Ian said as he stared at the puddle. "I don't think blood is quite this bright red."

"No?" I carefully kept all body parts away from the puddle but moved to my knees to get a better look. It wasn't the way it looked so much as the way it smelled. "I know exactly what it is."

"Yeah?"

I touched a fingertip to the edge of the red puddle, gathered a little of the stickiness, and put it on my tongue. "Sugar water—for hummingbirds. People make it red because hummingbirds are attracted to color. Well, I think that's why, anyway."

Ian followed suit and fingertip-tasted the liquid. "Well, that's good news, so far. Blood probably would have been bad news. Plus, I'd have to worry about your appetites if I'd just seen you reach willingly for a taste of blood."

I smiled a return of his. Okay, this was weird in many different ways. We were here to talk to Abner, not flirt awkwardly over spilled sugar water. I stood and looked someplace other than at Ian.

"I don't see a feeder or container for the syrup anywhere."

"Maybe it's inside." Ian stood, too.

"No, wait. Look at the greenhouse. There's a ton of feeders hanging on it."

Ian looked toward the greenhouse and then seemed to scan the entire property. "Uh-huh. Abner's probably just inside or in the greenhouse." He turned, kept to the side of the puddle, and knocked on the door. "Abner! Hey, Abner, are you in there?"

The hollow silence that followed made the back of my neck tingle. I turned to scan for the pair of eyes that I felt was watching us, but didn't see anything suspicious.

"Go inside?" I asked.

"Yeah, maybe." Ian moved to his left and peered into a front window next to the door. "Yeah, for sure." He stepped back to the side of the puddle, jumped over the syrup, opened the door, and disappeared into the house. "Abner. Hey, Abner."

Woof! Hobbit exclaimed from the open window of the truck.

"Nope, you stay right there. I'll be cleaning your paws all night if you step in this stuff."

Woof.

"Sorry, girl."

Hobbit sighed and rolled her puppy-dog eyes at me.

The light and shadows were just right that I couldn't see much inside the open doorway. I jumped the puddle and found what had caused Ian to hurry in.

"Abner!" I added my voice. There was no answer.

Abner's house was decorated in the style of single-man-who-hadn't-purchased-furniture-in-about-forty-years. His couch was covered in green material that made me itch just looking at it. He had two nonmatching chairs at the sides of the couch, one of them threadbare and probably the place where he spent most of his time when he wasn't in his greenhouse or at Bailey's. Next to the chair was a small side table that held an old-fashioned phone—the kind you plugged into a phone outlet but didn't require electricity to work. But it was the coffee table, worn and decorated with water rings and tipped on its side, that gave the whole room a sense of something gone wrong.

"He's not in the house," Ian said from the hallway in the middle of the structure. "I don't see anyone, anywhere."

"Damn." I needed to see for myself that Abner wasn't around, so I followed the path of Ian's search.

The kitchen was furnished in a predictable manner: Formica table and counters, old cabinets that were at one time probably a clean cream color but were now dingy.

"Dishes in the sink, but nothing is broken—it doesn't look as though there was any sort of struggle in here," I said.

"Bed's unmade, but that might not mean anything, either," Ian said.

I hurried down the hall and stepped into the bedroom. There was a full-size bed with an unmatched dresser and chest of drawers. The furniture was adorned with the types of man-things that had become familiar enough; having a dad and a couple of husbands let me in on the secrets of coin-gathering spots, a good place to put a watch, lip balm, the unnecessary pile of receipts for small items, and so on.

"I don't see his wallet on top of either the dresser or the chest of drawers." I looked under the bed and saw a few pairs of shoes and fuzzy dust bunnies. "Nothing." I stood and pulled open the closet door; there were only a few pieces of clothing. "Nothing."

"His truck wasn't out front, either, and I haven't seen his keys anywhere. There's a spot behind the greenhouse where he could park, but I really don't think he's here." Ian stood in the bedroom doorway.

"Do you think we've overreacted?" My pounding heart whooshed in my ears. *Where was Abner?*

"Did you see the coffee table?" he said.

"Yeah, but the living room didn't seem messed up except for that."

"It didn't. I'm going to double-check."

We moved so quickly down the hallway that I was surprised we didn't pinball off the walls.

"What's that?" Ian said as we reached the front room.

He pointed to something at the side of the table. In my previous quick survey of the room, I hadn't noticed the three white squares lined up on the floor.

I reached for a lamp and flipped the switch, filling the room with gloomy, sallow light, and crouched down.

"Old pictures," I said as I peered closely, careful not to upset the layout—it was spaced so evenly that it seemed planned, and maybe important. The pictures were obviously from another time—they were black-and-white images, slightly yellowed and warped.

"That could be Abner when he was younger," I said as I pointed at a young man who had Abner's roundish face. The smile was familiar enough, but the Abner I knew didn't have the hair to compare. There was a young woman next to the younger Abner. She was very pretty, her hair white and poofy like Marilyn Monroe's. Even with the lack of color film, I could see that she wore a thick coat of lipstick, most likely red.

"His wife? Was he married?"

"I have no idea. Remember, until you brought me here, I didn't even know where he lived. But—though I hate to be stereotypical in any way—I don't think there's a woman on the planet who'd live here without at least covering that chair with a towel or something." I pointed. "Actually, I'm really beginning to wonder if we were friends at all. This house—even the greenhouse—all of it is part of a person I don't know. I can't make any of this fit."

"People can be pretty secretive."

"I suppose."

"The other two look like pictures of trees, or something," Ian said.

"Uh-huh." Flanking the picture of the couple were indeed pictures of trees. One was of three trees and the other one had just one tree. "Weird."

"Tell you anything?"

"No, except that Abner might have had a thing for both blondes and trees."

"Right. Come on. Abner's not in here. Let's check the greenhouse."

"Yep." I glanced at the pictures one more time, but they didn't tell me anything at all.

We both leapt over the sticky puddle again and then closed the door behind us. I couldn't stand the thought of leaving her alone, so I let Hobbit out of the truck and we made our way along the dirt path to the greenhouse. It wasn't terribly far away, but I couldn't make my legs move quickly enough. The sky was darkening, and though I didn't want to leave any wildflower unturned, I hoped that we could wrap this up quickly.

In truth, there was probably nothing creepy about Abner's property, but with everything that had happened that day, it seemed like we were in the midst of the set for some scary movie. Would a mask-wearing someone step out from behind the bluebells and run at us with a big knife?

"What was with the coffee table?" I said, thinking aloud.

"Don't know. At first glance, it looked so wrong, but

at second glance, it almost seemed placed—like the pictures."

"Doesn't make sense. Do you think there was a fight—that Abner was taken from his house or something?"

"Can't tell from what we've seen. It's all strange but not really violent."

When we were about ten feet from the greenhouse, our conversation was interrupted as an array of motion-sensor lights in between the hanging hummingbird feeders blazed on. Hobbit barked at the sudden change.

"It's okay, girl." I petted her neck.

"Hey, that could be the feeder that had the syrup from the porch in it," Ian said.

I followed his glance and saw a busted hummingbird feeder. It was on the ground, next to the door of the greenhouse. The clear tube was cracked open like an eggshell.

"It doesn't look like any of the syrup was spilled out here," I said as I inspected more closely. A few drops still clung to the plastic, but if this was the feeder that had once contained the syrup, it had been pretty well emptied on the porch.

"There are no footprints," Ian said.

"Huh?"

"There aren't any syrupy footprints anywhere. We leapt over the puddle. If there was anyone else at the house—including Abner—they must have leapt over it, too, or they would have left footprints."

"Where is he?" I said.

"Abner! It's Ian and Becca," Ian said loudly.

There was no response.

"Let's go in." With Hobbit close by, I stepped surely toward the door. I was ready to face whatever boogeyman was on the other side. Again with some sort of superhero-weird speed, Ian's hand was on the doorknob long before mine. "How do you do that?"

He shrugged. "Let's be careful."

"Right."

Ian pushed the door open.

The greenhouse was mostly dark, but there was still enough light outside to cast shadows everywhere. One small, illuminated, white lightbulb stuck out from the wall underneath the main light switches. Its light didn't travel far. There were so many switches—a dozen or so—that Ian had to partially reach under some thick twine that hung in a perfectly round ring on the wall to flip them up.

"Wow," I said as I looked around. I had honestly never seen anything like it—so much so that I wasn't even sure what I was seeing. "This is better than Oz."

"Abner!" Ian called again. His voice echoed, but didn't receive a response.

The greenhouse was half as long as a football field and probably not quite as wide. There were rows and rows of flowers that seemed to be planted in tables. All of the tables had deep bellies and were linked together by PVC piping. Beneath them, there was a grated irrigation runoff system that snaked up and down the aisles. Even with all the soil, the greenhouse was immaculate; the floor was spotless, and the temperature was controlled by some invisible machine that whirred quietly in the background. As time-warped as his house furniture had been, Abner's greenhouse was modern, practically futuristic.

"I'm beginning to think he's just not here, Ian."

"Maybe," Ian said, as he peered at the tables and underneath them.

Hobbit and I picked an aisle and began walking down it. The flowers were color-coded. On my right were red somethings and on my left were purple somethings. The flowers were healthy and bright. Where there weren't flowers, there was either bare, even soil or healthy sprouts peeking up cheerfully. The entire space was filled with the earthy aromas of soil and flowers, but there was nothing artificial about the scent, nothing perfumy. I sniffed deeply. No one would ever figure out how to bottle this. I kept walking, recognizing some of the flowers from Abner's booth, not recognizing others.

"How in the world?" I muttered. Hobbit nudged my knee lightly. "This must have cost him a fortune."

"I can't even guess," Ian said as he joined us. "He's probably been working on it a long time."

"Explains the old furniture—why spend your money on the house when you could spend it here and create this?"

"I agree."

"Oh, look, here are some of his favorite ones." I pointed to some flowers with white petals and bright yellow centers. The stems, though mostly hidden by leaves, were obviously thick with thorns.

"They look wicked," Ian observed.

"They are. They're called Carolina horse nettle. Abner can create a bouquet, placing one of these just right so that it doesn't ever touch the customer at all. It's quite a trick." I echoed what I had said to Allison earlier in the day.

"Look at these." Ian picked up some old kitchen oven mitts that reached to his elbows. They were pocked with little holes in the red outer fabric, the white stuffing branching out here and there.

"Yikes. I think that any flower that requires wearing those for maintenance should be banned from all gardens."

"Damn!" Ian said suddenly. He ripped off the oven mitts and stared at the ground behind me.

"What?" I thought maybe there had been thorns in the mitts, but once he got them off, he pushed past me, went to his knees, and looked at something under a table the next aisle over.

"Oh my God," I said as I joined him and saw what he'd seen.

Underneath the table full of beautiful flowers, on the pristine floor, was something that not only looked out of place, but was stomach-roiling horrific, too.

It was an axe, the handle old and worn and the blade dark and bloody.

I have no idea what made me do it, but I reached for the axe and pulled it from the floor.

"Becca, I don't think . . ." Ian said.

I ignored Ian's hand on my arm and held the axe close. It was real, heavy and substantial.

"I think Abner's in trouble, Ian," I said.

"And I think perhaps you lied to me, Ms. Robins," a voice said from behind us. "You really did know where Abner lived. Now, put the axe down and step away from it, please."

After I swallowed my heart back down to my chest, I did exactly as Officer Brion said. He was halfway down the aisle, still in his crisp uniform. He didn't have his gun drawn, but once I stood, I put my hands into the air, just like any common criminal caught in the act would do.

Five

I had no idea what time it was, but all I wanted to do was go home.

Officer Brion had allowed Hobbit to stay with me, but he'd separated us from Ian. We'd gone through another complete round of questioning. I sat on the hood of the police car, and this time it went something like this:

"Ms. Robins, explain how you're here after you told me you didn't know where Abner Justen lived."

"I'm worried about him, Officer. The bloody axe. Do you think he's okay?"

"Ms. Robins, I'm asking, you're answering."

"Ian created that art." I pointed. "He knew where Abner lived because he had to deliver and set up the artwork. I didn't find this out until long after I talked to you. I didn't even think about letting you know. Besides, you questioned Ian, so you probably got the address from him, too." I wasn't in the mood to be questioned, and though I respected the police and what they did, I was tired and angry that they'd perhaps missed something horrible happening to Abner.

"So, Mr. Cartwright supplied you with the information?" He tapped his pen on his notepad as he looked over at Ian, who was next to the front porch, talking to another officer.

"Yes."

"Wait here."

"Officer Brion, what about Abner? Do you think he's hurt? Do you think the axe is the weapon that was used to kill Matt Simonsen?"

For a moment, Officer Brion kept his stern face. I was ready for him to tell me again that it wasn't my job to ask the questions, but then the hard edges of his face relaxed—only slightly.

"Ms. Robins, we don't know where Mr. Justen is, but he's a person of interest in the murder of Mr. Simonsen. We came out here tonight to talk to him some more. We hope no one else is hurt, but we don't have that answer right now. As for the murder weapon, that's not something I can share with you."

I nodded as he turned and went to talk to Ian.

I waited for a long time.

Finally, we were free to go—well, told to leave. Abner never did show up. The officers searched the house and greenhouse and presumably found the same things we did, but they didn't share their observations with us.

"Were you the one who told Officer Brion where Abner lived? Earlier today, I mean," I asked as Ian drove us back to my house.

"No. Officer Brion wasn't the one who interviewed me. It was the other guy. He didn't ask if I knew where Abner lived."

"Oh."

"In case you're wondering, I'd have given up the address if they'd asked." Ian's voice had a smile to it.

"Probably a good idea."

"Yeah." Ian scratched behind one of Hobbit's ears. She was fast asleep, spread out over both of us.

"Do you think Abner's been hurt?"

"I have no idea. I hope not. The axe isn't good, though, no matter whose blood is on it."

I cringed.

"They'll figure it out. They're the police," Ian said.

"Uh-huh," I muttered. But I wasn't so sure.

We replayed the police questions, neither of us learning anything new. Well, other than the fact that Officer Brion hadn't been able to hide his displeasure at the way Ian had been questioned earlier in the day. We didn't know how they'd finally figured out Abner's address, but they hadn't learned it from Ian.

Ian dropped Hobbit and me off with the promise that we'd do something less criminal-like next time.

I fell into bed and slept deeply, without one bad dream, and woke up after the sun had risen—this was rare, but at least I'd gotten plenty of rest.

It was Wednesday—my day off—and I was grateful to spend the time around my farm. The entire day before had been emotional and draining; it was good to have tasks to keep me busy. And, of course, I had to call my sister and give her the previous evening's details, which I did as I worked the pumpkin patch.

"I'm very pleased that you weren't arrested," Allison said.

"Me, too, but it was close. We were trespassing, after all. And I picked up a bloody axe." I switched my cell phone to my other ear as I lifted a slightly green pumpkin and rearranged it so that it wouldn't flatten on one side.

"Picking up a bloody axe wasn't smart, Sis."

"I know, but apparently Officer Brion *observed* us discovering it and me picking it up."

"That probably saved you."

"Yep."

"Did he believe you were there out of concern for Abner?"

"I think so, but I don't think they're concerned for his well-being so much."

"They suspect him, huh?"

"Pretty sure. I think they think the axe was the murder weapon, but they wouldn't tell us."

"I don't like the sound of that."

"I'm sure you'd have told me this already, but Abner's not there—not at Bailey's today?" I asked.

"No. His stall is empty."

"I figured."

We were silent for a moment, both of us processing . . . well, everything.

"Hey, I have a pumpkin that looks like Richard Nixon," I said to break up the quiet.

"Really?"

"Yeah." I lifted Mr. Nixon and moved him slightly. "He might now transform into Gerald Ford."

Allison laughed. "I hate to do this on your day off, but can you come in for a meeting this afternoon? Vendors are still—understandably—upset about everything, and the customers aren't rushing back yet, so I thought we'd get everyone together to talk things out. And the Equinox Dinner is scheduled for this Sunday. I want to see if everyone still really wants to have it, considering the circumstances."

I'd forgotten about the dinner. It was Allison's yearly moment to shine, so to speak. She always put together a great party for all Bailey's vendors and their families on the Sunday night before the fall equinox. That Sunday was typically the last day at the market for the seasonal vendors, who wouldn't return until spring. The dinner was a time for socialization, farewells, and evaluation. Everyone looked forward to it. "Sure. What time?" Though I still had lots of work to do around the farm, Allison could probably use a positive attitude/force at her meeting. I'd work on attaining such. Plus, I wanted to ask some questions; I wasn't sure who I wanted to interrogate, but having lots of people together might help me figure it out.

"About three o'clock. Oh, and Ian will be there, too. Maybe he'll show you the rest of his tattoos."

"Now I'm sorry I told you." In working up to the horror of the night before, I'd told Allison what I'd learned about Ian, particularly the mystery number of tattoos over his body.

"Sorry, but the way you talk about him is very interesting. You sound . . . intrigued."

"I'm too often divorced to be intrigued with anyone. You're mistaking my tone."

"Okay," Allison said easily, not willing to bring the issue to an argument. "Hey, go ahead and bring Hobbit today."

"Thanks. See you then."

We signed off. I snapped the phone shut and slipped it into the back pocket of my short overalls. I knew from experience that my pumpkin-turning crouch could result in my cell phone being propelled out of a side pocket. And the big leaves of pumpkin plants hid phones very well.

"You've been invited to a meeting. Are you excited?" I

asked my ever-loyal farming partner. She knew how to stay close beside me and step carefully enough so that her long paws didn't tear the leaves or crush any of the pumpkins. When I worked with the strawberry plants, she stayed to the outside of the runners. It took only a couple of smushed berries for her to learn that her feet weren't made for avoiding the small fruit.

Hobbit winked, acknowledging either the fact that she knew going to the meeting would be the best part of her day, or that she knew she'd be invited all along.

She'd come into my life literally the second that my second husband left it. I'd driven the last box of his personal items to the 7-Eleven not far from the farm. Scott and I didn't hate each other, but once the relationship was over, it was uncomfortable having him in the house, so I planned to meet him and deliver the box.

As I sucked on the straw of a Big Gulp and watched him drive away in his newer-model truck, silently wondering how he was ever going to make payments on the truck and buy gas for it when he didn't have access to my checking account anymore, a child stepped in front of me and held up a very small brown puppy with very long feet.

"Hey, lady, want a puppy?"

I can't even remember what the child looked like because I was so busy falling in love with the dog. Hobbit and I had been together ever since—two years of the best relationship of my life. Her enjoyment of the pumpkin patch was a bonus.

As I'd read on bumper stickers about fishing—time spent among pumpkins should not be deducted from one's life. The gourds were easy to grow and they produced such wonderful orange fruit that cultivating a pumpkin patch was an easily satisfying experience.

Unfortunately, my usually peaceful task was more stressful than relaxing this morning. As I walked through the patch, rearranging those pumpkins that needed rearranging, watering the plants, and inspecting the large leaves for mold, I kept thinking about poor Matt Simonsen and his bashed-in head. It was probably the Richard Nixon look-alike that brought the human comparison to the front of my mind, but in just about every pumpkin I looked at, I began to see the disfigured part of the dead man.

Who was he? What had he and Abner really argued about? Did Abner use the axe to kill Matt? Did they know each other before Matt had come to work at Bailey's? Was Abner now a victim, too?

Beyond those specific questions, there was the whole idea of murder. Even with two divorces under my belt, I'd never felt particularly murderous toward either of my ex-husbands; crazed with anger enough to slam a door with destruction in mind, maybe, but never homicidal. How badly must someone want someone else out of their life to follow through with killing them? Had Matt Simonsen been such a large thorn in Abner's side that the only way to relieve the pain was killing him? And if Abner wasn't the killer, then who was? Last time I'd asked, Allison told me that there were fifty-something vendors at Bailey's—some were part-time, others full-time. Though it seemed the police didn't suspect anyone other than Abner, could another Bailey's vendor have disliked Simonsen enough to do away with him? I wanted to know who that might be. And why.

I was beginning to look forward to the meeting. It wasn't that I thought I was smarter than the police, but I wondered if maybe my insight into the people I'd worked with for so many years might offer me a clearer look. And

I really wanted to know what had happened. I was curious, but I was angry, too. Bailey's was a great place to work and shop—someone had brought their mess to my 'hood, and I wasn't happy about that at all. I didn't feel unsafe, but the egg vendor Jeanine Baker had, and customers were bound to be wary for at least a little while. The sooner this was solved, the better off we'd all be.

I finished with the pumpkins at about ten o'clock, still leaving me with plenty of time to trim back the strawberry plants and give them the good soaking that would contribute to another great crop in the spring. My strawberries had been healthy and hardy this year, but that wasn't unexpected. Even though many of my berry jams were made from the berries of other farmers, I had a special knack for growing strawberries that were plump, sweet, and juicy. I was the envy of many local growers who tried in vain to duplicate my methods. And I wasn't secretive about my ways. In fact, I told anyone who asked exactly what I did. But still, to this day, no one was able to grow them the way I could grow them. I liked to think that my strawberries were a result of my ability to understand my plants innately and know exactly what they needed when they needed it. Perhaps it was something cosmic—a life-to-life relationship coming together in perfect harmony. In actuality, it was probably the slight slope of my land and the way the sun fell on the plants in a perfect arc, angling just right throughout the growing season.

Well, whatever it was, I was either lucky or damn good at it, and proud to be so.

I didn't believe in just turning on a sprinkler or a hose, allowing the water to run freely. I insisted on hand-watering everything. Beyond the fact that there was something peaceful about spending time in a garden or working the land, it was my job, my responsibility, to make sure that I created the best products I could. Personal attention to each and every plant was the only way, in my opinion.

Though I cleaned my kitchen/barn and all my cooking items every time I used them, on Wednesdays I cleaned everything again, inventoried the freezers, pulled everything away from the walls, and mopped floors and corners that I couldn't reach otherwise; this was most successfully done with music turned up to wall-shaking volume and was probably the best part of my week—I called it my head-clearing therapy, and I definitely needed that form of therapy today.

Hobbit wasn't allowed in the barn, so she always napped on the front porch as I cleaned, usually to the sounds of Springsteen, Motown, or George Strait. It was an odd collection of favorites, but MP3 players had changed the world and made those mixed-music collections I used to create on cassette tapes a hundred times easier to put together. Today, the "Teen Pop for the Geriatric" playlist sounded appealing, so with the background of Shaun Cassidy, David Cassidy, Donny Osmond, and Rick Springfield, I inventoried and then scrubbed until there was nothing left to scrub. The therapy worked wonders, and I emerged from the barn in a deeply contented state.

Of course, my phone had to ring and spoil the moment.

I fished it out of my pocket and read the ID: Unknown.

"Hello."

"Becca?"

"Abner?"

"Yes."

"You're okay?! Where are you? How are you?" My mind and mouth both started to whir.

"Becca, I didn't kill anyone."

"Abner, I never thought you did." The axe hadn't helped with that belief, but I didn't want to lose him.

"The police do."

I took a deep breath and told myself to calm down. I had Abner on the phone and the police still wanted to talk to him. Maybe I could—what did they call it—talk him in? "Abner, they'll figure it out. If you're innocent, they'll figure it out. It's what they do."

"I saw you at my house last night."

"Okay. Well, I'm sorry we were trespassing. I understand if you're mad at me." In truth, I was mad at him. Why hadn't he let us know he was there? But now wasn't the time to scold.

Abner was silent.

"Abner?"

"I know who killed Simonsen."

"Who?"

"I can't tell you."

"Oh, come on, Abner. If you know anything, you have to tell the police. This needs to get solved—you owe it to Mr. Simonsen's family to tell what you know. Shoot, you owe it to yourself to clear your name."

"I saw the murderer plant the axe."

"Okay. Let's go tell the police."

Silence again.

"Abner?" I looked at my phone. The call had been disconnected. "Dammit, Abner!"

Hobbit nudged at my knee. And just like that, my head-clearing therapy was negated. I stood and pondered what to do next. Should I call Officer Brion? Allison? Abner hadn't told me anything, really, just that he hadn't killed Simonsen, but he knew who had. Why in the world wouldn't he share that with the police? Or with me—I could take it from there. Unless he really had killed Simonsen and just wanted me to play along.

Woof.

"I have no idea, girl," I said. And I didn't. I was confused to the point that I was shaking my head to myself.

I didn't call anyone. Not yet, at least. Abner wanted to talk to me. Maybe he'd call again and tell me more—either more truth or more lies, whichever. But if he did call again, I planned on being much better prepared.

Six

So, who killed Matt Simonsen? I thought as I looked around the tent.

Farmers' market meetings were an unusual sight, to say the least. First of all, meetings weren't standard operating procedure for a gathering of farmers and artists. We were a restless crowd, made up of people who didn't do much in a committee way. We each did our own thing and didn't bother with group decisions. Sitting around in a meeting went against our grain. But the good part of any rare meeting we might have was the treats—everyone brought a little something. I contributed some blackberry jam, and there was an assortment of fruit, cookies, pies, and breads. And Betsy, whose tomatoes were heavenly, brought a full basket, a couple good knives, some salt, and my new favorite topping for her fruit: peanut butter.

As the tent filled and people grabbed their food, I sidled my way next to Betsy.

"So, I heard that you heard the argument between Abner and Matt Simonsen." It wasn't subtle in the least, but I was never very good with subtle. Plus I didn't want her to later think I had greeted her with ulterior motives.

Her green eyes flashed and opened wide. She was the most granola person I knew, and it worked well on her. Her long, straight brown hair was thick and smooth—if I'd tried to grow my hair past my shoulders, my head would have been covered in blond frizzy, stringy things. Her skin was flawless and would have looked painted if she tried to wear makeup—I didn't wear much myself, but my skin was freckled, and when I occasionally spread on some foundation, the improvement was noticeable. She wore bohemian dresses in contrast to my overalls and jeans. She was also very smart, with a quick wit that often left me laughing and wondering where she came up with such stuff.

"Well, Becca, I think I heard the argument. That's what I told the police."

"What do you think you heard?"

"Hmm. The police have that information. I'd feel wrong about sharing it with just anyone."

"I understand. It's just that Abner is such a good friend. I hate thinking he actually killed someone—if he's innocent. You might ease my mind."

She smiled slyly. "Come on, Becca. What's up?"

I guided her to the side of the tent and bent close to her ear. "I just want to figure this out—it isn't that I don't have confidence in the police. I do, but they don't know us the way we know us." I waved my hand, taking in the world of farmers' market vendors we lived in. "We might be able to help things progress faster. While this is unsolved, I don't think our safety is in jeopardy, but I do think our businesses are."

That got her attention.

"Well, keep it to yourself," she said. I nodded in agreement. She hesitated another moment but finally spoke again. "They were yelling, and I heard Mr. Simonsen call Abner a stupid son-of-a-bitch. Abner then said something to the effect of 'If you'd died all those years ago, we wouldn't be dealing with this—I could just kill you now and we could all finally move on.' That's all I heard."

"What does *that* mean?"

"I don't know. That's all I heard."

"None of that sounds like Abner."

"I know, but he was very angry. I've never seen him like that."

"Me, either." I tried to imagine those words coming from Abner, but I couldn't. And I couldn't think of anything else to ask. "Well, thanks, Betsy."

"Sure. Let me know what you find out." She turned and went back to the other vendors.

I maneuvered to the food but found I wasn't hungry anymore. Hobbit stayed at my heels as though she'd actually been trained instead of treated like another human.

I glanced around the small crowd—of the fifty-something vendors who worked at the market, only about thirty had shown up for the meeting. Most of my friends were there: Linda, Herb and Don, Jeanine, Barry, and Brenton. I knew most of the others, too, but hadn't had the time (or taken it) to get to know them all that well.

As much as I tried *not* to look for him, I noticed Ian there, too. He was in a tête-à-tête with Barry. He looked in my direction when I took a seat. He half smiled and half waved as Barry commanded his attention. I wondered if Ian knew anything about corn or was being forced to learn.

I sat on the other side of the room. Not because I was being coy, but because all the chairs on his side were taken. I was pretty sure that Ian's wave and smile to me paled in comparison to the light his eyes took on when he saw Hobbit. I was glad she didn't see him. It would have been humiliating to have her abandon me to sit beside someone else.

"Thanks, everybody, for coming in this afternoon. I hope I haven't disrupted your day too much." Allison stood at the front of the tent. She was back to her normal self: beautiful and confident. I knew the murder had taken, and would continue to take, a huge toll on her, but she was the consummate professional and she knew that business for her vendors had to go on. In keeping with their respect for her, the crowd quieted quickly and gave her their full attention.

"Yes, thanks, everyone," she repeated. "We've had a rough couple of days and I wanted to bring as many people together as possible to try to address all concerns or questions. Of course, if you'd like to talk to me in private about anything, please just let me know.

"I know that some of you knew Mr. Simonsen personally. Our condolences have been extended to his family, and we offer them to you as well. I didn't know him myself for very long, but he seemed like a very nice man. I've already spoken to his wife—Mr. Simonsen might have only begun working at our market, but he worked at many others over the years. He and his son worked together over at Smithfield for a long time. His son, Jessop, will continue to run their peach business over there. Those of you who know him might want to send sympathy to him or to Mrs. Simonsen."

I glanced around, but no one had the shifty eyes of

someone who had murdered someone the day before. I was curious, though—who, other than Abner and Barry, in this group had known Matt Simonsen, and how well? It wasn't the appropriate time to interject such a question. I tried to figure out who was missing from the meeting, who was and wasn't there yesterday. So much had happened, and between talking to market vendors both in person and on the phone, I couldn't put together in my head who had been where and when. I silently chastised myself for not paying better attention.

"We will place a small plaque on the front of the office building honoring Mr. Simonsen." Allison cleared her throat. "It's always difficult to broach the subject of getting back to work when a tragedy occurs, so please forgive me if this offends anyone—but I just want to remind you that the police have given us the go-ahead to continue with our jobs. I'm not saying this to rush anyone. But I know that sometimes getting back to work can help—of course, do this at your own speed, but I want you to know that we're cleared to do so. Does anyone have a question? Don't be shy."

Jeanine raised her hand hesitantly.

"Jeanine."

"Well, I wonder . . . well, I can't help but . . . Allison, how safe or unsafe are we?" Jeanine's face was still pale and drawn. She probably hadn't gotten much sleep.

"I think we're very safe, Jeanine, but we should all be careful. The police think that the murderer came here specifically for Mr. Simonsen." Allison cleared her throat again. "They feel we're safe. I'd love to tell you that I'm one hundred percent sure that nothing else awful is going to happen at Bailey's, but the truth is, we should all be aware and perhaps use the buddy system. I've put together a list of potential buddy groups. It's based on your schedules and the locations of your stalls, and if you've told me you despise someone, I promise I haven't paired you with them." The room snickered along with Allison's attempt to lighten the mood. "Perhaps we could unload and load in pairs for a while. And we should all watch out for each other. I'll post the list after the meeting. If I need to make any changes, let me know."

"Who's my partner?" Jeanine said.

"Brenton."

Jeanine seemed to think a moment before she nodded. "Brenton, you good with that?"

"Absolutely, we'll trade eggs for dog biscuits."

"I don't have a dog," she said flatly.

"I know someone who can solve that problem."

Jeanine's face finally flooded with the color of someone not so petrified. She and Brenton were actually pretty good friends and had worked next to each other for some time.

"I like your plan, Allison," she said.

Leave it to Allison to have a good plan. The collective mood in the tent changed noticeably. Jeanine's smile was genuine, and Brenton leaned back on his chair and stuck a piece of straw in his mouth.

"Good. I suppose the other thing is the fall equinox party. You've all worked very hard this year, and I'd love to treat you and your families to dinner on Sunday night as planned, but in light of what has happened, does anyone think that would be an inappropriate thing to do? Should we cancel or postpone?"

At first everyone was silent, and then a low murmur spread through the tent. This was a rough question—a party after such a horrible incident didn't seem right, but the dinner was looked forward to and changing it to a day other than the Sunday before the equinox didn't fit with either the idea behind it or the fact that some vendors would be gone from the market after this weekend.

"Oh, hey, Allison, I have an idea," Brenton said as he pulled the straw out of his mouth and sat up. "Let's still have the dinner, but let's have it in Matt Simonsen's honor. I didn't know the man, but he worked the land like most of the rest of us. He'd have appreciated the spirit behind it, I'm sure."

The murmur turned into sounds of agreement.

"Does anyone object?" Allison asked. "Okay, then, we'll keep it scheduled. Any other questions?"

"Where's Abner?" a voice called from the back of the tent, but I couldn't tell who it was attached to.

"Abner is taking some time off," Allison said. I didn't point out that the official word for him was "missing."

"I don't think he should be allowed to come back to the market until we know for sure he's not a killer." Goddard McElroy stood and leaned on his cane. He was a part-timer who sold baked potato meals out of a cart. His cart held a variety of toppings that melted perfectly over the hot potatoes. I often wished he was at Bailey's full-time. He was only in his forties but had a bad foot that required him to use the cane. He was never outspoken, so his words caught us all by surprise.

Of course, Allison handled him perfectly. She kept her voice calm but firm. "He hasn't been arrested—please, let's not be judge and jury, folks. Abner has been here a long time. He's our friend, and until there's proof otherwise, he's as innocent as the rest of us."

Goddard hesitated for a beat but then nodded and sat down.

Bo Stafford raised his hand. Bo was a mystery to me.

He was a big wrestler-type guy who couldn't be much older than about twenty, and he hadn't worked at Bailey's for very long. He grew and sold onions—white ones, red ones, little ones, and big ones. They were delicious, but his introverted personality hadn't done much for his business.

"Bo?"

"I'd like to know more about Barry Drake's relationship with Matt Simonsen. I've heard rumors." Bo's neck was thick, and when he spoke, he pulled his chin back, as though he wanted to make it even thicker.

"What do you mean, Bo?" Allison asked.

"Well, I've heard that Barry and Simonsen had a feud a number of years back about some land on the other side of Monson."

"Bo, I'm sure that's not relevant to the current issues. Many of us have worked in the business a long time. We've all had our moments. . . ."

"No, Allison, I'd like to answer." Barry stood. His face was blazing, and I became concerned about his heart rate. I looked at Ian, who was looking up at Barry with his own concern.

"Barry." Ian put his hand on Barry's arm. "No one's accusing you. You don't have to . . ."

"Yes, I think I do, young man," Barry said to Ian.

"I understand," Ian said.

Ian's easy tone made Barry blink. He was revving up for a fight, but Ian wasn't biting.

"Yes, I knew Matt Simonsen," he said to the silent crowd as about thirty pairs of wide, curious eyes, mine and Hobbit's included, stared at him. Yesterday he'd told me that he couldn't remember exactly where he met Matt Simonsen, but that he was "more curmudgeonly than me and Abner put together." Had he lied about not knowing him well or not remembering exactly where he met him? "And he was not one of my favorite people. We did have a fight—a legal battle, to be exact—over some land. I won, he lost. He didn't lose well, especially when it came to something as important as land. I didn't kill the man. My issue with him occurred a long time ago—almost thirty years. I wasn't happy to see him at Bailey's, but I was willing to give it time to see if we could make it work."

"Thank you, Barry," Allison interrupted, her tone possibly as firm as I'd ever heard it.

The open-eyed wonder of the crowd stayed focused on Barry for another moment, but then everyone turned to look at my sister. I was sitting in just the right spot, and I was angry that Barry had lied to me, so my glance stayed on him longer than the others'. I hesitated just long enough in turning that I saw something else.

Carl Monroe, the tallest, skinniest, most soft-spoken man I'd ever met, sat at the back of the crowd. He leaned forward in his chair with his chin down to his chest—he wasn't looking at anyone. Allison continued as I looked at Carl, wondering why he wasn't looking up.

"Really, everyone, I want you all to feel safe to come to work. Bailey's is still the greatest farmers' market there is. I don't know who killed Mr. Simonsen, but I'm confident that the police will find the murderer. In the meantime, we have absolutely no reason to suspect each other." She paused. I knew her well enough to know that she wanted to say something like *even Abner,* but she kept it to herself. "Let's look out for each other, and you have my cell phone number. I'll be available at all times—call me immediately if you have any concerns. Now, does anyone have any further questions?"

Carl stood with the rest of the crowd, but he didn't look

at anyone. He kept his head down, thrust one of his hands into a pocket, and made a beeline for the exit.

I don't know why his actions struck me as particularly odd, but they did. I stepped over Hobbit and around some people I didn't take the time to acknowledge, and met Carl at the exit.

"Hey, Carl, how are you? I haven't seen you in a while."

My gesture surprised him. We'd always been friendly enough toward each other, but my greeting wasn't normal.

"Becca." He rubbed at his nose and then looked away from my eyes.

For the first time in my life I experienced the lightbulb effect. As I searched for something other than *hey, you look guilty* to say, an idea literally lit in my mind.

"Carl, you sell peaches, don't you?"

"Yeah," he said far too belligerently.

"So, I bet you ran into Matt Simonsen a time or two, huh?"

"Becca, I really have to go." Carl looked at his watch and then disappeared through the slit opening of the tent.

I pulled the canvas back and watched him practically sprint down the aisle, his long legs giraffe-like. I debated chasing him, but I figured he could move faster than me and he wouldn't talk any more right now anyway. I'd have to figure out another way to find out what he knew.

"You get to be my buddy. You're one lucky girl," Linda said as she came up behind me.

"Huh?"

"My buddy. The buddy list, remember?"

"Oh, sure."

"Well, don't get all mushy or anything," she said with a slight jab at my side.

"Oh, sorry. Lots on my mind, you know."

"Sure, I get it." She glanced around the tent. "So, not to be insensitive or anything, but tell me about your night with Ian."

"How did . . . ? I didn't have a night with Ian. That makes it all sound so . . . wrong. We went to look for Abner, couldn't find him, and were told by the police to leave the premises."

"Okay."

"We didn't find Abner."

"Okay."

"Okay," I said, attempting to stop the conversation.

"So, he didn't make a pass at you at all? Ian, I mean."

"What? No. And is 'make a pass' still a term that people use?"

"I don't know. I'm as old as you—I'd take a *pass* by someone as cute as Ian any day of the week, though."

I laughed. "You deflect plenty of passes." Linda was gorgeous, but very picky when it came to dating.

"Okay, I'd take the *right* pass any day of the week."

"Becca, don't leave without seeing me first," Allison called from the other side of the tent.

"You're being summoned. I'll see you tomorrow," Linda said. "Bright and early. Don't be late. Again."

"I won't." I cringed. I'd really have to pay attention to the time now that someone was depending on me.

Hobbit and I hovered until everyone was done with Allison. I lost track of Ian and told myself to stop looking for him, anyway.

"Hey, Sis, you okay?" I said when she and I were alone.

"Oh, I'm fine."

"And what about Bo's surprise?"

"Well, there have been rumors swirling everywhere. I like to put an end to as many as I can." Allison sighed.

"Hang in there."

"Such a horrible tragedy—I'm so sorry it happened, but I've got to find a way for the vendors to feel like it's okay to move on, without sounding coldhearted."

"You did a great job."

Allison laughed lightly. "Thanks for coming in today. I really appreciate it."

"Sure."

"Oh—the reason I wanted you to stay."

"Yes?"

"I'm going over to the Smithfield Market tomorrow—where Matt Simonsen used to work and his son, Jessop, still does."

"Really? Why?"

"The market manager and I have scheduled a meeting to talk about a statewide market promotion. I know you're supposed to work tomorrow, but I could use the company. Plus, we haven't had nearly enough sister time lately."

"Sure. Of course," I said. I'd have gone anyway, just to spend the day with Allison, but since Smithfield was where Matt Simonsen used to work maybe I could find out more about him.

"Good. I'll pick you up at seven. Gotta run."

"Okay. Thanks," I said to my in-constant-motion sister.

Hobbit and I did a quick search for Carl, but not surprisingly, he was nowhere to be found. Ian was too busy with a couple of customers to interrupt, even after I stalled for a while. Since I was going with Allison, I asked Herb to buddy up with my buddy, Linda, the next day. He agreed, noting that Don would work with Jack by himself. Most vendors were packing up from the slow Wednesday, hoping that the upcoming weekend would bring back the normal crowd.

My head spun as Hobbit and I drove home. Abner had called me, but hadn't told me much—I was ready if he called again, though. And not only had Abner had issues with Matt Simonsen, Barry had, too. And of them all, Carl had acted the strangest. What was that about?

I needed to make some notes.

Thoughts of organizing index cards were rudely interrupted as I pulled into my driveway. It was only about five o'clock and there was plenty of light, but my front porch faced west and when the sun was just low enough, the bright light could be blinding. I'd put up a canvas roll-up screen that I never remembered to roll up. Someone was on my front porch, behind that screen. They leaned against the house, but it was obvious there was someone there, just not obvious who it was. I stopped the truck and put it in Park just as Hobbit gave a gravelly growl.

"Hey, girl, it might be someone we know," I said. I leaned out my window. "Hey, who's there?"

The standing shadow disappeared as though the person went into a crouch. I decided that maybe my dog's growl was on the mark. I didn't want to have anything to do with someone who wasn't planning on identifying themselves.

"Shit." I threw the truck into Reverse, stepped on the gas, and screeched back up the driveway and onto the state highway.

Somehow, as I drove I found Officer Brion's card in one of my pockets. I dialed my cell as I kept one eye on the rearview mirror.

Fortunately, he answered after only one ring. "Brion," he said.

"Hey, yeah, it's Becca Robins. There's someone at my

house—someone who tried to hide. Aw, hell." I wasn't sure how to sound coherent. Fortunately, the officer remained calm.

"Where are you?"

"Driving away from my house."

"Meet me in the front of Bailey's. I'll send a car out to your place and we'll go back together."

"You got it." And, for the second time in as many days, I almost reached the speed limit as I pushed my truck down the highway and prayed that all farming equipment was safely off the road.

Seven

"Show me again," Officer Brion said as we stood on the porch. He was not in his uniform but dressed instead in jeans and an old shirt. He smelled of gasoline—he'd just finished mowing his lawn when I'd called, and he looked terribly human with a smudge of something on his cheek and his short hair free from its slicked-back stronghold.

"They were standing about here. I saw the shadow do this." I did a crouch maneuver.

"No one in the house, sir." Another police officer, in uniform, stepped out the front door. Her name was Vivienne Norton, and she had a soft voice but bigger biceps and wider shoulders than most men I knew. Her hair was bleached, and she wore her makeup thick and her uniform tight. She was an odd mix of feminine and masculine. I wondered if she carried a wallet or a bag. "Ma'am, it looks as if nothing was disturbed, but I'd like for you to take a look with me."

"Sure." I stood from the crouch and looked at Officer Brion. "Now?"

He nodded and then turned to scan my property as I went inside with the other officer. Officer Brion, or Sam, as he'd told me to call him, had reached Bailey's in record time. I'd mostly calmed by the time I got there, so I was able to explain what I thought I'd seen—and by that time, I seriously wondered if I really had seen anything. I'd left the house so quickly.

I also wondered if he'd be irritated that I'd called him, but he wasn't. He assured me that I'd done the right thing and we both drove back to my house, me following him in his old Mustang.

Officers Norton and Sanford met us. Sanford, a burly guy with a big mustache, was off looking through my barn as I followed the alert Officer Norton. She didn't have her gun drawn, but she kept her hand on her belt as she led the way and seemed to look at everything.

"Ms. Robins, please look closely and let me know if something doesn't look right. Anything. Even if you're not completely sure."

I looked everywhere. Nothing was out of place—well, nothing that hadn't been out of place before. My dining table was covered in paperwork—bills, statements, junk mail. I'd planned on cleaning that up soon—I'd always planned on cleaning that up soon. Last week's newspaper was still folded and wrapped in bright orange plastic, placed on the table next to the couch that I hadn't spent much time on lately. My house was too large for just one person, and weeks could pass when I lived only in the bedroom, bathroom, kitchen, and dining room. Mostly, I was in the barn.

Fortunately, both my kitchen and bathroom were spotless. I might not be tidy, but I was clean. Sadly, my bed wasn't made, but that particular habit wasn't going to change just because the police now knew about it.

"Nothing strange at all. Nope. Nuh-uh," I muttered as we did the walk-through.

By the time we finished both the house and the barn, I was convinced that there was no one unwelcome on my property and maybe I'd imagined the whole thing.

I stood on the front porch with Officers Norton and Sanford as we waited for Officer Brion to reappear. His Mustang was still parked next to the police car, but no one knew where he'd gone. I was somewhat concerned about him, but the other officers assured me that he was fine, just checking in some hidden cranny that no one else had noticed.

"It's what he's the best at," Officer Norton said, sharing a secret smile with Sanford.

"Yeah," Sanford added, "If there's a needle in any haystack, he'll be the one to find it."

"He's the best," Officer Norton repeated. "He'll figure out the Bailey's killer, we have no doubt."

I cringed at the words she used. Bailey's should never be associated with a murder. And yet, now it was—at least temporarily.

Officer Brion reappeared a moment later, carrying in his hands the one thing that would tell both him and me who had most likely been on my porch.

"Ms. Robins, did you notice these out by your strawberries?" He held up a bouquet of flowers—wildflowers, to be exact.

"No, this is the first time I've seen them." My heart hollowed as I realized that it had been Abner on my porch, and I'd not only sped away from him in fear, but called the police on him, too.

"I think I checked everything pretty well, but why don't the two of you look for further evidence out in Ms. Robins' strawberries and pumpkins?" he said to the other officers. "Ms. Robins, let's you and I sit down and get to the bottom of your relationship with Abner Justen."

We sat in my kitchen and I poured him a tall, cold glass of iced tea. He was very thirsty and didn't act as though he was going to light into me, so I relaxed. His tough police exterior seemed to be somewhere else, most likely with his uniform. He wasn't brusque as he asked this round of repeat questions.

"You didn't see the person, though?"

"No, just the shadow."

"So it might not have been Abner."

"No, but I know his arranging. He put that bouquet together. If it wasn't him on the porch, it was someone who'd gotten the flowers from him," I said.

"Why would Abner be at your house?"

"Well, like I told you, we're very good friends."

"But you still claim you didn't know where he lived until last night?"

"Yep."

Officer Brion glanced at me over his iced tea. He was a nice-looking man in that way you'd never notice when he was in uniform. He had almost generic features: medium brown hair and light brown eyes, but once his hair got a little messy, he wasn't so generic. He was probably in his early forties, in good shape but not as good as Officer Norton, and he didn't smile easily.

"I confirmed that Mr. Justen is secretive about the location of his property, but why do you suppose he told Mr. Cartwright the address so easily?"

"He must have really wanted one of Ian's pieces of art. They're pretty wonderful," I said, but I doubted that Sam had any use for yard artwork. Besides, we'd been down this road before.

"But Mr. Cartwright and Mr. Justen hadn't been acquainted before the yard art transaction?"

"I don't think so."

"Hmm. He must have really liked that art."

"Uh-huh." I sensed that he was trying to get me to say something specific, but I had no idea what it was—I worked much better in the worlds of obvious and blatant.

Okay, it *was* odd that Abner gave Ian his address so easily. Very odd. *Had* they known each other? I was under the impression that they hadn't, but I didn't know for sure. I hoped my face didn't show my sudden doubt.

"What else can you tell me about Mr. Justen? We can't find record of him ever being married. Do you know anything about his personal life?"

I sighed. "No, nothing. As well as I knew him, I really don't think I knew him at all, Officer . . . Sam. I'm trying not to be angry about that because everyone has a right to their privacy, but I at least tell my friends where I live and give them my phone number. Anyway, during our excursion last night, I did see the pictures. Do you know who the blonde was?"

"No, I was hoping you might."

"No clue."

Sam sipped at his tea and looked in the direction of the dining room. I decided to fess up.

"There is something else," I said.

"What?"

"Abner called me today."

"Oh?"

I gave him the details, sparse as they were. He took notes and said he'd check my phone record to see what he could find out.

"You know, Ms. Robins, this is a murder investigation. I'd appreciate it if you'd let me know if Mr. Justen attempts to reach you again."

"Sure," I said, appropriately subdued. I should have told him sooner.

"Now, what about tonight?"

"What about it?"

"Is there someone you can call—someone you can ask to come over or someplace you can go? I'll have officers drive by throughout the night, but I want you to feel comfortable."

"Oh, I'll call my sister." I wasn't sure if I would or not, but she'd welcome both me and Hobbit. I didn't think I'd be uncomfortable, though. Even though Officer Brion was pretty convinced that Abner had something to do with Matt Simonsen's death, I still had at least a little doubt. If Abner'd been on my front porch, he'd probably just wanted a friend to talk to. But I couldn't deny the chill that zipped up my spine as I thought about the axe—really, could Abner have used it to kill someone?

"Very good. Would you like me to wait while you call?"

"Oh, no. All is well. I actually have an alarm system." I did, though I hadn't activated it in years. I thought I still had the code written on a piece of paper in a drawer somewhere.

"Well, then, thank you for your time, Ms. Robins. I'll

be in touch, and please let me know if you hear from Mr. Justen again."

"Of course."

I watched the officers drive away. I kept Hobbit at my side as I locked everything and searched for the security system code, to no avail.

Finally, after about fifteen minutes of watching television in my bedroom and imagining all sorts of mysterious noises, I called Allison and told her we were coming over.

I still didn't sleep well.

It wasn't that I was concerned about safety at Allison's house, but I spent most of the night being angry. I was almost 100 percent certain that Abner had been the shadow on my porch. Why the mystery with me? Why hadn't he just shown himself? Why hadn't he called again?

I woke the next morning, anxious to get up and get to work—just not the work at my stall. Without question, I was determined to figure out who killed Matt Simonsen. That earlier jab of denial about the murderer potentially being Abner was lessening with every moment that passed. It wasn't so much that I believed he did it, but if he did do it, I was ready to face that reality and do whatever was necessary to bring him to justice. No matter that we were friends, this craziness had to stop.

Allison and I were up and out of her house early—Hobbit had no interest in rising from the guest futon we'd shared, and Allison's husband would get their son, Mathis, up, dressed, and fed. Large coffees and even larger donuts were our breakfast as I drove us along the highway, pre-crack-of-dawn.

"I understand your determination, Becca," Allison said in between coffee sips, "but be careful."

"I will. I won't do anything crazy, but we know these people, Allison—farmers' market people."

"Everyone's a mystery in some way or another. You've seen that with Abner. Maybe the murder had absolutely nothing to do with market people."

"That's what I'm going to find out."

After a moment of thought she said, "Okay, let me know what I can do to help."

I nodded in the darkness. I thought about telling her my observations of Carl Monroe at the previous day's meeting, but I didn't. There might have been nothing strange about his actions—I'd look into it further, though, then maybe tell her.

"So," she continued. "Jessop Simonsen should be working at Smithfield today. I called Mrs. Simonsen yesterday to let her know about the dinner and the fact that we would have a moment of silence for Matt. She was actually very happy that we were continuing with our plans, by the way. And she said that Jessop *has* to work. He can't deal with sitting around all day thinking about what happened."

"I guess I get that," I said.

"Do you want to talk to him?"

"I don't know. You?"

"I do. I'd like to tell him how sorry I am, but I don't know if the timing will be right."

"It's a tough situation, no matter how you look at it."

"Awful."

Fortunately, Allison and I never ran out of conversation topics, so in order to move away from such sadness, we used the rest of our thirty-minute drive to talk about Mathis and our hippie parents who were currently touring the country in an RV. Neither of us had heard from them in few weeks, but that was nothing new. They'd call when they wanted to talk.

We pulled into Smithfield Market at about 7:00 A.M., earlier than our original plan, but there was still plenty of activity. In line with my belief that Bailey's was the best farmers' market anywhere in the universe, I hadn't spent a lot of time at many others. I knew all about the big ones in South Carolina, and I knew they were just fine when it came to farmers' markets. But Bailey's was the best. Of course, I wasn't beyond knowing that the vendors who worked at other markets probably thought theirs was the best, too.

Smithfield Market was about thirty miles from Bailey's, but it felt like a different world. Bailey's sat on the edge of the town of Monson and was surrounded by hilly land, fertile and deeply green. The Smithfield-area land was just as fertile, but it was flat and tended to brown up a little bit by the end of summer. And, though the town of Smithfield was close to the market, it couldn't be seen, heard, or smelled from the inner sanctum of the market tents.

But Smithfield Market did have one thing that Bailey's didn't have—well, two: funnel cakes and a Ferris wheel. It was as if the two most popular items from the state fair were stored at Smithfield during the off-season. It was too early in the morning for the Ferris wheel to be fired up, but whoever sold the funnel cakes must have already turned on the fryer. The smell of rich dough almost put me into a coma of fried bliss.

We were greeted at the entrance to the market by a very friendly man with a ready smile and the fastest walk I'd ever seen.

"Ms. Reynolds, it's great to see you again," the man said as he pumped her hand.

"Good to see you, too, Jack. This is my sister, Becca. Becca, Jack Wilson, Smithfield Market's manager."

We shook hands, and then he and Allison took off to his office for their business meeting that would apparently include market managers from throughout the state. I was invited to come along, but I couldn't think of anything more boring so I declined, hopefully hiding my terror at the thought of participating in such an activity.

I also wanted to find Jessop Simonsen. Despite what I'd said to Allison, I wasn't hesitant in the least to talk to him. I needed to know more about his father, and he would be the one to talk to. There was nothing easy about death, particularly when murder had been involved, but I'd do my best to be sensitive.

It was still early, so as I walked slowly down the aisles in search of Jessop, I watched the vendors set up their stalls. I compared the tomatoes and corn with what was sold at Bailey's. There probably wasn't much difference, but I was certain that the superior products were most definitely being sold by Barry and Betsy.

A corner booth of one of the aisles stopped me in my tracks, as literally as possible. I stood still, probably with my mouth agape in wonder, staring at the pies that had been created by someone, according to the sign, named Mamma Maria.

Mamma was not your typical mother/baker-type person. Frankly, she reminded me more of a stripper. She was tall, blond, and built—*just like her pies,* I thought to myself. Mamma wore Daisy Duke shorts and a low-cut shirt that I'd probably at least have in my closet if I'd been gifted with such cleavage.

"Hi," she said in my direction. "Like lemon meringue?" She held up an oversize pie, the topping probably almost half a foot high. I'd never seen anything like it.

"I, uh," I stammered.

She laughed. "This is the first time you've seen my pies, huh?" She waved to the back of her stall, where a cooler displayed a number of pies, all of them tall and beautiful and moving in slow circles inside a mechanical case. I focused on one tent card that read Mamma Maria's Mmmm-Amazing Lemon Meringue Pie.

"Yes, actually."

"Well, I make them all myself. I try to get most of my ingredients from here at Smithfield's, but no one's grinding wheat and selling flour here, so I have to get some ingredients from the grocery store. Let me get you a sample. My name's Maria Christopher, but everyone calls me Mamma."

Mamma turned toward the display case and pulled out a pie that had already been cut into. With long red fingernails guiding the way, she sliced a thin but tall piece and put it on a paper plate. She handed me the plate and a plastic fork that had a pink ribbon tied around the end of it.

"Thank you. I'm Becca Robins." The fresh lemon scent filled the air right in front of my nose, and my mouth was already watering explosively. I dug in.

"Mmmm," I mumbled as I chewed and enjoyed the melting sensation of the treat. "This is fantastic." Everything about the pie was perfect: the tart lemon, the light but tall meringue, the flaky crust.

"Thank you."

"You're welcome. And I'll take one, if you don't mind keeping it in your cooler until I'm done shopping for the day."

"Not a problem." Mamma turned again and put a small piece of paper with the word *SOLD* written on it beside one of the pies in the case. "So, where are you from?"

"I live outside Monson, but I work at Bailey's Farmers' Market."

"Oh yeah, what do you sell?"

"Jams and preserves—berries and pumpkin."

"Those sound yummy. I've been meaning to make my way up to Bailey's. A friend of mine left here and moved up there."

"Who?" *Did she know Matt Simonsen?*

"Ian Cartwright. Do you know him?"

"Ian worked here?" I swallowed the next bite without letting it melt first.

"Yes."

Now wait, I wanted to say, *why didn't I know that?* Ian hadn't said a word about working at Smithfield. If he'd worked here, he would have at least met Matt Simonsen.

"How long did he work here?"

Mamma shrugged. "About a year, I guess."

"Really?"

"Yes," she said, her eyebrows together. She was probably wondering why I was having a hard time grasping the concept of Ian working anywhere but Bailey's.

"You were friends?" I finally said.

"Yes. Oh, not that kind of friends. We were *just* friends." She smiled.

She thought I was jealous—I might have been if my mind had gone that direction. She thought Ian and I were "involved" or I wanted us to be involved. In truth, I was just attempting to understand why he'd hidden the fact that he'd worked with Matt Simonsen from me—and maybe from Allison and Officer Brion, too. I squashed the desire to burst into the managers' meeting and tell my sister what I'd just learned.

"Well, I hope he's doing okay up there," Mamma Maria continued.

"I think so," I said, forcing my voice to be even.

"Yes, he was very popular here."

"Why did he leave?"

"Um, well, I don't really know. You'll have to ask him. He still has customers who ask about him, but maybe he felt like he'd saturated the market. Maybe Bailey's expands his customer base."

"Maybe. Well, Bailey's *is* a great place, despite what you might have heard lately."

Her eyebrows knit together again as she put her hands on her hips. "Yeah, I heard about the . . . the murder. Just terrible."

"Horrible." And it was, but I had come to get answers, so I pushed forward. "I bet you knew Matt Simonsen."

"Sort of. Didn't know him all that well. Simonsen Orchards has had a booth here for a long time. It's at the other end of the market and down the next aisle. Speaking of expanding market base, I heard they wanted to grow their business, so the father went to Bailey's. Jessop still works here, but he's extremely shy." She looked in the direction of the younger Simonsen's booth and her forehead crinkled. "We knew something had happened when Jessop didn't show up that day. The Simonsens—at least one of them at a time—were never absent. They don't take a day off. Ever. They're part of the old-timer group. When they worked together, one of them was always around. When Matt went to Bailey's, I did wonder how they were going to get their orchard work done if both of them had to be someplace every day."

And now there would be one less Simonsen to get the work done. We didn't say the words, but we both thought them.

"Matt only recently started working at Bailey's, so I didn't know him well, but I heard he was a hard worker," I said.

Mamma nodded. "Don't suppose anyone knows what happened? It's creepy, you know."

"I have no idea what the police think," I lied. "Did you know of anyone who disliked Matt—any enemies or anything? Other vendors, customers?"

Mamma bit at the inside of her cheek. "Gosh, I don't have the slightest idea. I don't . . . didn't know them nearly well enough to answer that. They kept to themselves. They are . . . were hard workers. Friendly to their customers, from everything I've heard."

As Mamma's cell phone rang, relief relaxed her pretty face. She was glad to have an excuse to end our conversation.

"Hey, thanks," I said. "I'll be back later to get my pie."

She smiled again and answered the phone as I took off toward Jessop Simonsen. I wanted to call Ian immediately and ask just why he hadn't told me about working at Smithfield. Surely he'd known Matt Simonsen. I slipped my questions for him to the back burner of my busy mind. I'd talk to him, but for now I had other people to talk to.

Someone had wanted Matt Simonsen dead, and I thought that if that person wasn't Abner, then the murderer might have something to do with the place where Matt apparently spent most of his time—Smithfield Market. Mamma had said that Matt went to Bailey's to expand his customer base, but that didn't sit right with me. It made sense that Ian might have needed to expand his market—really, a person needed only one of his products. But peaches brought repeat customers. Like my own products, if someone liked them, they tended come back for more. Something else must have happened to send Matt away from Smithfield and to Bailey's.

Maybe I could get the answers from Jessop. And if he wouldn't answer my questions, Mamma had shown me how easy it would be to ask other vendors. I'd get the story, no matter who I had to talk to.

The funnel cake cart was right next to the Simonsen Orchards stall. Hanging from the display rack were three fresh cakes, glistening with oil and powdered sugar. I was there to do a job, not indulge my sweet/fried tooth, so I ignored my salivating mouth and stood on the other side of the aisle, pretending to be interested in some hand-painted greeting cards as I observed the man I assumed was Jessop Simonsen.

He was tall, like his father, but didn't have the same wide build. Instead, he was almost skinny. He wore old jeans and a clean white T-shirt underneath a brown body apron emblazoned with a bright peach iron-on patch. My mind played back the horrible picture of the dead body, and I remembered that Matt had had dark, almost black, hair. Jessop had dark auburn hair, cut fairly short. He was almost gangly but still kind of handsome. He was packaging up some peaches into a recyclable bag, and the look on his face was intense and serious. A middle-aged couple stood in front of his stall and seemed to watch Jessop closely, saying things that prompted him to put down whatever peach he had in his hand and search for another one. He took the picky customers in stride and didn't act impatient or put-out in the least.

When he had filled the bag, he looked back up at the customers and smiled easily. This confirmed that he was definitely handsome—and that he had a beautiful mouth. I wouldn't have called him feminine-looking, but he had a lovely pair of lips.

Once the transaction was complete, Jessop went back to his table full of peaches and rearranged the mess he'd made. The look on his face wasn't quite so relaxed anymore. In fact, it was pained. He might have been working to keep from thinking about the murder, but he was certainly distressed about something. Apparently, there weren't enough customers to keep the horrible thoughts at bay all the time.

My heart sank. This man's father was dead, killed, maybe killed by someone I considered a friend. Anger soured my throat. Who had done this? And if it was Abner, I might not be beyond harming him myself. A family had been torn apart.

"Can I help you?" a young girl with long braids asked as she pulled her tired eyes up and away from a thick textbook.

"No, thanks. Just looking around."

She looked back down at the book.

I calmed my anger and gathered the courage to go talk to Jessop. It was much more difficult than I'd thought it would be, but I couldn't *not* talk to him.

As I walked toward the stall, Jessop looked up and flipped an inner switch that made his misery disappear.

"Hi, what can I get for you today?" he asked pleasantly.

"I . . . My name is Becca Robins."

"Nice to meet you, Becca. I'm Jessop Simonsen." He was attempting to keep his customer service mode flipped on, but my monotone greeting must have sounded strange.

"I know, Mr. . . . I mean Jessop."

"Yes? Can I help you, Ms. Robins?"

"Jessop, I work at Bailey's Farmers' Market. I just wanted to stop by and tell you how very sorry I am for your loss."

"Oh." Jessop looked confused, perhaps shocked. "Well, thank you."

There might never have been a more awkward moment in my life. Fortunately, Jessop saved me.

"It's very kind of you to stop by. Is that why you came here today?"

"Well, my sister manages Bailey's. She came down for a meeting. I came along to give her some company—I'm sorry if I disturbed you."

"Oh. Your sister—Allison Something?"

"Yes. Reynolds. Allison Reynolds."

"She talked to my mom. She sent some flowers, too . . . that was nice."

"We know the police are working hard to figure out who . . . what happened."

"Oh, I know who killed my father," Jessop said. Suddenly, his eyes filled with both anger and tears. He cleared his throat as he turned to rearrange the peaches again. The tears never fell down his cheeks.

"You do?"

"Yes." He looked at me, tear-free but full of dangerous anger. "Abner Justen killed my father as sure as I stand here today."

"Really? What makes you so sure?" My chest tightened. He sounded so certain.

"I just know, that's all."

"Have you explained to the police why you think that?"

"Of course. They'll find evidence, I'm positive, but for now they've got nothing substantial."

I nodded. "So, they had a history, your father and Abner?"

Jessop huffed. "I'd say. Fifty years or more."

"Wow, that's a long time."

"Well, if Abner wasn't such a sore loser, this never would have happened. By the time Dad started working at Bailey's, Abner should have been long over it."

"Sore loser?" I wanted to keep him talking. "What, a land deal or something?" It was the best I could come up with.

Jessop huffed. "Not quite. Aw, hell, I guess it wouldn't hurt to tell you."

"Only if you're comfortable with that, Jessop. I'm not a gossiper . . ." I should have been ashamed of myself—this was none of my business. *But it is my business*, I mantra'd silently. I'd made it my business, if nothing else.

Jessop sighed deeply. As he released the air from his lungs, I heard a hitch of emotion. He was hurting in ways I didn't ever want to experience firsthand.

"It was my mother," he muttered.

"Excuse me?"

"My mother. Abner was in love with my mother. He was dating her when she met my father. She dumped Abner for my dad." A nerve twitched at the side of Jessop's face. He looked down and away from my eyes.

"Oh my," I said with my own heavy sigh. "Did you tell the police?"

"Of course. They'll catch him."

"Oh my," I repeated. As far as motives went, I could imagine the organ keys of doom now announcing Abner's guilt. "I didn't know, Jessop. I'm sorry."

"S'okay. They'll catch him. Hey, could you excuse me, please?" His voice cracked.

"Of course." I watched Jessop turn and walk out the back of his stall. I felt terrible for being the cause of such emotion—it hadn't been my intention. I was also simmering with anger. If Abner had called me at that moment, I probably would have answered only so I could hang up on him.

I debated whether I should leave or stay and apologize to Jessop again for disturbing his day, but if I were him, I wouldn't want to see me when I came back. I turned to walk away, my appetite for funnel cake reduced to nothing.

The market was already getting crowded, which was normal for a Thursday at most markets. I dodged people at about every third step as my thoughts performed mental gymnastics. It sure seemed like Abner could have been the murderer. But—I had to remember—seeming guilty and really being so was always a matter of evidence.

What about those pictures—that woman, was she Jessop's mother? Was that evidence? Officer Brion had asked me if I knew who was in the picture—he'd acted like he didn't know. Did that mean he really didn't know, or that he knew and was just trying to get more information? Probably the latter. Did he know that Abner had been in love with Matt Simonsen's wife? It was a long time ago, but still . . .

And what did Ian have to do with all of this?

I didn't realize I had stopped walking until an elderly lady bumped into me.

"Oh, dear, pardon me," she said.

"No, I'm sorry. Are you all right?"

"Fine, fine." She waved me away and continued her walk/shuffle. As I watched her to make sure she was none the worse for wear, something down the aisle caught my attention.

If he hadn't been so tall, I might not have thought I was seeing Carl Monroe, the Bailey's peach vendor who seemed to want to give me the brush-off yesterday, moving quickly away from me.

I knew I was seeing a tall person with short dark hair zigging and zagging away through the crowd, but I couldn't tell for sure if it was Carl.

Suddenly, he stopped moving and turned. He looked directly at me, his eyes wide and afraid. I lifted my hand to wave hello, but he turned and hurried on his way. Again. The man was trying to give me a complex.

"What the . . . ?" I took off running, unfortunately bumping right into the woman I'd stopped in front of a moment before.

"Young lady, have you been drinking?"

"No, ma'am."

"Drugs, then?"

"No, ma'am. I'm very sorry. Are you okay?"

"Yes, I'm fine, but you either need to slow down or walk at a steady pace. You're going to hurt someone. And if you are doing drugs, get some help."

"Yes, ma'am. Thank you." I took a wide step to the other side of the aisle and continued the chase after Carl Monroe.

I thought I'd lost him, but then I caught sight of his dark hair again as I rounded a corner. He was so tall and I was so short that I had to resort to jumping every few steps to keep track of him.

If my short-term memory was correct, he was about to reach a sort of fork in the aisles. He would have two paths to choose from. I stopped jumping so that I could just run as fast as possible to try to get close enough to see which way he went.

Right before I reached the fork, I jumped one more time. I got lucky; I saw Carl Monroe turn to the right—he was so tall he couldn't really hide. I turned up my speed and ignored the looks and exclamations of irritation directed my way.

I moved as quickly as I could and got lucky again. Suddenly the aisle cleared; I'd be able to veer right easily. Unfortunately, all my jumping hadn't made me privy to the fact that after I turned onto the new aisle, I should have moved slightly to the left to avoid a collision with a man carrying two cases of huge, fresh, ripe, and beautiful tomatoes.

I'm not sure I've ever seen anything like the tackle I inflicted on the poor tomato man. I had just the right momentum to smack into him with my full body, propelling him backward and all of those lovely tomatoes even farther backward and airborne, splatting on tables, poles, tent walls, and people.

As I lay on top of the man I'd taken down, I looked up and around at the unbelievable mess I'd caused. It was as though time had stopped as vendors and customers looked at me, at the mess, back at me, and at the tomato juice that dripped everywhere.

"Becca?" My sister appeared from bchind somconc with a huge red splat on their white T-shirt.

From the ground, atop the poor man I'd assaulted, I waved feebly and wished for the earth to open up and swallow me whole.

Nine

The good news: no one was hurt.

The not-so-good news: Carl Monroe got away, I'd made a complete fool of myself, there was tomato juice everywhere, and the old woman was now convinced that I was definitely either drunk or doing drugs.

Garrett Martinez fortunately had a great sense of humor. I'd taken him down and ruined his tomatoes, but he managed to lasso in any anger he felt and replace it with something that reminded me of hysterical humor.

Not everyone who'd been hit by a tomato found it quite as funny, but between Allison and myself, we extended apologies and promises to replace their clothing, and I probably offered to give away all of my upcoming season's pumpkin preserves if they came to Bailey's and reminded me what had happened.

With wet towels, Allison and I cleaned up what we

could from product displays. The dirt floor would eventually soak in whatever else remained.

It was honestly one of my worst moments, ever.

"Garrett, you will take this money and you won't argue with me any further," I said as I handed him some bills.

"It was only two small cases, Becca. I have lots more tomatoes, and you're giving me enough money for about five cases."

"Please take the money. The inconvenience I've caused is beyond what this covers, anyway."

"Accidents happen." Garrett shrugged. "Here." He took the money, kept one bill, the denomination of which I couldn't discern, took my hand, slapped the rest back into it, curled my fingers, and smiled. "You've had a rough day. I'm not upset—no one is hurt. I'll come see you at Bailey's. My mouth waters at the thought of pumpkin preserves on my toast this winter." He turned and presumably went to get more tomatoes, or change clothes.

"It's all right, Becca. He's right, accidents happen." Allison pushed back a stray hair that had fallen out of her ponytail. "We've got things pretty well put back together here. And Jack isn't upset in the least."

"Good." That was the last thing Allison needed—a market manager angry at her for anything. "What a morning."

"Why were you running?"

"Carl Monroe." I took the wet towel she was holding, dipped it in a bucket full of water, and wrung it out for one more swipe over a table.

"Our Carl Monroe—peach seller?"

"Yep, the same one."

"I don't understand."

"Come on, let's put this stuff away and pick up my pie, and I'll tell you all about it."

Once we were on the road and had stopped talking about the pie and how it defied all logic and physics, I told Allison what I'd learned.

"Can you believe that Ian worked at Smithfield and he didn't tell me?" I said as I slowed my truck for a red traffic light.

"Becca, I knew Ian worked at Smithfield. I didn't think to tell you. I'm sure he told the police."

"Oh. Well, I suppose he doesn't owe me any sort of explanation, but still . . . we went out to Abner's together. It would have been a good time to tell me he knew Matt Simonsen."

"He might not have known him well enough for it to matter."

"Or he did know him well—too well."

"There is that, but I find it hard to believe that Ian—or Carl Monroe, for that matter—could kill anyone. You say you saw Carl leave the meeting suspiciously yesterday?"

"Yes, and then he ran from me today."

"I don't understand it, but there's probably a reasonable explanation. You can talk to him at Bailey's."

"I will."

"I think the item of most interest is Abner's past with Matt Simonsen's wife. I'm trying very hard not to suspect Abner—don't want to, definitely can't let anyone other than you think I do—but his past romance just adds another brick in the wall, if you know what I mean," Allison said.

"That plus his sudden disappearance don't bode well," I said.

"No."

"But there's one thing that I keep getting hung up on."

"What?"

"Abner is really short," I said with a slap to the steering wheel.

"Yes."

"Matt Simonsen was really tall and his head was bashed in—I think from the top, not the back or the side. Even if Abner had used the axe, he couldn't have reached the top of Matt's head. Do you know which it was? I didn't look closely enough."

Allison was silent, so I looked at her. Her eyebrows where high. "No, Becca, I don't know which it was. You could call Officer Brion, though, and ask. You and he seem to be spending a lot of time together."

"Good idea."

"I was kind of kidding, Becca."

"Not me. I'm gonna call right now."

Officer Brion first wanted to know if I was all right. I told him I was fine but had a question.

"I don't know why I'm telling you this, but the blow came from behind and landed on top of the right rear quad rant of the cranium," he said as though he had the file open in front of him.

"Thank you. Was the axe the murder weapon?"

"I'm not going to give you that information."

"Darn."

"Don't hesitate to call again if I can help in any way," he said with the same sarcastic tone Allison had used a moment ago.

I told Allison what he had and *hadn't* said and finished with, "See, whoever hit Matt Simonsen had to be tall, maybe as tall as Carl Monroe."

"Possibly," Allison said doubtfully, "but there are lots of ways someone can be higher up than another person—stand on a chair, a table, sprout wings, something."

"True, but I can't imagine how you could surprise someone and kill them from behind if you're standing on something."

"Dunno. But don't forget—no evidence, no guilty." Allison wagged her finger back and forth.

"Right," I muttered. I was leaning more toward thinking everyone was guilty, but I didn't say that to her. "Next stop, Bailey's."

I had lots of people I wanted to talk to.

Ten

I tried not to take it personally that everyone I wanted to talk to wasn't at work. No surprise that Abner wasn't there, but Carl wasn't there, either, his stall empty of even his display tables. It looked as if he'd packed up for the season, which was possible, but Allison hadn't heard from him so she had no idea.

And last but far from least, Ian wasn't there. He didn't necessarily keep to a strict schedule, so Allison thought he was probably in his garage/studio working on projects.

"Come on, Sis, he knows where I live. He won't mind me knowing where he lives. He told me it was a garage in town."

"He didn't answer his cell—I'm not going to give out someone's address if they haven't given me the okeydokey. You're out of luck. Sorry."

I sighed heavily and put my hands on my hips. She wouldn't budge; I was sure of it. But I had other methods.

"Fine. I get it," I said too willingly. Allison looked at me with obvious suspicion.

"You have another idea. Don't tell me what it is. Go. Out of my office. I have work to do."

I turned to leave.

"And thanks for the company to Smithfield this morning," she said to my back.

I turned. "Thanks for letting me and Hobbit crash at your house. I'll pick her up on my way home."

"No hurry."

I walked out of the office and took an immediate left. The market office was brick and mortar, but the tent walls began immediately on each side of the small building. I looked around, saw that I wasn't being watched, stepped through the tent opening, and was suddenly well hidden in a small enclosure. I was at the back of Herb and Don's stall, where they had a small area walled off for storage—that was where I'd gone. I loved their oregano, but in this small space the scents from their herbs were a bit much. I crouched down, knowing I could watch the office door from my secret spot and Allison wouldn't see me lurking.

I did take a moment to debate the intelligence associated with my plan. I was sure Ian would eventually call either me or Allison and gladly tell one of us where he lived. Maybe.

What if he didn't call? And what if he was somehow involved in the murder? The fact that he hadn't told me that he'd worked with Matt Simonsen sat wonky in my gut and made me think he was hiding something. If I could find out where he lived, I could surprise him with a visit. And since he wasn't in the phone book, I'd resorted to hiding and breaking and entering.

I pulled out my phone and called Linda.

"Hello, there. Where are you?" she said.

"Hey, Linda," I whispered from my crouch.

"Becca, why are you whispering?"

"I'll explain later. I have a favor to ask."

"Sure. What's up?"

"Yes, ma'am," I heard Don say from the other side of the wall to the storage area. "Let me see if I've got enough in the back."

Really? You've got to be kidding.

"Hang on, Linda," I said. I could either go out the way I came in or lie flat behind a taller stack of boxes. Don would surely see the tent wall flap if I left, so I chose to crawl and flatten myself into the dirt floor.

"Becca, Becca, what's going on?" Linda said.

Don pulled back the booth's wall in a flourish, sending a bunch of dirt flying directly into my nose. I swallowed and rubbed the roof of my mouth with my tongue, doing everything I could to stifle a sneeze. I was flat on my stomach and I planted my face into the floor. Direct from the ostrich school of hiding: if I couldn't see him, he couldn't see me, right?

"Becca?" Linda said again. I'd kept the phone at my ear while putting my face in the dirt, and this made me want to giggle. So now I had to stifle both a sneeze and a giggle.

Don whistled as he moved boxes somewhere on the other side of the storage area—right where I'd been crouching. I had no idea what tune it was, but he hit the high notes with style.

"Here it is," he said. "I found plenty, ma'am."

In only another second he was out of the storage area and back to the front of his stall.

I sat up and wiped the dirt off my face.

"Linda."

"Becca, what the hell . . . ?"

"Hey, could you just call Allison and ask her to come over to your stall and help you with something?"

"Uh."

"Please."

"Okay. Sure. I'll come up with something."

"Thank you." I closed the phone and crawled back to the other side of the storage area. If Don had to come back there again, I wasn't going to hide. There was a better way to do this, I was sure, but I didn't take the time to figure it out.

I peeked out of the side opening and waited. A short moment later, Allison hurried out of the office building.

"Good job, Linda," I muttered. She must have come up with something good to put Allison in such a hurry.

I looked around again—this side of the tents and the office building were facing the main parking lot and there were people walking here and there, most of them toward the entrance to the market that was on the other side of the office. But it wouldn't be too strange to see someone appear from the back of a tent, so I stood straight and walked out, making sure I looked like I knew what I was doing.

I stepped back into the office building and turned the knob on Allison's office door.

Of course, it was locked. But that was easily overcome. Allison kept an emergency key on the frame above the door—I'd seen her use it only once, but the moment had made an impression. Allison was über-organized—the fact that she needed an emergency key made her more human than I'd previously given her credit for.

I swept my finger over the dusty frame, found the key, wiped it on my T-shirt, unlocked the door, and closed and locked it behind me.

"*Phew*," I whispered to myself.

Allison's door was probably circa 1970-something, and it had a window on the top. The pane was made of frosted glass so no one could see through it in either direction, but the fact that it was there made me feel exposed. I hurried to the desk.

I wasn't exactly sure where Allison kept the vendor files, but after a quick opening and closing of a couple of metal drawers, I found a file tab that read Vendor Applications.

There wasn't time to be nosy about anyone other than Ian. He was right there, the first one in the C section.

I grabbed a pen and a Post-It and jotted down the address. I was familiar with that part of town—all of the streets were named after Ivy League universities. Ian lived on Harvard Avenue. I hurried the file back into place and closed the drawer, grabbed the Post-It, and put it into my pocket. If Allison wasn't on the other side of her door right now, it looked as though I'd managed my cloak-and-dagger maneuver.

But just as I put my hand on the doorknob, another idea popped into my head. Allison had mentioned that Abner had listed his sister's address on his application. That address suddenly seemed like something I needed to have.

I went back to the drawer and fingered through the files to the Js.

Abner did, indeed, list an address other than the one I now knew was his—and it just happened to be located on Yale Avenue. I thought I was imagining things, so I double-checked Ian's address.

Both of them lived in the same part of town—one street away from each other.

"Well, that's interesting."

Coincidence?

There wasn't time to ponder the question, so I wrote down Abner's sister's address and put it in my pocket, too, and then went back to the door.

The office building wasn't large, and even though Allison's door was a few steps in from the building's front door, she had a window that faced the front parking lot.

A blind was closed over the window, so I couldn't see anything but I could hear some sort of diesel vehicle pull up right next to the window. There wasn't a parking space, but I'd seen people stop there when they wanted to talk briefly to Allison or someone else in the office.

The diesel engine sputtered loudly outside the window. I wanted to leave the office, but whoever belonged to that truck would no doubt see me. I didn't want that, so I stood still, my hand almost on the doorknob, and waited.

Someone approached—I could see the shadow through the frosted pane. I stepped to the side of the door so they wouldn't see mine. The person knocked forcefully.

"Ms. Reynolds! Ms. Reynolds!" The male voice sounded urgent and maybe angry.

I didn't really recognize the voice, but there was something familiar about it. I wanted him to speak again.

Instead, he reached for the knob and started to shake it. The maneuver sent me back to the desk, and though I didn't think he could get the locked door open, the whole building was old enough that a good yank or shove might do the trick. He shook the knob more forcefully, sending the entire frame into a stiff warble.

I didn't know what else to do, so I crouched and hid under the desk.

"Ms. Reynolds!" he yelled this time. Now I thought he must be angry, but I couldn't be sure. He was silent long enough that I crawled out from under the desk. The shadow wasn't on the other side of the door any longer. Outside the office window, the slam of a truck door sounded just before the diesel engine revved and tires sprayed gravel.

I leapt over a chair, went to the window, and pulled back the blind, but I was too late. I could only see the brown truck from behind. There was no way to distinguish who was in the driver's seat.

But at that moment, two things became very clear in my mind—the shadow had been very tall. And Carl Monroe drove a brown diesel truck.

I had one more address to gather. And if Carl Monroe lived on Princeton Avenue, I'd know I'd gone beyond coincidence.

But just as I turned away from the window, I heard Allison's voice as she walked back into the building. She was talking on her cell phone, and the volume of her voice increased as she got closer. My gut got mushy.

She was my sister and she wouldn't hate me for long, but I didn't want to be caught by anyone. And the fact that I was sneaking around on my own twin made me feel worse.

But other than throwing myself out the window, I didn't have much choice but to wait and confess my sins.

Eleven

Somewhere in my youth or childhood, I must have done something good. Though it hadn't felt like it over the last few seconds of panic, I must have been living right somewhere along the way. Allison finished her phone call before sliding the key into the lock. Then, just as I was ready to throw myself at her mercy, her phone rang again. I couldn't make out her words precisely, but I thought I heard her say that she'd be "right there."

She left the small building, and I left her office as though the fires of hell burned at my feet, which in actuality they probably did. I'd later feel the heavy weight of guilt about my illegal and disloyal activities, but for now, I was grateful for the addresses I'd acquired and wasn't willing to push my luck further for Carl's. Ian and Abner's sister would be a good start.

I locked Allison's door and hurried out of the building, only to be greeted by Barry and a wagon full of corn.

"Hey, there, Becca. Where're you off to in such a flurry?" he said.

"Oh, hi, Barry. I'm just going to run some errands." I ignored the desire to sprint to my truck. I also ignored the anger I felt about Barry's lies about just how well he knew Matt Simonsen. What he'd told me the day of the murder and what he'd shared in the market meeting didn't jibe. Another day, another time, a time when I wouldn't be afraid of getting caught, I would have a bunch of questions for Barry. As it was, I just wanted to get away and get to the Ivy League neighborhood.

"Don't you usually work on Thursdays?"

"Yeah, but I hung out with Allison today—we went to a meeting."

Barry looked at me like I was speaking Martian. He was probably wondering just what meeting I would willingly attend that he hadn't been invited to. He was also smart enough to be suspicious that I hadn't pushed him regarding his lies.

"Oh, well, all right, then. I needed to ask Allison a question. Is she in there?"

"No. Not at the moment. She got a call and hurried off somewhere." I waved my hand through the air and then swiped a wisp of hair off my forehead. If Officer Brion had been watching, he'd have known I was guilty of something. Body language was probably one of his specialties. "Hey, Barry, have you seen Carl today?"

"Uh, nope. Come to think of it, I wondered about him, too. It seems kind of sparse in there. We have to move past this tragedy. You know that, don't you, Becca?"

"Sure. Yeah, I'm sorry. I'll be back tomorrow. I'm sure Carl will, too."

"Uh-huh."

"Hey, gotta go, Barry, but I'll see you tomorrow. Promise." I needed to get out of there before Allison returned. She'd know I'd been up to something.

"Good. Well, I guess I'll see you later, then." Barry's nostrils flared roundly and he took off with the wagon.

I didn't run, but I walked at breakneck speed to my truck. Once there, I took a deep breath and calmed my heartbeat down to something that wouldn't attract vampires. I didn't have the constitution for criminal behavior.

The short trip to the Ivy League neighborhood of Monson al-lowed me to clear my head—I hadn't gotten caught, that was good.

I needed to find out what Ian really knew about Matt Simonsen, and I needed to attempt not to be irritated at him for not telling me the information sooner. He wasn't obliged to. But still, he should have said *something*. And perhaps I could get something useful out of Abner's sister. I wasn't quite sure what I wanted to get out of her, but I'd figure that out.

The Ivy League neighborhood was one of my favorites. I'd often thought that if I ever got tired of my wide-open spaces, which was unlikely, I'd want to live in one of the old homes on Harvard, Princeton, or Yale. The yards were filled with tall trees and there was nothing cookie-cutter about the houses, most of which were made of brick. My favorite coffee shop and bookstore were also nestled quaintly on one corner. "Nestled" was the best word to use when describing this neighborhood.

Ian's was my first stop. I turned onto Harvard and searched for the address. The house was spectacular. It was tall, with lots of windows, a line of small ones across the second—or was that the third?—floor. The architecture was French Tudor and made me think of pastries. I parked in front and headed for the driveway. If Ian lived in the garage, it must be somewhere along that path.

I debated whether I should stop at the house and announce myself, but I decided not to. The garage was, indeed, at the end of the long driveway, and Ian's truck was parked to the side of it.

I didn't see anyone else as I made my way, but as I approached the garage, I heard the rumble of music. It wasn't loud enough to reach the house or any of the other houses in the area, but it vibrated the aluminum garage door.

There were no windows in the front, but there was a side door that had a window at the top of it. I shaded against the glare with my hand and peered in.

Ian was there, working on something that required the use of a large polishing cloth. He was shirtless, so I was getting to see some of his tattoos.

I pressed my nose closer.

He was working on a round piece of metal, flat and about the size of a basketball. The large cloth moved quickly over the surface. The force of his efforts caused the muscles in his arms and chest to expand and contract enough that the starlike design on his right forearm and the lines of a design I couldn't quite distinguish on the left side of his chest moved. The tattoos were both only in black ink, and they blended with his skin more than they stood out.

Ian was thin, but there was nothing skinny about him. And even more than my voyeuristic enjoyment of looking at his body, I liked watching him move. He was athletic; smooth, with the ability to make his body do sports things. I'd never quite gotten there, having given up on sports after a terrible childhood experience with kickball. From my vantage point, I concluded that Ian probably hadn't ever had a bad day of kickball. Most likely, he'd ruled the field.

He had on jeans, so if there were any other tattoos, I'd have to get to know him better to see them. I pulled my nose away from the glass and lifted my hand to knock.

"Can I help you?" a voice said from behind me.

"Oh!" I turned, fully expecting to see Officer Brion. But it wasn't a police officer at all. An old man, in a bow tie and suit, held his hat in his hand as he inspected me, the intruder.

"I'm sorry. I'm a friend of Ian's. I was just about to knock. Should I have stopped by the house first?"

"Not at all, dear. You were standing there for so long I wondered if there was some problem."

My cheeks heated from the blush that must have been close to neon. I didn't know what to say.

"It's all right. I understand. Believe it or not, I was young once, too. I'm George McKinney. Your friend is making good use of an old man's garage. Had my driving rights taken away from me a couple years back." He tapped his glasses. "Peepers don't peep as well anymore. Now I take the bus everywhere." He sighed as though he'd resigned himself to the task. "Ian's good for the garage and good company for me."

"Nice to meet you. I'm Becca Robins."

We shook hands. "Pleasure to meet you." He inspected me for a beat more and then nodded. "I'll be off, then. If that young man gives you any trouble, my back door is always unlocked. You can run in there and either use the phone or grab a knife to slice him open."

"Oh. Well, all right. I appreciate that."

George nodded, put his hat on, and then took off in

a spry walk down the driveway. I turned and knocked. Knocked again, with enough force to be heard over the music this time.

Ian looked up from his work and squinted toward the door. I waved. His face was first full of question, but then softened into a smile. He gave me the one-second sign, turned off the music, and pulled on a gray T-shirt.

"Becca?" he said as he opened the door. "Good to see you."

"Hey, Ian. Thanks."

The awkward silence didn't last long.

"Well, come on in. My shop isn't spotless, but it's been much worse."

During my earlier spying, I hadn't noticed just how wonderful the garage was. But now I took the time to look around. There were parts of Ian's sculptures everywhere. Spires, tubes, balls, starbursts; the designs were endless. Everything was placed on large tables, and though I hadn't noticed them before, there were windows all along the back and one of the side walls. There were two large machines against the garage door, both with big belts.

"This is something, Ian," I said.

"It's a good space."

"Yeah."

"So, uh, can I get you something to drink? You thirsty? You okay?"

"I'm a little thirsty, but I'm fine. Why?" I said. He was peering at me strangely.

"You look like you might have had a rough day or something."

"Really?" I looked down at myself. Tomato juice splatted over almost every inch of my shirt, overalls, and legs.

Over the tomato juice, there was a layer of dirt from my body plant in the back of Herb and Don's tent. "Oh, I'd forgotten all about this." I laughed. I must have been a sight.

Ian licked his thumb before wiping it over my jawline. "What's all this?"

"Uh, well, it's tomato juice and dirt. Long story." I thought I should tell him that touching me, especially with his saliva attached, wasn't appropriate, but I didn't want to.

He smiled. "You have adventures that you don't even realize."

"Something like that."

"Well, how about a soda? You're more than welcome to clean up in my bathroom, but you don't have to."

"Actually, that would be great. Thanks." I was suddenly self-conscious about my state. How could he take my questions seriously if I looked like I'd had a rough day drinking Bloody Marys on a beach somewhere? And why, all of a sudden, did I not feel angry at him or the urgency to ask the questions? His spit must have magical powers.

"This way." Ian turned and walked toward the back of the shop. "It's just a ladder, but it's pretty sturdy. My landlord's an old guy, and he had it reinforced so he'd feel safe climbing it." Ian pulled down a ladder that unfolded as it fell from the ceiling.

"I met him."

"George?"

"Yep. I was spying on you before I knocked, and he caught me. He gave me full permission to use one of his kitchen knives if you were trouble."

Ian blinked his dark eyes and then laughed. "Well,

George is a murder-mystery fanatic. Loves talking about anything bloody. His eyes aren't so great anymore, so I sometimes read to him at night."

"You do?" I couldn't imagine it.

"Uh-huh. You were spying on me?"

"Uh-huh." We looked at each other for a beat, both of us wondering things that weren't ready to be spoken. "I wanted to make sure you didn't look murderous."

"Okay. Apparently I didn't?"

I nodded. "So's the bathroom up there?"

"Yep." Ian led the way and then helped me as I reached the top rung and stepped into the apartment.

I knew that later I'd have to describe to Allison what it looked like, so I registered my first impression and went from there. It was masculine, but cute and cozy and well lit, with lots of windows along the back wall. There was one large room divided into different areas, everything either brown, tan, or navy blue. We'd stepped into the TV area, where a worn brown leather couch faced a television as small as my own. The coffee table in front of the couch was covered with organized stacks of paperwork and a laptop. The kitchen area lined the wall behind the couch. Everything was small—the stove, the refrigerator, and the two-place table. On the other side of the room, closed off by a tall three-panel divider, was the bed. Even though it was mostly hidden, I could tell it was made.

"Bathroom's over there." Ian pointed to our left.

"Thanks."

"There're towels and stuff under the sink."

"Thanks." I hurried into the small room and closed the door. It was spotless, which was a pleasant surprise. There was no tub, but there were a shower, a toilet, and a sink, and clean towels and washcloths right where he said they'd be.

There was also a mirror—the image in which would haunt me for years. How had I not realized that my face was covered with tomato pox? Why hadn't Allison or Barry said something? But ours was not a clean career—maybe it was just the world we lived and worked in, and they saw nothing unusual in it.

Farmers' market careers aren't for the dainty or those who don't want to get a little dirty. The nature of our work is physical, and it frequently takes place either in the out-of-doors or in open spaces. It's wonderful and full of fresh air, but it's also grimy.

I rinsed off my face, arms, and hands and called it good. The damage had been done anyway. Then I decided I needed a good mental talking-to, so I sobered my face and looked directly into the mirror.

That's enough flirting. You're here to ask serious questions. Get serious. The look of doubt that was returned did not instill the confidence I'd hoped for.

At least my face was cleaner, I thought, as I left the bathroom.

Ian was staring inside his open refrigerator.

"It's a good thing your landlord can't see well. He'd have probably called the Centers for Disease Control if he'd noticed all the stuff on my face."

Ian turned and smiled. "Or he would have wanted the gory details on how you became infected. So, diet or regular soda? And I don't suppose you like beef jerky? That's all I have at the moment."

"Regular soda, and I'm not hungry, but I like beef jerky just as much as anyone else."

"Ice or not?"

"Straight from the can or bottle is perfect."

Ian shrugged, pulled out two cans of soda, and walked around the couch.

"Have a seat." He waited until I sat on one end of the couch before he sat in the middle of it. He handed me the soda. "So, what's up, Becca? I can't imagine you're here just to say hi, though I'm glad to see you."

"Yeah, actually I do have a question," I said as I popped the top of the can.

"Shoot."

"How well did you know Matt Simonsen?"

"Oh. Not well at all."

"Did you work at Smithfield Market?"

"Yeah, for about nine months."

"Then how come you didn't know him well?"

Ian's brows came together. "Becca, have you taken a part-time job with the police?"

"No, I just want to know. And . . ."

"And what?"

"Why didn't you tell me this before?"

Ian gave one of those knowing half-smile things as he looked away from my probing glance. He looked back up soon enough, though.

"Becca, I didn't think about you not knowing. I thought everyone knew I'd worked at Smithfield before, so therefore I must have at least been acquainted with Simonsen. I wasn't trying to keep anything secret. Especially from you. I guess I just didn't think it needed to be talked about. I told the police everything I knew about Simonsen. He and his son kept to themselves. I don't think they looked favorably on my art, but they weren't ever rude to me—just distant, like they didn't have much time for my silliness, but that was fine. They were hard workers, old-timers, you know.

There before the sun came up and gone only when their product was sold out or the market was closing. I never had any real conversations about the Simonsens with the other vendors, so I couldn't tell the police anything more than that."

"Oh."

"Have I satisfied your questions, Officer?" Ian said with another smile.

"Well, maybe. I have one more question, though."

"Ask away. I'm an open book."

"Did you know that Abner's sister lives one block over from you?"

"I had no idea," Ian said. But he suddenly sat up on the edge of the couch as though he'd heard something.

"What?"

"Well, you might just be cut out for this questioning thing. You made me remember something. I can't believe it didn't come to me before."

"I did? What?"

"Right before I left Smithfield, I saw Abner there."

I sat up, too. "What happened?"

"I knew he looked familiar. I just couldn't place him when I first got to Bailey's. He was at my Smithfield stall, looking at my art, asking me all kinds of questions. Someone called his name, but I can't remember who it was."

"Male or female?"

"Female, I think. I was busy with a few other customers, so I didn't pay attention, but he left right after that."

"I wonder who it was."

"I have no idea. Maybe more will come back to me if I think about it. I don't think there's much to what I'm remembering right now, but I'll call Officer Brion and let him know. Good job, Becca," he said.

We both took sips of the sodas.

"Thanks."

Because we'd both sat forward on the couch, we were now very much in each other's space. So close that I hoped my breath wasn't bad. His wasn't.

I really don't think either of us intended for what happened next to happen. It was one of those moments where some other force takes over and just pushes two pairs of lips together.

We each leaned toward the other. Ian put his tattooed hand on my cheek and hesitated, giving us both a moment to make sure this was the direction we wanted to go. It was. We both leaned farther and then kissed. It was almost like an extended junior high first kiss—gentle and practically innocent. Except that my heart rate didn't think it was so innocent.

Ian stopped first. He sat back slowly and pulled his hand away as though that magnet was still working hard to keep it where it had been.

"Hey, Becca, I'm sure it was way too soon for that, but, well . . ."

"It's okay. Really, it is."

Ian's eyes squinted as he inspected my own.

"You . . . um, well . . ." he said.

I laughed lightly. "I'd better go."

"Yeah, one of us probably should, huh?"

"And you live here. I'd better go," I repeated, forcing myself to get off the couch and get out of Ian's garage.

I don't know whether I scampered or scurried, but I know I was quick about climbing down the ladder. Our kiss had done something to me that made me want to run away from Ian as much as it made me want to stay. I needed to clear my head—again.

Using the lightning-quick movements I'd become accustomed to, somehow he reached the door before I did. He pulled it open and stayed out of my way as I stepped over the threshold.

"Ian," I began.

"I know, I know. That was a mistake—you think you shouldn't have allowed that to happen." His smile was far too knowing for someone in his mid-twenties. His tone wasn't whiny. Instead, I thought he was trying to make me laugh.

"Actually, no, that's not what I was going to say. I don't think it was a mistake. It was an impulse, but from all I could tell, we both had the same impulse. No harm done."

"Really?"

"Yes."

"Hmm, I can't figure out if your analysis is positive or negative for the potential of doing that again someday."

I shrugged.

"So what did you want to say?" He leaned on the door frame and crossed his arms in front of his chest. His eyes were way dangerous, and I liked that.

"I was just going to say that I'll see you tomorrow, if you're working."

"I'll be working."

"Good. See you then."

"Great."

I turned and walked down the driveway. I didn't look to see if he was watching me go, but I hoped he was.

As I drove toward Abner's sister's house, I realized that Ian had answered my questions, but for all I knew, he was a serial murderer who hypnotized those who suspected him by first poisoning them with a bit of his spit and then kissing them. When my head was on straight, I'd have to go over what he'd said and figure out if it made sense. I couldn't let his kiss overshadow my ability to think clearly.

Right.

I drove down Harvard, heading toward Yale. Higher education suddenly had a whole new meaning.

Twelve

Yale Avenue was similar to Harvard in that trees and big, beautiful older homes lined the street. But there was one house on Yale that stood out from the others.

Abner's sister's house was small and squat. It was adorable, but still small compared to the others surrounding it. It looked like a dollhouse cottage with its clean brick exterior and soft pink painted trim.

I had no idea what I was going to say to Ms. Helen Justen as I climbed the steps and knocked on the screen door that had a puppy figure sculpted from thick aluminum in the middle of it.

I heard and felt the fast pitter-patter of someone running to the door. It swung open and a very old woman with wild hair and a wild look in her eyes said, "I'm busy in the kitchen with my preserves. Who are you, and what do you want?"

"Ms. Justen, my name is Becca Robins. I happen to

know a few things about preserves. Would you like some help?"

"Abner's friend Becca?"

"That's me."

"Come in and back to the kitchen." Helen turned and hurried away. Her flowered housedress flapped behind her, and her pink slippers sent sparks of static electricity up from the shag carpet.

I was impressed with the timing of my visit as I entered the house. I couldn't think of another time in my life when I'd happened upon a preserve "situation." I hurried back to the kitchen, but not without first noticing all the pink: pink furniture, pink pillows, pink knickknacks. Everything was neat and well placed, and somehow didn't remind me of Pepto Bismol.

"I'm stirring," Helen said as she looked up from a large pot. "I'm close to the boil." Even though she was old and small, there was nothing feeble about her.

"Smells good. Where's the pectin?"

"Over there." She pointed to a counter on the other side of the small kitchen. I grabbed the pectin and took it to her.

"Thanks, dear." Helen smiled. "So, you're Abner's Becca? I've heard so darn much about you. All good. Abner thinks you're the cat's pajamas."

I laughed. "Abner and I are very good friends. He helped me a bunch when I first started my business."

"Really? That proves it, then—he adores you. He's not one to offer help very much."

"I think you're boiling," I said, looking down into the pot.

"So I am. Dump that pectin right in. I'll keep stirring."

I dumped as she stirred. We both looked at the beautiful red mixture.

"Strawberry, huh?" I said.

"Yes, a friend has some of those plants that have more than one crop a year. I think she said she has three full crops—you heard of those?"

"Sure. I don't have that kind, though. I think they're called Everbearing. My plants just bear fruit one time per year."

"What's the difference?" she asked as we watched for the mixture to come to a rolling boil again.

I shrugged. "My plants have longer runners—vines. Some say there's a different taste, but I think if you take care of your plants, the berries can all taste great."

"Boiling. One more minute." Helen pushed a button on the stove, and the timer showed the number 1.

I hadn't timed this last boil for years. I'd developed an inner timer. I just knew when it was ready.

"Grab another ladle out of that drawer." She pointed. "We can both fill."

I did as she asked and surveyed the readied jars on the table. Her system seemed efficient enough except for one fault that caught my attention. From the looks of things, she had hand-cut all of her strawberry pieces. I preferred to throw mine in for a fast spin in the food processor. It was quicker, of course, but I also liked the more evenly sized fruit pieces that came from the processor. It was a delicate balance, though. Too much processing wasn't a good idea, but just enough could make each bite of the preserve mixture have just the right amount of correctly sized pieces of fruit.

I wouldn't say anything, though. I might be the expert, but she had probably been doing this for many more years than I had.

The timer beeped, and Helen slid the pot next to the

sink. She skimmed off the top foam and then lugged the pot to the table. We each went to work with our own ladles and measuring cups.

"So, Becca, tell me why you came to visit me today," Helen said as we both ladled and poured.

"Ms. Justen . . ."

"Helen, please."

"Helen. I'm worried about Abner."

She looked away from my eyes. "You know, the police were here yesterday."

"Oh yeah? What did they say?"

"They wanted me to tell them where my brother was, but I wouldn't. Though the officer—Brion, I think it was—was a very nice man. It seems that Abner has gotten himself into some trouble, doesn't it?"

"Yes, it looks that way. Do you know where he is?"

"I have some idea, but I don't know for sure."

"Don't suppose you'd tell me where you think he might be?"

She looked back into my eyes, her own glimmering with the sparkle of having a secret. "Probably not, but not because I don't think Abner wouldn't want to see you. I just think it's best if his location is kept secret until all of this nastiness is worked out."

"Helen"—I stopped ladling—"I'm not sure how it's going to get worked out. The evidence is stacking up against him. He needs to tell the truth to the police."

"Keep filling, dear," she said. I resumed the job. "Abner is innocent. I promise you that. He wouldn't hurt a fly."

I didn't know exactly how much she knew, so I didn't bring up the bloody axe.

"Well, then he definitely needs to turn himself in. Justice will prevail."

"Not if he's being framed."

"Who's framing him?"

"He won't tell me, but I have my suspicions."

"Tell *me,* then. Who would frame Abner?"

Helen sighed and inspected my face again. She wanted to tell me—tell someone—what she knew. She was the type of person who found it challenging to keep a secret.

"Well, Matt Simonsen was a thorn in his side for years. They were not friends."

"Why's that?" I asked innocently. I wanted her version, untainted by what Jessop Simonsen had shared with me.

"Abner was, at one time, very much in love with Simonsen's wife, Pauline."

"Really? When? This is about love?" Again, my tone rang with sincerity.

"He'd have to give you the details; it was when they were very young. Pauline promised herself to Abner but Matt became very sick with pneumonia, and once Pauline had helped take care of him, she claimed they fell in love. They got married, and that was that."

This was some new information, though Betsy had told me that she'd heard Abner say something like *If you'd died all those years ago . . .* to Matt. Was that what he was talking about? The pneumonia?

"So maybe he finally snapped and killed the man who took his woman?" I said.

"No, I don't think so." Helen shook her head slowly.

The wheels in my mind turned. "So what about Pauline? Do you think she could have killed her own husband to finally be with Abner?"

"I don't think that's possible, either. She had her youthful wild moments, but she never struck me as homicidal.

Plus, it's been many years. I think if she was going to kill anyone, she would have done it before this."

"What do you think, then? Who could have killed Matt Simonsen and would frame Abner for it?" If I asked enough times, maybe she'd answer.

"Again, I only have my suspicions—I want to be surer before I tell anyone. I do know this, though. Pauline was not only a beautiful young woman, she was rich, too. I wonder if that doesn't have something to do with it. With her hand in marriage came lots of money."

"A dowry?"

"Not really. It was her money. She was rich, but everyone knew about it. Everyone knew that whoever married Pauline would be marrying the most beautiful woman in town and would become instantly rich. Anyway, whether it was her beauty or her money, she had a number of suitors. I think one of them killed Matt—even after all these years, maybe the killer couldn't let go of his love for Pauline."

"But you're not speaking about Abner?"

"No, a different suitor altogether. Another one who happens to work at Bailey's." She gasped and put her hand to her mouth. She was about to break—not that she hadn't wanted to, anyway.

"Another one! No! Who?" I accidentally dropped the ladle to the floor, making yet another red splatter of the day. "Damn! I mean . . . Sorry, Helen. Stay put, I'll get it cleaned up. But tell me who you're talking about." I put the ladle in the sink and took a wet cloth to the floor.

She laughed at my butterfingered antics. "Really, you don't need to worry about it. I can clean it up later."

"I got it. But tell me who you mean," I said from my

hands and knees. I didn't want her loose tongue to tighten up.

"You have someone there named Barry? He sells corn?"

"Yeah."

"He was in love with Pauline, too."

"Nuh-uh."

"Yes, pinky-swear."

I stopped cleaning midswipe. The list of Barry's lies was growing. He hadn't been straight with anyone.

"Helen, I thought I heard that Barry was involved in a land dispute with Matt Simonsen years ago. Is that true?"

"Not that I'm aware of, but that doesn't necessarily mean anything."

Barry had lied to me, then later claimed he and Matt had been involved in a land dispute. I'd seen him on my way out of Bailey's. Had he been the one who'd knocked on Allison's door when I was hiding? I didn't think so—he was tall, but surely I'd have recognized his voice. Barry's truck was white, not brown. And the person who was knocking might have absolutely nothing to do with any of this. But something nudged at me, telling me that he *was* involved. But how?

"Becca?" Helen said, pulling me from my thoughts.

"Huh? Sorry about that. So, Barry? Really?"

"Well, I don't know anything for certain, but I remember that they were all very much in love with Pauline. There were other suitors, of course, but those three men loved that woman with a strength that they almost couldn't control."

"All three of them?"

She nodded. "And I know what you're getting at. You

still think Abner might be involved, but I don't think he is."

"And you won't tell me where he is," I said as I finished cleaning.

"No, that's up to him. He's my brother, Becca, the only family I have left. I could never . . ."

"I understand." I'd have gone to any length necessary to protect Allison.

"Time to seal the jars," Helen said pleasantly. She was ready to change the subject.

I tried to ask her more questions, but she was done speaking about anything that had anything to do with her brother.

We sealed and then wiped the outsides of the jars in record time, and then put the filled jars into the boiling water canner and let them process. Two people on the job made a huge difference, though I knew I wouldn't be hiring a helper anytime soon. I loved my alone time in my kitchen with only preserves and loud music for company.

A noise sounded from the front room just as we finished pulling the preserves out of the water.

"Yoo-hoo, Helen."

"That's Liz. Come on."

I followed Helen to the front room. Liz was young, with a pretty face framed in red curls. She wore a white nurse's dress under a light blue sweater. Her feet were encased in unflattering white oxfords, but the entire ensemble worked on her.

"Oh, sorry, I didn't know you had company," she said as she inspected me. I remembered the mirror at Ian's. I'm sure I was a horrifying sight. Frankly, I was surprised Helen had let me in the house.

"Liz, this is Becca. Becca, Liz."

"Nice to meet you," I said. She responded with only a quick nod.

"Liz is very protective of me. She helps me around the house and with a little physical therapy on my old shoulders," Helen said. "Liz, Becca is a friend. Be nice."

That loosened up Liz a bit. She smiled, but not with her entire face.

"Well, I should probably go, anyway. Let me finish in the kitchen and I'll be on my way." I really didn't want to go. I had enjoyed talking to Helen and playing Super Preserve Woman, but there was really nothing else for us to discuss, and Liz's arrival put a damper on the mood.

"Come back and visit, Becca," Helen said as I made my way out the door. "I've heard so much about you. And Abner was right, you're delightful."

"So are you. I'm glad we met. I look forward to seeing you again."

I left the house and Helen closed the door behind me, but then it opened again.

"Becca, I almost forgot. Abner thought you might be stopping by and he wanted me to tell you something."

"Really? Okay, what?"

"He wanted me to tell you that though he doesn't dislike them, he doesn't have a thing for hummingbirds. Is that some sort of code or something?"

"Uh, I don't really know, but I'll think about it." It *was* some sort of code, but I didn't know how to decipher it. There had been lots of feeders on Abner's greenhouse and syrup on his porch. If he wasn't fond of hummingbirds, why would he have all that stuff? *And that was the question, wasn't it?*

"Well, take care," Helen said before she closed the door again.

"You, too."

In a haze of distracted thought, I made my way to my truck. Just as I put the key in the ignition, my cell phone rang. Unknown name and number. I flipped it open. Another coincidence? I didn't think so, as I looked at the house. A pink curtain fluttered. I'd have bet that Helen made a phone call the second after she closed the door.

"Abner?"

"Becca?" he said.

"Listen to me, Abner, I don't want you to call me ever again unless you agree to meet with me in person first. I've had it with your mysteriousness. I need some answers. Where are you?"

For a long few moments, I thought I'd lost him. In truth, I didn't want to lose him—I wanted to help him, but to do that, I needed to talk to him in person.

Finally, he responded. "Okay, Becca, tomorrow afternoon. Go to my house at about three, and I'll call you and give you instructions from there."

"Abner, I don't . . ." I began, but there was a distinct silence on the other end. "Abner?"

He was gone.

I turned the key and revved the truck's engine. I decided that if I actually went to Abner's house and followed his cryptic instructions, he'd be lucky if I didn't bring my own axe to bloody.

Thirteen

I drove directly home, made sure all the doors were locked, peeled off my filthy clothes, and stepped into the shower. As I watched grime swirl down the drain with steamy hot water, a million thoughts crashed around in my mind.

What a day!

As much as I'd have loved to stay under the water until it ran cold, I had too much to think about and write down. So much had happened, and I didn't want to forget one detail.

I didn't know if it was the call from Abner or everything else that sent me into the creepy zone, but after putting on my most comfortable flannel pajamas, I turned on a bunch of lights, found the alarm code, set it, and then parked myself at the dining room table/desk. I found some light green index cards that were still wrapped in tight plastic, tore them open, and began my notes.

I titled the first card Abner. I listed what I could. He'd been the one to find Simonsen's body; he'd been overheard in an argument with Simonsen—death threats and all; he'd been cagey to everyone (except Ian) about where he lived; there was a bloody axe in his greenhouse (I made a note to ask Officer Brion about fingerprints on the axe); he was missing in action, except for the flowers he put in my pumpkin patch and the calls he'd made to me; he'd been in a long-ago love triangle with Simonsen—I scratched that out and wrote *love square*—now, according to Helen, Barry was involved, too. Finally, I noted that he didn't care for hummingbirds, though it sure seemed like he did. And he wanted his sister to tell me that specifically. Again the urge to wring Abner's neck if he didn't give me more information at our meeting made me clench my teeth.

I reread my notes. He sure seemed guilty on paper. Love was motive enough, and had been the reason for more murders than anyone would probably ever know for certain. But still, something didn't fit. I turned the card over and wrote:

But Abner is gentle—feisty, but gentle. He's claiming he's being framed, but won't tell by whom. His romance with Pauline was apparently a long time ago. Could he possibly still love her? Could she be the one framing him? I thought I'd heard somewhere that most murders were committed by loved ones.

"I need to know about Pauline and Matt's marriage," I said aloud. How was I going to find out about their relationship? The only realistic way I could think of was to talk to Pauline myself. I'd burdened their son enough with my surprise visit—he probably wouldn't give me a straight answer about his parents' relationship, anyway. But it was too soon for me to interview the grieving widow, wasn't it? I'd have to figure out a way, or . . . I made another note on my Officer Brion card—I'd ask my new friend, the police officer, if he knew anything. It wouldn't be strange for the police to have asked her such questions. Maybe Sam had shown Mrs. Simonsen the picture, too—maybe she was the blonde. I'd for sure ask Sam, I just didn't know if he'd give me a straight answer.

Satisfied with my progress on Abner's card, I grabbed another one. This one was titled Carl Monroe. My notes were about his strange behavior at the meeting and the fact that he'd been at Smithfield and, while there, had run from me. What was he doing? And why would he run? That's pretty much always a sign of guilt, but guilty because he'd killed someone? Or was there another reason? If so, what was it?

I turned the card over and scribbled about not knowing him well enough to make any real judgments. He'd always been quiet, nice, and tall. Tall. Presumably, so was the person who killed Matt Simonsen. So was the person who'd knocked on Allison's door when I'd been stealing information. Could that have been Carl's voice I heard? Maybe.

I grabbed the phone book and looked up Carl's address. Maybe his would be easier to find than Ian's and Abner's.

"Nuh-uh," I said aloud. "No way." There was only one Carl Monroe listed in the thin phone book. Though I wasn't familiar with the area, the address seemed to be right on the other side of Abner's property. On a separate card, I jotted down Carl's address. How could this new address be just a coincidence? How well did Abner and Carl know each other? How close friends were they really?

If Carl and Abner were good friends, I never saw it. I'd have to ask Allison or some of the other vendors.

My next card was about Barry. I noted what Helen had said about his love for Pauline. I listed his lie about how well he knew Matt Simonsen, which seemed to change every time I talked to him or to someone else about him. I also wrote down what he had said to me on the morning of the murder. It had been something about thinking the police didn't suspect him because he didn't have any blood on him. At the time I'd thought he was just being Barry, but now I wondered if maybe he was "protesting too loudly." Barry was also tall. He was big and tall, and had a difficult time maneuvering his body, but he could probably still swing an axe. I turned the card over and added:

Barry's a pain, not a bad guy, but of all the people I'm looking at, I'd say he was the closest to being a killer. Why would he lie if he had nothing to hide?

This was an awful thing to say about anyone, but I had to be honest with myself.

Though I could have devoted a card to Helen, I had no suspicions that she'd killed Matt Simonsen. I moved to my last card: Ian Cartwright. I smiled as I wrote his name, but then forced myself to be sober and focus on what I knew about him.

He'd worked with Matt Simonsen at Smithfield; he hadn't told me, but he hadn't thought that he was hiding something from me; he learned Abner's address in record time while working at Bailey's—though he said it had been because of the sculpture that Abner purchased. He lived close to Abner's sister. I turned the card over.

The words I wanted to write weren't appropriate for a murder investigation, so I allowed myself a moment or two of personal thought instead.

Ian said he was from Iowa, but I was curious, for personal reasons, to know more about him. His darker skin and ink-black hair made me think he might be at least partially Native American. Maybe African American? Shoot, maybe just a very olive-skinned Caucasian. I had no idea, but I was curious, just because. And I wanted to know even more. What did he do when he wasn't working or reading to his landlord? And why did I suddenly have a picture in my mind of him reading in front of a fireplace, wearing only his jeans, as I'd seen him today? And why did I suddenly wish our kiss hadn't been so innocent? And wasn't I too old for all this nonsense?

I cleared my throat, put the pen to the back of Ian's card, and wrote: *I've been married twice and must remember that relationships are not my strong suit. But the fact that I find him attractive (despite his younger age) and would like to inspect his tattoos further could cloud my judgment as to whether or not he's a murderer. Must keep on my toes around this one. And not allow his poisonous spit to touch me again.*

I suddenly realized that I'd been asking a bunch of questions, but leaving out an important one. Did these people have solid alibis? I'd been investigating, but trying to hide the fact that I was doing so. Apparently, Ian and Barry had been at Bailey's, but I didn't know exactly what time they'd arrived Tuesday morning. And I didn't remember seeing Carl at all that day. I was searching for something that would tell me who had killed Matt Simonsen, but I needed to get more aggressive. I was just going to have to ask my possible suspects what they were doing at the time of the murder. Or I would have to ask Officer Brion what he'd learned. Or both.

The doorbell chimed, making me jump an inch or two off the chair. Allison had said she'd deliver Hobbit, but my nerves were on edge.

As dogs will do, Hobbit greeted me as though she hadn't seen me in a month.

"She's so fickle," Allison said. "She acted heartbroken

to leave Mathis, and now you'd think she was relieved to be away from the awfulness of our place."

"Hey, girl. Treats," I said as I rubbed her neck and dodged her slobbery tongue. The word "treats" always sent her directly to her bowl. I'd already placed her favorite bacon snacks over her regular food. After she'd pattered away, I turned to Allison. "Thanks for bringing her home. I needed a shower something fierce."

"Sure, not a problem, but since you owe me and all"—she smiled—"tell me what you did with the rest of your day. How's your investigation going?"

I cringed, but I didn't think she caught it. Did she know I'd been in her office?

"Come on in. I'll give you all the details," I said as I crossed my fingers behind my back. Someday I'd admit to sneaking into her office, but it probably wouldn't be until we were both old and gray and she could no longer run faster than me. Allison valued what she did, and the fact that I'd done something to betray her trust would make me feel guilty for about a hundred years or so. That was probably enough punishment, or so I rationalized.

We sat at the table as I lied and told her that Linda had known where Helen lived and that Ian had called me with his address. I told her the truth about what was discussed at both places, except that I left out the kiss and the call from Abner. My feelings for Ian were still too new to discuss, and she'd have made me call Officer Brion to tell him about Abner. Though I still might—I'd told him I would—I wasn't sure yet.

"Did you know that Carl and Abner live close to each other?" I said.

Allison shrugged. "I never thought about it. We work with farmers in a fairly small geographical area. Some of them are bound to live by each other. Carl's behavior is strange, though—running from you? He's one of my easier vendors—never asks for anything special, shows up when he's supposed to, does well. I like him a lot."

"Me, too, but . . . do you know if they're friends?"

"The only person I've ever seen Abner be truly friendly to is you. Other than that, he's the same to everyone."

"He's always been good to me."

"Becca," Allison said in her serious I'm-one-minute-older-than-you voice, "I want you to be careful."

"Oh, pshaw, there's nothing to worry about. I'm fine." I stood. I wasn't hiding anything—I was sure she saw that I'd armed my alarm. "Hey, I still have some of Mamma Maria's Mmmm-Amazing Lemon Meringue Pie. Want some?"

"Absolutely, but quit trying to change the subject. I know you have some concerns, or you and Hobbit wouldn't have come over last night."

"That was just Abner—who else would have left the flowers? And yes, I admit I was a little freaked," I said as I cut thin but bouffant-high pieces of pie and brought them to the table. "But Abner's no threat to me, Allison. He probably just wanted to talk. No big deal."

"Okay, what if Abner isn't the killer?" She slid a bite of yellow heaven into her mouth, her eyes closing in appreciation as she let it melt on her tongue.

"I know, it's delicious, isn't it?"

"I've never tasted anything quite like it—Linda bakes amazing fruit pies, but this is amazing in a whole different way. Anyway, if Abner is the killer, he's dangerous, and if he isn't the killer and the real killer realizes you're out there asking questions, well, you could be in danger, too." She pointed at me with her fork.

I thought about that as I let my own bite of pie melt. I

didn't want to comment on the fact that if Abner was indeed the killer, I was going to meet him in person the next day.

"I'll be careful," I finally said. What else was I going to say? The truth was—yes, I'd attempt to be careful, but I wanted this crime solved and I was going to do whatever it took to help solve it. Too much rode on a good conclusion. But, frankly, my sister probably couldn't handle that truth.

"Good. Now, is there anything I can do to help?"

"Hmm. I don't know." I hadn't thought about asking Allison for help for the same reasons that she'd just lectured me about. I wouldn't want to put her safety in jeopardy. She was a mom and had a family of her own—it would be beyond irresponsible of me to put her in any sort of danger. Our hippie parents hadn't believed in much discipline while we were growing up, but they'd often shared their ideas about karma—whatever I put "out there" would come back to me a hundredfold. If something bad happened to Allison, I'd think it was the result of my own poor decisions. But perhaps there was something that wasn't so dangerous. "Wait, maybe there is." I looked at my watch. It was dark, though it was only seven thirty. "Want to go for a ride?"

"Um, sure. Where to?"

"Let's drive by Carl Monroe's house. I can show you where Abner lives, too, plus I'd like to get a feel for how far apart their properties are."

"Okay," she said, only a little doubt lining her voice.

We finished the pieces of pie, practically licking the plates; I put on real clothes, and rounded up Hobbit before we took off in my truck. I know Allison noticed as I re-armed the house alarm, but she didn't say a word, for which I was grateful.

The night was cool but clear, and the air smelled crisp

with fall. The moon was full and bright, lighting the world just enough as we moved down the traffic-free road.

"What will it mean if Carl and Abner do live right by each other?" Allison asked.

"I have no idea, but the coincidences of everyone's addresses sit funny with me. Maybe you're right and it's just because we live in a fairly small community, but I'm curious. I don't want to just sit at home being curious. A quick drive-by wouldn't hurt."

"Got it. Did you come up with anything else today?" Allison asked around Hobbit.

"I need to ask more questions. I've got to be less sneaky about what I'm doing—I won't announce that I'm trying to find the murderer, but I need to know if Barry, Ian, and Carl have alibis, so I'm going to have to ask them outright."

"Maybe I can help with that."

"Tell me."

"Carl wasn't there Tuesday morning, but Barry and Ian were. I didn't see Barry until we were all together, but I saw Ian unloading a piece of his art."

"This was all during the time the murder was taking place?" I asked.

"Presumably. Officer Brion said the murder took place very early—maybe before 6:00 A.M. Barry's an old-timer; he's always there early. And though Ian might not have been in the business for long, when he's there, he has to be there early to set up his stuff. I was there at six fifteen and saw both of them. Neither acted strangely at all."

"But there are fifteen minutes of unknown. A lot can happen in fifteen minutes."

"I suppose."

"Anyway, I need to ask more questions."

"Okay, I can still help."

"Awesome. How?"

"The Fall Equinox Dinner will be a perfect opportunity to talk to almost everyone. No one likes to miss it. Everyone will be in a good mood, so they might not care if you start nosing around. I had my doubts about still having the dinner, but I'm glad we're doing it. It'll be good for everyone. How about that?"

"I think my sister is a master of human behavior. That's a great idea."

"I have another one." She smiled.

"Okay. You're on a roll."

"I think you should bring Officer Brion as a date."

"What?"

"Yeah, tell him to wear real clothes so he isn't so recognizable. He could be there to observe and make sure you don't get yourself in trouble. He might get some good clues, too."

"I think you've fallen off that 'roll' I just put you on. Having the police there would just scare people into not talking—he'd be recognized. And—here's my biggest concern—as my date?"

"Yes, just a pretend date. He's not married, I know that. And I get what you're saying, but the point here is to try to solve a murder. I think having him there is more than worth the risk."

"How do you know he's not married?"

"I'm not sure," she said too innocently. "What? Do you think Ian will mind?"

I hesitated a beat too long. "No, not at all."

"Uh-oh, something happened at his apartment, something you didn't tell me. Spill it."

"Nothing really happened. Just a very innocent moment, that's all."

"You two kissed, didn't you?"

"Like we were in junior high and had never done such a thing before."

"That's adorable."

"He's ten years younger than me, Allison. Actually, that might have been his first kiss. Ever."

Allison laughed. "I highly doubt it. And his soul is so much older than yours that the body age doesn't matter in the least. And, more important, his soul is kind."

Our parents' influence was showing again. Soul age versus body age was a recurring discussion in our home. And kind old souls were always considered the biggest winners.

"Unless he murdered Matt Simonsen," I said.

That stunned her silent for only a brief instant. "I can't believe that's what happened," she finally said.

"I'm sure of this—neither you nor I want to believe that, but we still don't know."

"Hmm."

"Yeah, hmm."

"Well, just let Ian know it's a fake date with Officer Brion. He'll understand."

"But if, by chance, the police suspect Ian even a little, I can't tell him that I'm going on a date, fake or not, with the investigating officer."

"I believe this is what we call a sticky wicket."

"I believe this is what I call 'I'm screwed.'"

Allison laughed again. "It's a good idea, though. Call Officer Brion if you think it's the right thing to do. I could just invite him, but people might get freaked to see a cop there if he isn't with . . . well, with you. People like you and always find your love life intriguing. It'd be a good diversion measure."

"Nice. Let me think about it." I sighed. "Right down there is Abner's." I pointed at the first back road Ian had taken me onto. I was glad we were getting closer to Carl's. I'd never been comfortable talking about my personal life. There'd been too much drama, and I was to blame for lots of it. Pointing out my faults was much less fun than investigating a murder.

"I'd like to see Abner's greenhouse, but we'll save that for another day. Or night," Allison said.

"Sure. So if I understand Carl's address, there'll be a road ahead about half a mile. It should be more obvious than Abner's—a road sign and everything."

"What's the street name?"

"Ridge Way."

We both sat forward and peered ahead. Hobbit stuck her neck out, too. The headlights were helpful, but the moon was so bright that we probably could have turned them off and driven without being seen. But there was nothing I could do about the engine noise from my old truck, so turning off the lights would have probably drawn more attention.

"There. There it is," Allison said.

I cranked the steering wheel and turned down a road that was better traveled than the one leading to Abner's farm. This one was paved, though it was only a two-lane state road; dead weeds and cracked pavement advertised that it wasn't a high priority on the road repair lists.

"How far?" Allison asked.

"Shouldn't be much farther. I think it'll be on the left."

The moonlight played over empty fields for a short time. Soon, the light illuminated the manicured rows of Carl's peach orchard. If I had any artistic ability, I'd have wanted to paint or draw the scene. The orchard was set in a bowl of land, so as we drove down the road, we saw only the tops of the seemingly perfect trees; it was like we were seeing an ocean of leaves.

"He has a beautiful place," Allison said.

"And look at that house," I said.

The house was huge—a mansion that reminded me of the Munsters' place, only nicer and not scary at all. Commanding and beautiful, but not creepy. It sat close to the road at the end of the orchard.

"Carl must do very well," Allison noted.

When we were still a good hundred feet or so from the house, I stopped the truck and pulled to the side of the road.

"What are you doing?" Allison asked.

"There are lights on in the front of the house, and it's so close to the road, Carl might see us if we drive by. I'm going to get out and walk."

"What? I thought you just wanted to see where he lived."

"I want to get a look inside where he lives."

"Why?"

"I want to see what television shows he watches at night," I said as Allison rolled her eyes. "Actually, I don't really know why, but something tells me I should."

"Not a good idea, Becca. I'd recommend just knocking and talking to him."

"Hmm. No. Stay here with Hobbit. I'll be right back."

"Be . . ." was the last thing I heard before I got out of the truck and scampered into Carl's lovely bowl of a peach orchard.

Fourteen

"Honestly," Allison said in my ear. She must have gotten out of the truck right after I did. "I don't understand the need to do this."

"Where's Hobbit?" I asked as we wove our way through the short peach trees.

"Still in the truck, like a good girl. I grabbed the keys and locked the doors. She'll be fine for a few minutes. But why are we doing this?"

"Carl evaded my questions and then ran away from me. There's something up with him. If he saw it was me knocking, he probably wouldn't answer the door. I just want to peek in. I'm not going to linger in a voyeuristic state or anything."

"I could knock."

Maybe, but I didn't want to take the chance. The word "knock" made me remember the earlier visitor to her office.

"I don't think that would work, either. Hey, did Carl come visit you today?"

"No, I haven't seen him at all. Why?"

"Just wondered."

I pulled on her arm and we crouched in the middle of the orchard, the smells of fresh night air and cool earth all around. My heartbeat whooshed in my ears, and I knew my eyes were wide with excitement. This new life of crime I'd been dabbling in was both scary and exhilarating at the same time. More scary than exhilarating, but still . . .

"Why are we crouching? We're in a bowl. I don't think anyone can see us. Come on, I'd like to get home before midnight." Allison pulled me up by my arm.

We continued through the trees. I'd worked the land enough to spend at least a moment wondering how Carl was able to make his orchard produce such lovely fruit. Did the trees sitting in the bowl make for good irrigation or perfect sunlight? Or was he like me, lucky in what he produced though he was never quite sure how he did it?

At the edge of the trees and up the side of the bowl was Carl's mansion.

"They're ooky and they're spooky," I sang quietly.

"It does remind me of that, too, except that it's very well taken care of—no cobwebs or monsters."

"Look, there's someone in the front room."

From the low angle, it wasn't possible to see any exact features of the person in the room, but a head bobbed up and down as someone paced.

"We've got to get up higher." Allison took a step up the slope.

"Al, we're too close to the house. Carl could see us if he looks out the window at just the right moment, and I don't want him to see us coming from the orchard. I especially don't want him to see you." I suddenly realized that what my sister was doing could put her job in jeopardy. She was the manager of Bailey's and was always the perfect picture of integrity. Any sort of funny business on her part, particularly with someone who worked at the market, could get her fired.

She looked at me, the bright moonlight shining off her dark eyes. As twins sometimes do, we shared my thought in silent communication.

"Right. You're right. Well, then, you climb up there and have a peek. Just keep low."

"I have a better idea. Look. These trees aren't peach trees." I pointed to a line of taller, stronger trees bordering the orchard but still sitting in the bowl. "Boost me up into one. The leaves will hide me."

She had a million reasons why my plan was a bad idea, but she had the chance to vocalize only a couple of them before I supported myself against a trunk and lifted my foot in expectation. Pavlov's reaction set in, and she cupped her hands to give me the perfect step. A couple of seconds later I'd made my way up to a branch.

"You okay?" Allison whispered. She really wasn't that far away, but the drop to the ground was breathtaking.

"Fine."

"Can you see anything?"

"Give me a minute." I could almost see something. If I could just get a bit closer, I thought I'd be able to see all of Carl's front room. I was on top of the branch, on my stomach. I lifted my behind in the air and inchwormed my way about a foot. The branch wavered and wobbled, and then drooped almost too much for comfort. But I could see perfectly.

The bobbing head did indeed belong to Carl, and he was

most definitely pacing. The room was filled with large, dark wood bookcases and lots of furniture that looked as though it had been made for reading comfort. There was richness to the whole space that confirmed that Carl did very well selling peaches, or else he had money from somewhere else.

I couldn't see the floor of the room, but Carl must have been wearing a path into whatever covered it. His lips were moving, so he was either talking to himself or there was someone with him.

"See anything?" Allison whispered again.

"Yep. Carl," I answered. The limb I was stretched out upon gave another wobble as I spoke. I sucked in my breath and held tight with my hands and knees.

"What's he doing?"

I dared to speak again. "Give me a minute, Al. I can't talk and hold on at the same time."

"Okay."

Carl looked purposefully at something just to the right of my field of vision. He stopped pacing and crossed his arms in front of his chest. As he spoke, his line of vision didn't falter. He was talking directly to someone. And, if I could only go another foot or so, I'd see who it was.

Slowly this time, I lifted my behind again, my knees digging into the branch. I pushed myself forward, my hands scraping on the rough bark. The limb was not happy I was moving again. This time it not only wobbled, it creaked with displeasure.

"Becca?" Allison said, this time not whispering. "What're you doing?"

I ignored her as I focused on the last few inches I needed to traverse. The limb wasn't going to hold for long, so I knew I'd have to get a quick look and then move backward or prepare myself for a body-bruising fall.

"Becca?"

The last inch wasn't quite all the way there, but I thought that if I stretched my neck, I could accomplish my mission. I stretched and turned and stretched a little more. It was to no avail; I still couldn't see who Carl was talking to.

Then, with a sudden start, Carl threw his arms into the air and turned. I got lucky because the person he was talking to stood and followed him. And though he was significantly shorter than Carl, I was up high enough that I could see exactly who it was.

Abner held his hands together in a plea as he followed Carl. His face was strained with his words, and I could only guess that he was begging for something.

The limb creaked and groaned in what I now thought was a pre-snap warning.

"Becca, come down now!"

I'd seen what I needed to see. I wanted to move my body backward, but the tree wasn't having any of that. The branch was about to go. I realized that if I fell from this angle, I'd hurt myself, but if I managed to get my barely more-than-five-feet-tall body over the side of the limb and held on to it like the bars on an elementary school playground, I'd probably be okay. Somehow, I did it. I swung myself over and swooped backward and held on to the limb, shockingly not scratching my hands too badly. I swung once for dramatic effect and then landed on my feet. The tree was still intact. So was I.

"That was interesting," Allison said.

"I saw Carl talking to someone."

"Who?"

"I'll tell you in the truck."

"Fine. Let's go." Allison turned and led the way out of the orchard.

I took one more look around. If I hadn't taken that extra moment, I would have definitely missed something I thought might be important.

To the side of the house, but outside the bowl, there was a lift in the land; a hill. On top of that otherwise bland hill of grass were three trees, evenly spaced and lonely in their moonlit dismissal from the crowd in the orchard. It took only a second to realize that I was seeing the three trees in one of the pictures at Abner's house.

"Becca!" Allison whisper-yelled from the edge of the orchard. "Let's go."

Allison probably would have called the police if I went to investigate them, so I tucked the idea to the back of my mind and hurried to my sister.

Fifteen

"Abner? Are you sure?"

"One hundred percent sure, Allison." We were still in the truck, parked on the side of the road. We'd locked the doors but were exposed in the bright moonlight. I resisted the urge to fire up the engine and screech the tires in a speedy escape. Something in my gut made me want to wait and see if someone would come outside. Another part of me wanted to march up to Carl's front door and demand that he and Abner tell me what was going on. These two feuding choices froze my fingers around the key and my right foot poised above the accelerator.

"Becca, we should call Officer Brion," Allison said. "It's our responsibility to do as much."

I reached over and touched her arm.

"Yes, we probably should. But, Allison . . ."

"I know, Abner's your friend. He's a friend to all of us, Becca, but he's either gotten himself into something awful or is being thrown into something awful. Either way, murder is involved, and that makes it dangerous. Plain and simple—dangerous. You aren't—we aren't—qualified to solve a murder. That's what the police do." Her voice was firm, but she still hadn't reached for her phone. When I'd seen Abner in Carl's house, I'd decided that I wasn't going to let Officer Brion know about my meeting with Abner the next day. Whatever Abner had to say, he was only going to say it to me, I knew that. If he was the murderer, I was fairly certain he wouldn't kill me. If he wasn't the murderer, I'd be more willing to listen to his story than the police ever would. I had to talk Allison out of calling them.

"How about this, Al? How about I ask Officer Brion to the dinner, we see what shakes out from that, and then we play on the up-and-up with the police? If we get Abner arrested before the dinner, we might miss out on something important. If he killed Matt, it was because of something specific. He's not going to kill anyone else."

"Do you think Carl's in danger?"

I looked toward the now-spooky house that glowed in the spooky moonlight.

"No, Allison, I really don't. Carl seemed agitated and Abner looked like he was pleading, but I don't think there's any danger there. I don't." I didn't. If I had, that would have been enough for me to call the police and officially hand over my unofficial part of the investigation. As it was, I still thought I stood a good chance of getting at the truth.

"If you're sure."

"I'm sure."

"You'll call Officer Brion and ask him to come to the dinner? If it would make things uncomfortable for you and Ian . . ."

"It won't. It'll be fine. I'll call."

"Okay. Let's go home."

As the distance from Carl's house increased, our moods improved. Once over the adrenaline rush of our entire adventure, we were both pleased at our seemingly fine-tuned skills to spy and not be caught. And Hobbit, at first irritated that we had left her in the car, enjoyed our triumphant attitudes.

By the time we pulled into my driveway, we were back to our normal selves, discussing our wayward parents and the group health plan that an insurance agent had pitched to Allison. The conclusions we came to were that our parents would be fine, and the health plan might be a good idea. Allison would hand out information flyers.

Once Allison left for her home and Hobbit and I had secured ourselves in the house, deep sleep came easily for me and my dog. I was always grateful that she didn't snore, but I doubted anything would have awakened me that night. The security of the alarm wasn't the only reason I was able to relax so deeply. I was plain old pooped out.

I woke the next morning at my usual early hour, got dressed, and headed out to the barn. It was good to have a normal routine, except now I kept checking my phone for the time. I wasn't going to let Linda down. I was going to be a good buddy and be at Bailey's right on time.

I packed a supply of preserves for the day. I didn't pack a full load because I had every intention of leaving no later than about two o'clock, so I could easily get to Abner's place by three o'clock. As I worked, I wondered about the conversation I'd seen between Abner and Carl. Abner could have been pleading for a number of things. It wasn't fair to speculate, but I couldn't help it.

Before last night I hadn't known they lived so close to each other, let alone had any sort of friendship, or partnership, or whatever it was. Why was quiet, shy, peach-selling Carl in the middle of any of this? And what the heck did those three trees have to do with anything?

I loaded up the truck and made my way to Bailey's. I pulled into the unload-load area right before Linda. She flashed her lights and gave me a thumbs-up when I looked in the rearview mirror. She was impressed that I was on time. So was I, actually.

"It's good to see you," she said as we opened the tailgates of our trucks and started to unload.

"You, too. And it's good to be here," I said. It was great to be there. I loved working at Bailey's and it was great to be back in the routine.

"So, you going to tell me why you had me call Allison out on a fake emergency yesterday?"

"Was that only yesterday?"

"Yes, it was."

I caught a glimpse of one of her pies. The crust, as usual, was the perfect light brown and I could almost taste it with my eyes.

"Yeah, I'll tell you, just not before I confess to her. Give me some time?"

"Well, sure," she said with a crooked smile. "I see you ogling my pie."

"I'd better buy that one," I said.

"All right." She laughed.

Sometimes we traded, but I was short on items she could use. The strawberries from my own crop were dwindling, and I didn't trade the other fruit I purchased for my products—she usually purchased some of the same fruit for hers. However, when I started bringing the pumpkin preserves, everyone would want to trade with me. Linda had once told me that the entire population of Bailey's used my pumpkin preserves for their Christmas gifts. I couldn't help but be thrilled by that.

I set up my stall quickly, almost carelessly. I needed to talk to people before I could focus on selling.

"Hey," I said to Linda as I craned my neck around the tent wall. "I need to run and talk to someone for a minute. Can you watch?"

"Of course," she said hesitantly.

"What?"

"Becca, whatever you're up to, be careful."

"Always." I winked.

I hurried first toward Carl Monroe's stall. Not to my surprise, but to my disappointment, he wasn't anywhere to be seen. I was a little worried about seeing him with Abner the previous night, but I still held fast to my initial instinct—Abner wouldn't hurt Carl. I called Allison, nonetheless.

"Becca? What's up?"

"Carl's not at his stall."

"Oh, I know. He stopped by to see me earlier this morning—and I thought maybe he'd caught us. I panicked a bit, but that wasn't why he stopped by."

"What did he want?"

"He's low on product, so he wanted to let me know that he wouldn't be in his stall today and was saving the inventory for Saturday, and that he'd for sure be at the Equinox Dinner. He asked if he could bring a date."

It was the end of the season and lots of vendors who sold only what they grew were either done selling or almost done selling for the season.

"But he was fine?"

"Perfectly. He was shy about asking to bring a date, but that didn't surprise me. He's a shy man."

"Yeah," I said. *Unless he's a murderer trying to act shy.* Was he the one who'd knocked on Allison's door? Maybe he'd just stopped by to tell her about his product?

"Anything else, Becca?"

"No. Talk to you later." We hung up.

Next stop, Ian's. His stall was empty, too. I didn't remember who his buddy was, and I stood at his stall with my hands on my hips. I was becoming irritated at the world. Why weren't people where I needed them to be?

"Becca?"

I turned to see Barry making his way slowly down the aisle.

"Hey, Barry," I said. "How are you?"

"Fine. You? You were sure in a hurry yesterday."

"Oh, yeah, sorry about that. Hope I wasn't rude. Hey, let me help you." I reached for the wagon handle he'd been pulling. Though he often struggled with simple walking, he looked the worse for wear today. I wanted to confront him about his lies, but there was something about the way he seemed to be hurting that made me suddenly want to be gentler in my questioning. Plus, I'd already thought about how best to approach Barry. Accusing him of lying, even when he clearly had, was not the best way to get him to talk. Now, offering to help him with his wagon, that might work better.

"Normally, I'd say no, but I think I'll take you up on that today. My hips are acting up and my shoulders seem to want to act up right along with them." He let me take the handle and then reached for his right shoulder, digging at it with his knuckles. His face was pasty white and his eyes were pinched at the corners. He was clearly in pain.

I pulled the corn wagon deftly down the aisle as I formulated the best way to ask Barry if he was a murderer. We pulled into his stall and both started lifting the corn from the wagon to the display table.

"So, Barry," I began expertly. "I was wondering . . ."

"What?"

"Well, guess who I met yesterday?"

"Is this a knock-knock joke or something? You sound odd, Becca."

"No, it's not a knock-knock joke. I met Helen Justen."

Barry froze in place, his hands full of corn and halfway to the display table. I was surprised that his face became even paler.

"Now, there's a name I haven't heard in an eon or so. Helen Justen. Well, well, well." He put the corn on the table and then sat on a stool. He took off his straw hat and wiped at his temples with an old handkerchief. He smiled. "How was she?"

"Fine. I helped her with some preserves." I had no idea why I said that.

"A long time ago . . . oh, shoot, you don't want to hear an old man's stories."

"Yes, I do. What were you going to say?" I'd finished unloading the wagon, so I leaned against the table.

"Well, Abner and I were pretty good friends when we were young'uns. Oh, we caused some trouble, yes we did."

"I bet."

Barry looked up. As his eyes landed on mine, his face clouded. He'd connected the dots: I met with Helen Justen, which meant we talked about Abner, which meant we talked about Abner's connection to Matt Simonsen. Of course, Pauline Simonsen came up in conversation. And finally, we must have discussed the love that every man currently over the age of sixty who was associated with

Bailey's seemed to have had for the younger version of Mrs. Simonsen. That thread inevitably led to Barry.

"What was it about that woman, Barry? She must have been something. Why didn't you mention your long-ago love for her to the police? Or to me?" I asked.

Barry's mouth pinched. He looked like he needed a moment. Would he tell me to leave? I didn't think so. Should he lie? Should he shut up? He would come to the right conclusion in a minute, I just had to give him the time.

"Aw, hell," he muttered as he stood from the stool and pretended to arrange some corn. "Aw, hell."

I attempted a sympathetic smile, but I was never good at that sort of thing.

"Becca, you have to understand how long ago all this was. None of it matters in the least, but if I'd brought it up to the police, they might have thought it did."

"I understand."

Barry looked around as though he didn't want anyone else to hear his next words. It was still early enough that the crowds hadn't come yet.

"We were so young and . . . well, everything that goes along with being young, you know what I mean?"

"Yes."

"The three of us were friends—Abner, myself, and Matt—we called him Matty, that's how young we were. We went to high school together." Any reservations he'd felt a moment ago were now replaced by a reminiscing tone. Allison, the brilliant human nature expert, always told me that people loved to talk about themselves. If you wanted to know something about someone, sometimes a little nudge was all they needed. "It was the sixties, a crazy time. But we weren't part of the sixties crowd. We were farmers. All three of us came from farming families. We got up before the sun, did chores, went to school, went home, and did more chores. But when we weren't working, we were together, raising our own versions of a ruckus." His eyebrows lifted as he smiled. "Not the same as your parents; they were more, uh, in tune with the sixties."

"You went to high school with my parents?"

"Yes, but I didn't know them well."

"Huh." I was the one who hadn't connected the dots—of course my parents were the same age as Barry and his buddies. I couldn't imagine that meant anything to the murder of Matt Simonsen, but I'd see if I could contact them and ask them what they remembered. "Tell me more about that time. When did you all meet Pauline?"

"Oh, yes, well, Pauline Nelson moved to Monson the summer before our senior year. She was something to behold."

"Beautiful?"

"No, she wasn't beautiful, she was spectacular. Next to her, beautiful didn't mean much. She was pretty, sure, in that young, fresh-faced, bright-eyed way, but she was more. She was smart and funny and made everyone else feel like they were smart and funny. She was someone new, Becca, and she was, probably still is, a wonderful person."

He looked off into the distance, into the past, certainly. "She liked me first," he said quietly.

"Tell me."

"Aw, shucks, Becca, before my body got old and too big to wrangle around with some sort of grace, I was something."

"I bet." I smiled.

"Anyway." Barry's cheeks reddened. "Anyway, anyway. I asked her out first and I was the first one she went out with. It was the best two months of high school."

"Two months. That doesn't sound like very long."

"Naw, I was bound to lose. She had an eye for Abner, even when she was dating me."

"That had to be pretty tough on your friendship."

"It was, but there was nothing to be done. No one understood it. Abner was a handsome enough fella, but they just didn't seem right together, you know? And Abner had nothing, barely a pot to pi . . . well, you know."

I nodded as though I agreed, but I didn't really. Abner had a heart of gold, I knew that much. He'd built an amazing greenhouse and what seemed to be a profitable business. But who was I? I hadn't known him then. People usually turned out pretty different from their high school selves.

"What was it about him that attracted her?" I asked.

"Never did understand it. They just hit it off, like they were meant to be together. She saw something the rest of us didn't."

I shrugged. "The laws of attraction are more abstract than definite in my life. I suppose it's hard for anyone to completely understand why people love who they love."

Barry nodded.

"So what happened? Why did she marry Matt Simonsen?"

"Now there's the question of the century. I didn't understand it then, and I still don't. The three of us, our friendship, fell apart after high school when Pauline married Matty. Before that, Matty got real sick with pneumonia and Pauline, being the friend that she was, helped take care of him. All of a sudden they were in love. After that they went their way, I went mine, and Abner went his. I even gave up peaches," Barry huffed.

"What do you mean?"

"My family was a group of peach growers. Since Matty and Pauline went into the peach business, I gave it up. Couldn't bear being in competition with them. That seems very silly now after all these years. I'm happily married, Becca, with two wonderful kids. I wouldn't trade any of my family for another moment with Pauline."

I didn't want to divert the conversation, but something occurred to me that I quickly filed to the back of my mind. Carl Monroe must also be in competition with Simonsen Orchards. Carl seemed to be pretty successful. Had competition with Simonsen Orchards perhaps led him to do something horrible? I'd have to think about it later. For now, I had to stick with getting whatever I could from Barry.

"That's good news," I said. "But what about Abner, Barry? He never got married, as far as I know. Was he not able to move forward?"

"I always wondered. Like I said, we all went our own ways—even after all that time and these recent years when Abner and I have worked at the same place, we still aren't close like we used to be. After high school, we never had one discussion about it. But I still don't know. He loved her something fierce. Maybe we all did, but I always thought he loved her the most."

Now came the hard part. Had I waited long enough into the conversation to ask the question? Was I going to do this right?

"Barry, where were you Tuesday morning, during the time that Matt Simonsen was killed?" Subtle as a brick. Even though Allison said she'd seen him, there was still some unaccounted-for time.

His mouth twitched, but he must have seen the seriousness in my eyes. I wanted an answer.

"Becca, I didn't kill Matty. We hadn't been friends in a

long time, but I would never have killed him. For what it's worth, I don't think Abner killed him, either."

"Helen Justen said she thinks you might have been the killer."

Barry's belly jiggled with his laugh. "Of course she did, Becca. I broke up with Helen Justen so I could ask Pauline out. That was just another ugly part of the whole ugly matter."

"Oh." That did put a different twist on Helen's accusation, though I'd have to find out if it was true. "Then where were you?"

"I told this to the police, Becca. I was here, but if you must know the details, I got up extra early, picked up Jeanine and her eggs because her truck was in the shop, and we set up our stalls together. Go on over and ask her. I'm sure the police already have." He pointed at Jeanine, who was deep in thought about something. "We live by each other and we often come in at the same time—earlier than any ole bird lookin' for a worm."

"I've been to your house. You live on the far side of town, right?"

"Have for a long time."

I nodded. My thoughts needed to catch up with my mouth. Barry lived nowhere near the Ivy League neighborhood; he lived nowhere near Abner and Carl. Barry's address was the one that didn't seem to fall in line with the other coincidences. That in itself didn't clear him, but his alibi probably did.

"Hmm. Well, I didn't know that Jeanine lived by you."

"A long time, Becca. And the stuff you're talking about, it was a long time *ago*. I really think you're barking up the wrong peach tree, darlin'. I don't know for sure if Abner killed Matty, but I don't think he did. He might have held a torch for Pauline, but after all these years . . . well, you just move on."

I nodded again, but I wasn't so sure I agreed. "Barry, what about Carl Monroe?"

"What about him?"

"Are he and Abner friends?"

"Becca, I don't know. Abner and I have worked together civilly for a lot of years, but as I told you before, we aren't good friends. I know Carl, but not well enough to know who he's friends with. Now, I've got to get to work. Scoot along and let me get my stall put together." He sniffed. "We all moved on," he muttered.

Again, I wasn't so sure, but there seemed to be nothing else I needed to know. "Yeah, thanks for your time, Barry. See you at the dinner?"

"See you there," he said as though I hadn't just accused him of murder. Maybe he liked telling his story—getting some of it out. Maybe.

I made my way back to my own stall, wondering if Helen could still be so angry about being dumped by Barry that she falsely accused him of murder. If so, then contrary to what Barry said, not everyone had moved on. Helen hadn't struck me as vengeful, but when it came to love, who knew anything for sure? I also wondered if Barry had told me more lies or if I was finally getting the truth out of him. I'd check with Sam—I knew he had to have talked to Pauline Simonsen. But would he tell me what she said?

I did one more walk-by of Ian's stall, found it still empty, and then hurried to my own.

It was good to sell my preserves. It felt normal and right. The crowd numbers were still low, but that wasn't a surprise. I sold, I chatted with Linda, sold some more, chatted with Herb and Don, sold some more. Not one customer asked about the murder, no one mentioned it. No one even looked over their shoulder funny, like they were concerned about someone running at them with an axe held high. I saw Allison a few times, though she didn't stop by my stall. She was in her manager mode, handling manager-type things like customer complaints, power issues, or whatever. It was a good day.

And when I sold out of product by one o'clock, my meeting with Abner came to the front of my mind—Abner my friend, not Abner the murderer. Hopefully.

"You done already?" Linda asked as she saw me packing up my portable table.

"Yeah. I didn't think we'd have a normal crowd today, so I didn't bring enough to last the day." It was a perfect excuse.

"Yeah, it's still slow."

"Uh-huh."

I said good-byes to the normal group and, because I couldn't resist, checked Ian's empty stall again and left in my truck, as though meeting with a murder suspect was as normal as selling preserves.

Sixteen

There were two reasons I hadn't asked Officer Brion to the din-ner yet. First, I wanted to talk to Ian. Our kiss hadn't been something that an exclusive relationship might be built upon, but I decided it was only polite to give him a heads-up. And I wanted to talk to him in person—that effort being thwarted today, even though I thought he'd told me he'd be at Bailey's. Second, I didn't want to talk to Officer Brion until I'd talked to Abner. Officer Brion seemed like a pretty good police officer; he'd know something was up by the guilty tone of my voice. He'd track me down before I could make the meeting.

The trip to Abner's was easy this time around. I slowed at just the right moment to turn easily onto the hidden back road, and my truck rumbled over the bumps without too much argument. All these years, and I'd never known where Abner lived. Now I knew where his sister lived and where he'd created his magical greenhouse. I also knew where Barry and Carl Monroe lived. And it might all mean squat. But I didn't think it did.

"It matters," I said to myself. "I just don't know why or how, yet."

Abner's house and greenhouse had a distinctly empty look to them. There was plenty of light left in the day, but there seemed to be a shadow over the property; a sadness, a longing.

"Just your imagination," I muttered.

I stopped in front of the white house at two fifty-eight. My phone rang exactly two minutes later.

"Abner?"

"Becca?"

"Where are you?" I demanded.

"Park behind the greenhouse. There's a path into the woods. You'll have to walk. You'll be here in about seven minutes."

"You're kidding, right?"

No response. The timer on my phone had stopped counting. The call had taken ten seconds.

"Damn." There was no way I was going to walk into the woods, alone and unarmed. Why would anyone do such a thing?

The seconds ticked by as I sat looking at the phone in my hand.

Somehow my mind twisted reality and worked to make sense of Abner's request. I came to the horrible conclusion that I was not going to miss this opportunity. I was going to do as Abner had instructed. I was going to walk into the woods and meet him. I knew he wasn't a murderer. I just hoped I was right. I pulled the truck behind the greenhouse. To prove I wasn't totally insane or stupid, I dialed Officer

Brion's number. I'd never received his voice mail before, so I was surprised to hear his business-like greeting.

After the greeting, I spoke quickly. "Uh, hi, Off . . . I mean Sam. Becca Robins here. I'm at Abner's. He called, said he'd meet with me. I'm parked behind his greenhouse and I'm going to walk down some path. He said it should take me about seven minutes to get there. Uh, just thought I should let you know. And thanks."

I'd probably just killed him with a heart attack, which meant he wouldn't be able to help me. But if he recovered in time, he'd head this direction and hopefully be here before the next axe fell.

"What's wrong with me?" I mumbled as I propelled myself out of the truck. I had a tool kit behind the seat that contained a screwdriver and a hammer, or so I thought. At some point I must have needed the screwdriver for something, so all that sat in the metal box was an old hammer. I threaded the hammer handle through a belt loop on my jeans and realized I looked like I was heading out to do some carpentering. I was not only being foolish, I looked the part, too.

I headed toward the well-worn path and tromped down it as I muttered to myself. There wasn't anything spooky about the heavily treed woods. And no matter what direction I looked, in the distance I could see part of someone's farm. Abner's to one side, Carl's to the other, and then two others, the homes of which I hadn't yet broken into or spied upon. But the day was still young.

After an approximately seven-minute hike I came upon a cabin smack-dab in the middle of the surrounding properties. It was small, made of wood planks and with a rock chimney shooting up from the the left side. The path opened up, both toward the cabin and farther past it. The continuing path opened wide and smooth, so that I thought a vehicle could it drive on it easily. I couldn't see Carl's property as well as I could a few minutes earlier, but I thought that this wider path probably led right to his big house and the orchard-in-a-bowl.

"Abner?" I cupped my hands around my mouth.

Before I could call again, the cabin door opened. Abner walked out and smiled sheepishly. He pulled his handkerchief out of his pocket and wiped his bald head.

"Come on in, Becca. Thank you for coming."

He sounded resigned and sad, but also truly grateful that I'd shown up. I wanted to hug him and then slug him in his arm, but instead I sighed and made my way to the door.

"Abner . . ."

"I know, I know. We'll talk." He stepped back and motioned me through the doorway.

"There's not a murderer in there, is there?" I asked.

"There're no murderers either in there or out here, Becca. It's just you and me, and neither of us have ever killed anyone."

"I'm counting on it." My hand on the hammer like it had a trigger, I walked through the door. The cabin was one big room with a bed, a couch, and a small table and chairs beside a half-wall kitchenette.

"Thanks again. For coming out here. Should I leave the door open?"

I looked at him and knew again, knew more deeply, maybe, that he wasn't a killer. He was my friend Abner.

"No, you can close it. Is this cabin yours?"

"Yes, this is still my land. I built it a long time ago. It's my idea of a vacation. I get away from everything and everyone, but I don't have to travel far to get back home." He laughed. I didn't laugh with him. "Please sit down. Want something to drink?"

"No, I don't. Is this where you've been staying?" I sat on one of the chairs.

"No. The police know about the cabin. It's not smart for me to be here for very long. I'm staying somewhere else, but this seemed like the best place for us to meet."

"Are you okay, Abner?" I asked. I was a mix of emotions. The murder, Abner's possible involvement, his running away, his asking me to meet him in a cabin in the woods—it was causing a tidal wave in my gut, but still, first and foremost, Abner had been my friend for a long time, and I knew he wasn't a murderer. I held on to that thought most of all. Or tried to.

"I'm fine, Becca," he said. "I don't like what's happening, but I'll get through it."

"How? The police are looking for you. How are you going to get through this? You know who the murderer is?"

"I do."

"Then why won't you tell the police?"

"Because the murderer is very clever and is good at making all the evidence point in my direction. I'm hiding until I can figure out how to solve that problem. If I'm in jail, I'll have no control."

"Abner, I admire your need to clear your name, but this is what the police do. They know how to search for evidence, including evidence that someone is being framed."

"Becca, I don't doubt their skill. I just think the murderer is cleverer than anyone gives them credit for."

I took a deep breath. "Okay, then tell me who it is. I'll do what I can to help you."

I meant what I said, I would help; but mostly, I had a deep need to know who was awful enough to take an axe to Matt Simonsen's head.

"Not going to do that. Yet."

"But you will at some point?"

"Maybe." He sighed. "But the real reason I asked you out here is because I want you to stop asking questions about the murder. Please."

"You want me to what?" Anger shot through me, red and hot, and choked my throat and burned my face. I was trying to help him, and he wanted me to stop?

"You talked to my sister. You shouldn't have done that."

My fingers went to the hammer again. It wasn't really in me, but the urge to beat this man senseless did cross my mind.

"First, Abner, friend, you don't get to tell me what to do. Second, I'm trying to save your butt. Third, this murder—though the person who got the worst of it was Matt Simonsen—has affected lots of people I care about. Bailey's reputation could be in question. Allison's job and the businesses that all the vendors have worked so hard to create could be jeopardized."

Abner's face fell as I went through my list. He was smart enough to have thought of all of these things. I wasn't telling him anything new, but he waited patiently as my blood pressure spiked with the tone of my voice.

"Becca, I shouldn't have said it that way. I'm sorry. I'm concerned for your safety, that's all. Hey," he laughed, "you just said a second ago that this is what the police do, not regular citizens like us, right?"

I took another deep breath. "Why are you concerned for my safety?"

"Because I don't want you to get caught in the cross fire."

"I can . . ." I was going to say that I could take care of myself. I could, but it sounded like something someone said right before something awful happened to them.

"I know you can, but, still . . ." His voice was kinder this time.

"Abner," I said with a sigh.

We were silent, both of us gathering this strange anger that wasn't really real—it was a misplaced product of fear on both our parts, I knew that much.

"Abner?" I broke the silence.

"Yes?"

"Why didn't you show yourself at my house the other day?"

"I don't know what you mean."

"When you hid on my porch and left the flowers in my pumpkins?"

Abner stood, a redness coming to his face. "I wasn't at your house. I swear to you. See what I mean?" He wiped his head again. "The murderer knows what you're up to. You have to stop."

Did I believe him? If so, there was a good possibility he was right and I might be in danger. If not, he was doing a great job of acting the part—*scare her and she'll stop.*

"Abner," I said, "if I'm in danger, give me something; something I can work with. I'll be careful. Tell me . . . well, tell me what Carl Monroe has to do with all of this."

That got his attention again. His eyebrows lifted high. "Nothing. Why would Carl have anything to do with any of this?"

"He's your neighbor; you've worked together for a long time. He's been acting funny, too. And when I saw him at

Smithfield Market, he ran from me." I left out the part that I'd seen Abner at Carl's house. I don't know why; it just seemed like something I needed to keep to myself a little longer.

"Why were you at Smithfield Market?"

"I went with Allison. She had a meeting with the manager. I thought it might be a good opportunity to see where Matt Simonsen worked, see if anyone there might give me some insight. My 'investigation' got diverted when I saw Carl."

"Becca, you have to believe me, I have no idea why Carl was at Smithfield, no idea at all." He pondered it for a moment.

"What, Abner? Is Carl the murderer?"

"What? No, Becca, Carl couldn't hurt anyone. I don't know why he was there, but it had nothing to do with Matt Simonsen, I assure you."

I wondered, but I said, "I met Jessop Simonsen. He seems like a nice man."

"I don't know him well, but I'm sure he's a nice man."

"Why? Because though you might have hated Matt Simonsen enough to at least threaten to kill him, you know that Matt's wife, Pauline, is a nice lady? Perhaps a lady you might have loved at one time?"

And there—I'd just offered him the biggest shock of all. He sat down again. "I knew you'd talked to my sister, but I didn't know you'd learned so much."

"She didn't tell me everything, Abner. Barry told me some, too. He told me something about your younger days."

"Barry," Abner muttered as he shook his head.

"Is Barry the murderer, Abner?"

"No, Becca, it isn't Barry. Barry's version of the past

might be tainted with time, though, you need to know that."

"Were you in love with Pauline?"

His chest puffed as he pulled in a deep breath. He let it go with another wipe of his forehead and said, "Yes, very much so."

"Are you still?"

He didn't answer quickly, which surprised me. "No, not really. It's been a long time. We had a great love and I'll always look back on that fondly, but I haven't loved her and she hasn't loved me for a long time."

"Was she the one in the picture?"

"What picture?"

Did Abner not know about the pictures and his upturned coffee table? If not, then he hadn't gone in his house before Ian and I and the police got there. I told him what we'd seen.

He nodded. "That was probably Pauline. I think I know what pictures you're talking about, but I don't know why they were there. They aren't mine. I didn't see them. I didn't go back into the house that day."

"Are they Pauline's?"

"I don't know, but I don't think so. She sent me all of our pictures when she left me for Matty. Being youthful and romantic, I burned them in my own little ceremony."

"But being youthful and romantic, too, maybe she kept some pictures."

"Maybe. I don't know."

"The killer must have put them there."

"Maybe."

"To somehow add to the case against you?"

"Maybe."

"Why did Pauline leave you for Matt?"

The hum of an engine outside rattled loose glass in one of the front windows. Was Officer Brion here already? And did he drive to the cabin? If so, he must have known about a different path. There was no way a car could have come the way I did.

Abner stood up and looked out the window. "Dammit," he said.

"Is it the police?" I asked. I wished I hadn't called Officer Brion. I might not have been getting much information, but I had Abner in a question-answer mode, and now it looked like I was going to be the one to turn him in. I felt awful.

"I don't know. Come on, let's go out the back. We'll have to use the window."

I stood and looked around. I might not have been happy with my choice to call the police, but I didn't like the idea of running from them.

"What?" I said. Abner's eyes were wild, but I realized they weren't the *right* kind of wild. "Oh, wait, it's not the police, is it? It's the killer."

I headed toward the window. I was going to see who was driving toward the cabin.

"No, Becca, don't!"

But I didn't listen. That is, until a sudden explosion rocked the world.

In one very fast move, I flattened myself on the ground, the hammer pounding into my hip bone as I landed on the dusty floor. Abner was on top of me in the next split instant.

"What the hell was that?" I yelled.

"A shotgun. Stay down, Becca," Abner said.

I was torn between staying down like he said and pitching myself out the back window like he'd suggested. *We were being shot at?*

We stayed on the ground, him on top of me, for what must have been less than a minute, but in soul-aging time it was a year or so.

The engine of the vehicle fired up again. I heard wheels turning on the dirt road and then spinning out before taking off again. Even though Abner tried to hold me back, I squirmed my way out from under him and crawled to the front door. On my hands and knees, I reached for the knob, opened the door a crack, and peered out. I saw a cloud of dust and the back of a nondescript brown truck.

"Abner, you'd better tell me exactly who that was," I said as I closed the door and glared back at my horrified friend.

"Police, open the door!" Officer Brion yelled from outside.

I have no idea how what happened next happened, but apparently Sam didn't have the patience to wait for me to turn the knob again. He either put a good shoulder into the door or kicked it. His maneuver slammed it open, and it caught me in my side. I was propelled through the air and farther into the cabin, landing on my back. As I saw the pretty white stars circling above, I was conscious long enough to be grateful I hadn't landed on the hammer this time.

Seventeen

As I came back to consciousness, I experienced that "where am I, who am I?" sense of discombobulation. The first thing I saw when I opened my eyes was the sky. It was lovely—mostly blue with a few clouds. The sun must have been pretty low, because I couldn't find it.

In a delayed reaction, the pain came next, and all at once. My left hip, my right arm, and the right side of my head hurt in ways I hadn't ever experienced, even when I broke my leg in high school after falling down a flight of stairs.

"Ohhh," I groaned involuntarily.

The pain also reminded me of where and who I was. But where was Abner? And Officer Brion? I lifted my head from what I realized was a pillow, and I looked around.

I was on a stretcher next to an ambulance. There were another ambulance and three police cars in the space around me. There were lots of official-looking, uniformed people, too—police officers and EMTs.

"Miss, you okay?" someone said as he appeared next to me. The EMT, who had a buzz cut and friendly eyes, looked very young and very concerned.

"I think so."

"You need to rest. You don't have a concussion, but you're pretty bruised. We put an IV in you with some pain medication."

"I don't think it's working."

The young man checked the mechanisms that made up the IV and said, "You should feel it kick in any second. You haven't been out for long, that's the good news."

"Okay. Where's Officer Brion?"

"Right here, Becca," he said as he appeared on my other side.

"Sam." I sat up again as the EMT put his hands lightly on my shoulders to push me back down. "Where's Abner?"

"He's on his way to the jailhouse, Becca. How're you doing?"

"Fine, but how is he, how is Abner?"

"He feels terrible that he put you in a dangerous situation, but I think he was probably glad we found him. It's not easy to hide all the time."

"Damn, I had him talking, Sam. He hadn't told me much yet, but I thought I might get him to give me something." I put my hand to my tender temple. "Hey, did you see that brown truck?"

"No. I walked to the cabin from Abner's house. I heard the gunshot and ran, but by the time I made it to the cabin, the vehicle was out of sight. Did you see anything else about it—license plate, bumper sticker, broken light, anything else?"

"No, it was a very plain brown truck."

Sam looked at the EMT, who nodded, apparently giving permission for him to continue asking questions.

"Becca, I know you don't feel well, but I need you to tell me everything you can about what you and Abner discussed, and I need you to do it now, before you forget anything and before they take you to the hospital."

"I'm not going to the hospital."

"It's for the best," the EMT said.

"Did I break any bones?"

"No."

"I don't have a concussion?"

"No."

"I'm just a little beat-up?"

"A lot beat-up," the EMT said.

"I'm very sorry about my part in that," Sam said, sounding more human than he ever had.

I glanced at him, at the EMT, and back at Sam.

"I'm not going to the hospital. I'll tell you about the entire conversation if you get this IV out of me and help me off this stretcher."

The corner of his mouth quirked as he and the EMT shared a look that made me angry.

But the EMT took out the IV, and Sam helped me off the stretcher and to his car. I got to sit in the front seat with the door open as he, obviously in charge, spent a few moments giving directions to other police officers and telling the EMTs that one ambulance could leave but one should remain just in case I changed my mind and did need a fast ride to the hospital, or if the search of the woods and cabin turned up someone else who was hurt.

Other than Allison, he was probably the most efficient person I'd seen in action. He knew how to take charge without being annoying and he knew what to do—in my experience, so many people who want to be in charge don't ever have a real plan. I suspected that Sam Brion, like Allison, always had a plan.

"He's not married, you know." Officer Vivienne Norton and her muscles had come up next to me.

I blinked. "Well, that's probably a good thing, because I think I'm going to ask him out to dinner."

Officer Norton smiled and winked. I wasn't about to burst her bubble by telling her that the date wouldn't be real, but just a way to further investigate the murder.

"Does he date much?" I asked. I was suddenly curious about the non-law-enforcement side of Sam Brion.

"Not really. Some. He moved here only about a year ago. No one knows much about his past, except that he's never been married and has no children. There was either a fiancée or an almost-fiancée or something, but no one can get the details."

"Where did he come from?"

"Chicago."

"Interesting," I mumbled.

Officer Norton excused herself and got back to work.

"Okay," Sam said, as he got into the driver's seat. "I think I can take your statement now. How're you feeling?"

"Fine, really," I lied.

"Good. Well, Becca, tell me the events that led up to you going into the woods to meet with a *murder suspect*, and what happened while you were there—talking to a *murder suspect*—and what that *murder suspect* had to say."

"I know, it was stupid."

"Yes, it was. You know I could have you arrested?"

"For what? Being stupid?"

"I'd think of something, and I'd make it stick." His mouth twitched again. "But I'm not going to arrest you. In fact, I'm so relieved that you're okay, I think I might actually find a way to forgive your stupidity—if you never, ever do it again."

"Pinky-swear." I imitated Helen Justen's promise.

"Good. Now tell me everything."

And I did. I told him *almost* every single thing that I knew. I even told him about Ian working at Smithfield for a year. He knew Ian had worked there and didn't act as though he had any particular suspicions about him, which was good. He listened, asked a few clarifying questions, and took notes. He told me that my job of investigating murders was coming to a close. The one thing I didn't share with him was the fact that Ian thought he remembered Abner being at Smithfield a little while back. Ian said he would call Officer Brion and share that detail. If he had, great; if not, I didn't want to mention something that might make Abner seem even more suspicious. Oh, and I didn't tell him about kissing Ian.

"Sam, did you talk to Pauline Simonsen about her past with Abner? Did you show her the pictures?"

He thought about it a moment before answering. "I did and I did, but I'm not able to share her answers with you. She said some things that lead me to . . . well, lead me to need to investigate some things further. I'm not just being difficult, Becca, but I can't tell you what she said."

"Okay. But Sam, if Abner was the murderer, then who shot at us? That must have been the murderer."

"Becca, most of the evidence points toward Abner. I don't know who shot at you, but I'll figure it out. I won't keep Abner under arrest if I can find any evidence anywhere that gives me a better suspect."

"But what about Abner's insistence that he's being framed?"

"That's a common thing for people under arrest to say."

I sighed. I was suddenly very tired.

"Oh, hey, let's get you home. I'll drive you, and have Officer Norton bring your truck."

"That's not necessary."

"It's either that or the hospital."

"Okay, take me home."

The arrangements were made, and in record time we were on the road.

"Sam," I said, "I know I'm out of the investigation business"—I wasn't, but it was better that he thought I was—"but I have an idea."

"Okay."

"Allison has planned a dinner for all the vendors and their families for Sunday night—it's a fall equinox thing, but it's mostly a time for the vendors and their families to come together before many of them leave until next season. It's a yearly event and very important to many of the vendors. They get to relax and socialize with the people they work with. Anyway, Allison thought she might need to cancel it in light of the murder, but everyone still wanted to go, so we're going to take some time to honor the memory of Matt Simonsen."

"Sounds like a good thing."

"Anyway, maybe we, uh, maybe you could go, well, would you like to go? We'll do some undercover investigating. It could be . . ." It didn't feel right saying that it wasn't a real date, but I didn't want him to misunderstand, either. I searched for the right words. Fortunately, he saved me.

"I get it. It would be a good idea for me to be there, but if I just showed up, people would think of me as the police. If I'm with you, maybe everyone will relax."

"Yes, that's it."

"Great idea. I accept. I'll pick you up at . . . ?"

"The dinner starts at six."

"Okay, I'll come get you about 5:30."

"No, come get me at four. I'm sore, but the dinner isn't until day after tomorrow. I'll be fine, and I want to be there early to help Allison set up."

"Deal," he said doubtfully. He looked at me as though he thought the date might not happen at all. I was probably a scary mess, but I wouldn't miss the dinner no matter how banged-up I felt.

We pulled into my driveway and were greeted by a very happy and annoyed dog. Hobbit had expected me home much earlier, and her entire body shook with irritated love. I pulled my sore body from the car and attempted to look like I didn't hurt all over. The EMT had given me some pain medication? I couldn't imagine how bad it would have been without it.

"I'll check your house, and then I want you to lock up and set the alarm," Sam said.

"Thanks." I considered going to Allison's again, but the way I felt, I knew there would be no better place for me than my own home, my own tub, my own bed, and next to my own dog. I'd make double sure the alarm was set.

I waited outside with Officer Norton, who had followed us in my truck, as Sam searched the premises. There was no more talk of Sam Brion's personal life. Officer Norton, probably a pretty good police officer in her own right, stood beside me but kept her eyes moving over my darkening property.

"All clear, Becca. Come on in," Sam said from the front porch.

Surprisingly, my leg didn't fall off my bruised hip bone as Hobbit and I walked forward. Sam helped me in and made sure I was okay before he turned to leave.

"Thank you. I guess I'll see you Sunday night," I said.

"Yes, ma'am," Sam said, without batting an eye.

"Hey, Sam, really, thank you for today. I'm sorry I didn't call you sooner, and I appreciate you getting there so quickly."

Sam smiled in yet another way I hadn't seen before. "I think I just might have you convinced that investigating a murder isn't wise for someone not properly trained—not to mention licensed or armed with something more effective than a hammer."

"Yes, you have," I lied, but I smiled before I closed the door all the way.

Hobbit and I armed the alarm and watched the police officers drive away.

"What a day, Hobbit. Hot bath for me, and then I guess I'd better call Allison."

Because of the wonder of cell phones, I could take the hot bath and call my sister at the same time. Before I sank into the water, I inspected the newly bruised me. The side of my face looked like I'd been punched, my shoulder had an interesting starburst-pattern bruise, and my hip had a hammerhead-shaped bruise that actually might have made an awesome tattoo. Maybe I'd show that one to Ian.

As I was in the tub of relief, I called my sister. Once she got over lecturing me, she expressed her concern and told me to get over to her house or she'd be at mine in warp speed. I explained the tub and alarm situation, and we agreed I was probably just fine where I was. All in all, she wasn't too mad, but I was sure I'd hear more from her after I healed.

There was one more call to make. I really needed to talk to Ian, but it was getting late and I didn't want to bother him. He beat me to the punch. My phone buzzed, his number showing up on the caller ID.

"Hey, Ian," I said cheerily. This hurt my face, but I didn't groan.

"Becca. How are you?" His words weren't laced with concern, so I figured he just meant it in a friendly way.

"I'm fine. You?"

"Good. I wanted to let you know why I didn't show up at Bailey's today after I told you I would. A new customer had a hard time making up her mind where she wanted her sculpture placed. After about a hundred different spots, she chose the first one we'd looked at. Naturally."

"Sounds challenging." I laughed lightly. This hurt my face, too.

"Goes with the territory."

"Yeah."

"Anyway, I know this is really late notice, but I wondered if you wanted to go to the Fall Equinox Dinner with me Sunday night." He cleared his throat.

"Oh, Ian, thanks for the invitation, but strange circumstances have occurred and I already have a date. Of sorts."

"Okay." He tried to hide the question in his tone.

I debated what to say next. "Ian, do you have a few minutes? I'd like to tell you what happened today."

"Sure. I'm listening."

Because I easily gave him the details of the day, I hoped

my instincts about his innocence were correct. And as we spoke, I realized that I really liked this man, my potential new boyfriend who was ten years younger than myself, an artist, and tattooed in a number of places.

My hippie parents were going to be very proud.

Eighteen

Unfortunately, I wasn't in any shape to go to Bailey's on Sat- urday morning. I didn't feel horrible, but I woke up stiff and sore, and colorful. I was sad to miss the last Saturday for many of the vendors, but I'd have to be content with seeing them on Sunday.

My bruises were transforming, and some of the black was turning yellow and purple. Lying around or sitting still made everything stiffer, and the idea of making jam seemed overwhelming—I could see getting halfway done and then losing the energy needed to finish it.

So I did light chores around the garden, barn, and house, fielded calls from the entire world regarding my well-being, and made Hobbit happy by giving her too much attention.

I even took a nap, which was a rare treat.

But when I woke up at midafternoon, I was restless. My body felt a bunch better, and I had enough energy to be irritated that I hadn't made the day more productive.

I debated what I could do for the next couple of hours to burn off energy. There was always something to do, somewhere. It was far too late to go to Bailey's with some product. My barn was spotless—I hadn't made enough jams or preserves this week to dirty it; my crops were in great shape and I'd given more than enough attention to the ripening pumpkins; my dining table still had stacks of paperwork, but I was in no state of mind to try to figure out what to do with all of it.

"Want to go see Allison?" I asked Hobbit.

She wagged her tail in the affirmative, so we got in the truck.

I had every intention of going to Bailey's and visiting my sister and everyone else, Ian included, but I stopped at the top of the driveway. Going to Bailey's required turning right, but something didn't want me to go that direction.

I'd promised Allison, Ian, and Sam Brion that other than my upcoming "date" with Sam, I was done investigating murders. On our call the previous evening, Ian had said he was going to come to my house and keep me out of trouble today, but I convinced him that I'd just be resting and he should take advantage of the Saturday crowd at Bailey's. And I told them all again today, when they called to check on me, that I was fine and was going to take it easy. I hadn't been lying on purpose; I just hadn't known I'd feel such an urge to turn left.

"You up for a different drive?" I asked.

Hobbit again wagged her tail affirmatively.

"You're so easy."

I turned left.

Something had been eating at me, and I didn't know how I was going to ease the pain other than go check things for myself.

The trees. What was with the trees? I wanted—no, I *needed*—to see them for myself. Sam had told me he'd investigate, but he wouldn't promise to share details. I needed details.

It was daylight, so I wasn't going to go to the trees via Abner's house and the woods; I'd walk over Carl's more open property and I'd have Hobbit with me. I still had Carl in my "potential murderer" category, and I knew without question that he was at Bailey's—Allison had confirmed as much when I asked her that morning. Apparently everyone was at Bailey's except me. In many years, I didn't think I'd ever missed a Saturday, but as I pulled in front of Carl's bowl orchard, I felt like it was meant to be. The big house was clearly empty, and the trees in the orchard seemed to beg for my company.

"Let's go, girl." I parked on the side of the state highway again.

Hobbit followed me toward the bowl. She remembered that the last time she was here, she was forced to stay in the truck. She lifted her nose to the wonderful smells all around and looked at me as if to say, "See, I could have handled this the first time."

The only realistic way to get to the trees was through the bowl. The orchard smelled heavenly—this was something I'd noticed on my previous visit, but hadn't taken the time to appreciate. But it wasn't peach smells so much—most of the peaches were gone—as it was healthy trees and soil. I had a nose for such things, and the smells around us seemed to tell me that Carl took very good care of his orchard.

Carl was one of the vendors who probably wouldn't be back to Bailey's until next season, and I wondered if he did something else to supplement his living from selling peaches. Why didn't I know the people I worked with as well as I thought I did? I always missed those who weren't lucky enough to have a pumpkin patch or be able to freeze enough product to have a year-round operation, but I didn't really *know* many of them well enough at all.

Hobbit and I climbed up the other side of the bowl and walked back into the warm sunshine that cut through the slight chill in the air. The pain in my hip was escalating slightly, but I tried to ignore it.

Allison's words from our morning conversation came to me as I realized I was breathing heavily.

"Don't overdo. Even if you feel better, you've been through trauma; you need to make sure you get lots of rest," she'd said.

The trees were only a small hill away so we continued on, though I was slow.

When I got there, I was no longer certain that these were the trees in the pictures. They might be, but so much time had passed, and though the setting seemed the same, the trees were definitely bigger. I thought they were some sort of maple; they weren't huge, but they were full with leaves that still didn't hint at a color change, yet that wasn't unusual for this time of year in South Carolina.

I looked back at Carl's house, which I could clearly see, but I couldn't distinguish any other properties from this vantage point. That seemed odd, because I was higher up, but nonetheless I couldn't see any part of Abner's house or greenhouse.

I went to the other side of the trees and realized that without question these must be the ones in the pictures. Each of them had a heart carved into its trunk and words carved inside the hearts—not just initials, but whole words.

One said Pauline Loves Barry but had an X over it as

though to cross it out. Another tree, the middle one, said Pauline Loves Matty, and it, too, had an X over the writing. The last tree was the most disturbing, though. I think it said Pauline Loves Abner, but I couldn't tell whether or not those words had been negated by an X. Someone had recently taken what must have been an axe to it, and the only part I could read was Pauline Loves A; everything else was chopped up. I wondered if Sam had seen the trees yet, and if he had thought to check the axe for wood pieces along with blood and fingerprints.

"Weird," I said. "Why?"

Beyond the fact that chopping away at the words was childish, the tree probably wouldn't survive, and that irritated me. The Xs had been done a long time ago, carved with the same sort of thing that had carved the initials. The trees had made it through the carvings. But the chopping was a recent addition, something violent and thoughtless.

"It's some sort of clue, Hobbit, but I have no idea what it means," I said as I touched the exposed innards of the beautiful tree. "Who did this?"

Hobbit didn't answer but made her way back to the other side of the trees. She barked lightly to get my attention.

Someone was pulling into Carl's driveway. We were far enough away that they might not think to look in our direction, but I didn't want to risk being seen.

"Come here, girl," I said.

Fortunately, she listened and we hid behind the middle tree.

It was a truck, but not a brown one. In fact, it was white and maybe only five years old or so. It also had a topper over the bed. It had come from the opposite direction than we'd come, but I didn't like that my bright orange truck was on the side of the state highway, right there for everyone to see. I didn't have any advertising on it, but the color was an announcement in itself.

Since the house was so close to the road and the driveway was so short, once the white truck was all the way in the driveway, I couldn't see it. I really wanted—no, *needed*—to know who was driving it.

"Damn. Hobbit, come on."

We came out from behind the tree and hurried to the bowl. I ran like I'd been beaten up the previous day and my hip in particular had been injured. Even Hobbit looked at me like she wasn't sure if I was serious or not—my gait was far from even and pain free, but I trudged along.

Finally we reached the bowl, and I practically slid on my behind down the side. I hurried (well, to the best of my ability) to the slope of the orchard from which I'd previously spied on Carl. There was no climbing the tree today, but I crawled up and peered over the side of the bowl. Hobbit, good sport that she was, lay on her belly next to me, her long paws sticking up over the lip of the bowl like rabbit ears.

The truck was empty and my breathing was more labored. If someone had come at me with an axe at that moment, I would have told Hobbit to run and save herself; there was nothing I could have done to protect my aching body from anyone or anything.

Ten minutes or so passed before the person attached to the truck emerged from the house.

I was shocked from the top of my bruised head to the bottom of my sore toes.

Mamma Maria, the pie lady from Smithfield Farmers' Market, came out of the house, looked around as though she was trying to spot someone watching her, and then snuck a key into the lock. She wore jeans and a white T-shirt, but she was still . . . what was the term? Oh, yes, she was *hot*. She was a beautiful, sexy woman who baked amazing pies—if I wasn't so curious about her involvement in Matt Simonsen's murder, I might have been jealous. She hurriedly slid the key into her back pocket, got in the truck, and drove away. She didn't look in my direction once.

What was she doing at Carl's house? Why wasn't she at her own market on one of the busiest days of the year? When could I get another one of her pies?

For a long time, I leaned against the edge of Carl's orchard bowl and tried to come up with some answers, but nothing came to me except more questions. I couldn't call anyone and tell them what I'd discovered. I'd pinky-sworn that I was out of the business of investigating murders and that I would take it easy all day. Even Allison might have had me arrested if she knew what I'd been up to—if only to keep me out of trouble.

"Come on, Hobbit, let's go home," I finally said.

I gathered my stiffening self and my dog. We made our way out of the bowl—my crawl wasn't pretty—and into my truck.

So, for the rest of the afternoon, I did as all my friends/family/pretend-doctors said. I thought my busy mind might prevent me from relaxing, but I was wrong. I didn't just rest, I slept—another long nap. As I was dozing off, I hoped any upcoming dreams would help sort out the questions. But as far as I remember, I saw only black nothingness.

Nineteen

Surprising myself, I woke up in a good mood. I felt a bunch better and was well rested. Hobbit thought this suspicious, and for a while she followed me around the house with doubting eyes.

I still wasn't going to Bailey's, but I was ready for some serious time in the barn. I needed to get my inventory built back up to a respectable size. I planned on working the next week with a pain-free body, a good attitude, and lots of jam. Plus, I had a party to prepare for, and my bruised face would require a slab or two of makeup. That would take time.

Blueberries called to me from the freezer. Of my frozen fruits, they seemed to be most ready to be transformed into jam. This relationship I had with my plants and fruits, this intuitive communication, was probably something I got from my hippie parents, but it was real to me.

I pulled the berries out of the freezer to thaw while I

readied everything else. First, I loaded jars into the dishwasher. My modern kitchen had been fitted with modern appliances, and my dishwasher had a Sterilize cycle. I still prepared the lids via the old-fashioned method: boiling on the stovetop.

There isn't really anything more satisfying than the mashing of blueberries. Well, to me at least. Once they'd thawed enough, I placed the berries in the bottom of a pan and took a potato masher to them, happily smushing them just enough, and to perfection. Other fruit worked in the food processor, but the potato masher was the only way to go with blueberries.

My job was in so many ways my sanity. The process, from growing the crops to selling final products, was satisfying at every step. Working at Bailey's, with my sister and with other friends, was a life that I wouldn't trade for anything. As I worked the jam that Sunday morning, I realized that I wasn't going to let a murderer or a few bruises ruin what had become a really terrific life.

Besides, I was close to figuring out . . . well, something. Whether it was the murderer's identity or something else, I wasn't sure. A realization of some sort kept trying to spark in my mind, like I was staring at something that I wasn't really seeing. I'd mentioned as much to Ian when he called a couple of nights earlier, and he'd tried to add some flame to the spark, but neither of us had been able to get any closer to what I was missing.

Sigh.

Between attempting to organize my thoughts and enjoying some Motown classics as I worked, the time flew. Before I knew it, I was on the last step of processing the jam-filled and sealed jars in boiling water. Some people didn't follow through with a complete boil, but to reduce any chance for spoilage, I not only boiled the jam-filled and sealed jars, but did so for a little longer than needed. After about seven to ten minutes, I used tongs to pull out the jars and set them on a cooling table, careful to not let them touch one another or bang into anything. They'd cool throughout the day, and I'd be able to add them to my next week's inventory. I was excited about the possible predictability of next week's schedule. It would be good to get back to Bailey's.

I left the kitchen at about two o'clock, a good day's work accomplished. Hobbit greeted me happily and stayed at my side as I went back into the house. She waited as I showered and dressed. I kept telling her I was fine, but she held fast in her mission.

I wanted to take her to the dinner, but that wasn't a reasonable idea. I'd lock her in the house when I left, and she wouldn't be happy. I'd owe her big, but I'd find a way to make it up to her.

At exactly 3:41 P.M., a knock sounded on the front door.

"He's a police officer, Hobbit, he's trained to be early," I said as I put in an earring. I'd had my ears pierced when I was eleven and had worn jewelry consistently until I'd started in the farming/preserves/market business. Casual, with no time for accessories, had been my fashion statement since then. But I was sure that Allison had worked hard to make this dinner upbeat, and that made me think I should spruce up a bit. And though the makeup had been necessary to cover my bruised face, I'd made it look pretty natural.

I opened the door with a smile and then froze in place. Officer Brion—I mean Sam—froze, too.

I know what was going on in my mind. I can only guess

what was happening in his. This time it went something like this:

"Hi," I said to the man whose oil light must have been blinking. Whatever he used for his slicked-back style was noticeably gone. In its place was a head full of clean, wavy brownish hair, somewhat ruffled. His short-sleeved shirt had a bright print; something almost Hawaiian but not quite. His muscular calves stuck out from below some casual shorts. He looked positively . . . playful.

"You're wearing a dress," he said as his eyes opened wide.

"Yes, it's the only one I own." It was a sundress, not really appropriate for the cooler evening weather, but I'd planned on wearing a sweater, too.

"You look . . . nice."

"Are you sure?" I laughed.

He smiled, almost laughed, too, as his cheeks reddened.

"Yes, I'm sure. I just wasn't expecting a dress."

"You look nice yourself. And you don't look a thing like a police officer."

"That's the plan, isn't it?"

"Yes, it is," I said. "Did you have to go buy that get-up?"

"No, believe it or not, my clothes aren't always unicolored, wrinkle free, and intense. Well, I can't help the intense part so much, but I like a wrinkle or two sometimes," he said, his mouth fighting another smile. To prove his intensity was never far away, he didn't take his serious eyes away from mine. He could probably put a hole in steel with that stare if he wanted to.

"That's good to hear." I cleared my throat.

We looked at each other another beat or two. I suddenly

wanted to know more about him— Why had he come to Monson, and what had his previous life been?

"Uh, well, we should probably go," he said, breaking up the strange moment.

"Of course." I grabbed the sweater I'd thrown over a chair and turned to Hobbit. "Be a good girl."

She switched it on big-time. She was a pro eye-drooper.

"Let's take her," Sam said, being totally taken in by lesson one of Dog Charm School.

"I'd love to, Sam, but think about it. It's probably not a good idea. It's a dinner."

"You're right, but I hate leaving her. Will she stay in the car?"

"Only if we stay in it with her."

Rough decision of the day made—Hobbit would miss the party. But I had on a dress, some earrings, and a thick layer of makeup—I felt very girly, and though it wasn't something I needed to feel all the time, it was fun every now and then.

I was used to trucks, mostly old trucks. Sam's vintage Mustang convertible was a welcome change. With the top down (by my choice—he asked which I preferred), my hair felt like it blew just right.

"Sam, I didn't hear anything new yesterday. How's it going with Abner? Allison was surprised that no one has said a word to her."

"Believe it or not, I've kept it under wraps, which in a small town is no easy feat."

"How?"

"I have my ways, but you probably don't need to know the details. Suffice it to say that the news will be out by morning. The best thing is that Monson only has a weekly paper, not a daily. Monday's—tomorrow's—edition will have the story. The larger cities are interested in our small-town murder, but they'll pursue it more after the *Monson Gazette* lands on porches tomorrow."

"Allison and Ian know, Sam. I told them both," I said, experiencing a rare moment of telling the truth.

"I figured as much, but they must not have spread the word, either."

"I don't think so. We'll probably find out when we see how we're greeted at the party."

"It'll be fine, either way." Sam paused. "So, how are you, Becca? How're you feeling?" he asked once we were on the state highway.

"I'm fine," I said.

He looked doubtful.

"You were shot at, you hammered your own hip, and I threw you across a room with a door. Those sorts of things can cause pain."

"I know, but really, I'm fine." I was. Mostly. I was much better than the day before, but I didn't go there. I wasn't ready to tell him about my excursion. I wasn't ready to tell anyone. Besides, Sam had said he'd check out the trees. He'd probably already seen them. Mamma Maria's surprise appearance also wasn't something I was ready to share. I wanted more details, hopefully from Carl and hopefully this evening at the party.

"Well, even tough police officers like myself"—he winked—"are required to talk to someone after being shot at."

"A psychiatrist?"

"Yes, or psychologist. There are lots of people you can

talk to if you need to. I'm not one of those 'ists,' but you can always talk to me."

"Thank you. I appreciate that, I really do, but it was one shot and I don't think I was the target. I'm not freaked-out in the least."

"Okay."

"Thanks, Sam," I said.

"You're welcome."

"So, you've been a police officer for a long time?" I asked.

"You're changing the subject, I see."

"Yep."

"I've been a police officer all my life, or at least since finishing college. It's all I ever wanted to be."

"So it's a passion?"

"Complete and total."

"Where did you grow up, come from?"

Sam paused long enough that I glanced at him. When he finally spoke, he said, "Chicago, the one in Illinois." He tried to make the tone of his voice light so I wouldn't notice the pause. It didn't work.

"Why did you leave Chicago for South Carolina?"

"Have you ever been to Chicago?"

"No, I don't think I have."

"It's a wonderful city, but it's big and there's a lot of crime—some of it very violent. I was ready for a change."

"Crime like murders at farmers' markets?"

"Good point."

"Hmm."

"What?"

"Well, you don't have to tell me or anything, but I know you're not giving me the whole story. You said you love being a police officer, so enforcing the law in Chicago was probably wonderful. And South Carolina? There's something else behind why you chose here, I can hear it in your voice."

Sam laughed. "You definitely have a keen sense of observation. Very impressive. If you ever get tired of farming and farmers' markets, I bet you'd make a good cop."

"I'll never get tired of what I do, but you still haven't answered my questions. Tell me what you're leaving out."

Sam guided the convertible down the open road. There was no traffic, and the fields and intermittent dwellings on both sides of the road were part of what I loved most about where I lived. I thought I might lose my mind if I ever tried to live in a big city.

"Well, why I left is a very long story that I'm not ready to share with anyone quite yet, but maybe someday. Why I came to South Carolina, though—well, that's easy. My grandparents lived here. I was born and raised in Chicago, but my parents brought me here to visit frequently. When I wanted to go someplace other than where I was—Chicago—I chose the place that had the best memories for me."

"That's a pretty good reason," I said.

We drove in silence for a few minutes. Sam seemed to need a moment of introspection.

"So, how many murders have you solved?" I broke the silence.

He laughed again. "That's an interesting question. Let's see, I helped solve four in Illinois. Unfortunately, I worked on a number of others that didn't get solved while I was there. This is my first murder in South Carolina. I'll have it solved—or you'll have it solved for me—shortly."

"You're confident?"

"Yes."

"Is there a possibility that the murderer is someone other than Abner?"

"Anything is possible, but I have to find the evidence."

"What can I do to help?"

"Quit putting yourself in danger, and don't 'forget' to tell me anything else."

"Point taken, but really, I want to help. Tonight, at least. At the dinner. Is there something I can do? I know you'll be investigating, even though you won't look like it."

"I don't know, yet. Let's see what happens. Follow my lead, whatever it may be," Sam said as we pulled into Bailey's parking lot.

"Deal."

There were still customers, since the market didn't close for another two hours, but there weren't many. We got a parking spot close to the front entrance. I looked around for brown trucks. There were six that I could see with my quick survey. Except for one that seemed like it was fresh off the showroom floor, they all looked pretty much the same.

"I have a few officers around here tonight. They'll never be far away," Sam said.

"You do? Are you worried about our safety?"

"Not particularly, but precaution is good. No one will notice. I've got them outside the market and at key road intersections. I can't tell you *all* my secret police stuff."

"Share whatever you want. I like secrets."

Sam got out of the car and walked quickly to my side. He opened the door and offered me his hand. "I noticed. Shall we?"

"I believe we shall." I was feeling much better, but my hip was still sore enough that the help was nice.

Probably noting my slightly off gait, Sam crooked his elbow. I happily put my arm though it as we entered Bailey's. Of course, the first person we saw was the one I didn't want to see me arm in arm with another man.

"Mr. Cartwright," Sam said as he extended his hand.

"Officer. Becca," Ian said as he shook Sam's hand and sent a conspiratorial pinched smile in my direction. "Nice to see both of you. How're you feeling, Becca?"

"Hey, Ian, I feel pretty good, much better, thanks," I said. I'm sure he didn't look any different than he had the day I'd gone to his apartment, but he looked different to me. Or maybe I looked at him differently. He seemed older than I'd remembered, or my mind played a trick to make it so. I'd already explained my fake date with Sam to him, and he'd taken it in stride, but I suddenly felt guilty about kissing Ian and then going out with Sam.

I realized that, if nothing else, my social life had changed dramatically because of the murder.

"Mr. Cartwright, I'd like to spend some time at your booth. I think I might have a great place for one of your sculptures," Sam said.

"Really? Anytime. You're even welcome to come to my apartment and see my workshop. I allow all law enforcement to visit and search the premises undeterred. Becca might have told you that," Ian said, focusing on me as he finished the comment.

"That might be a good idea," Sam said, as he patted my hand and looked at me. "Ian called and told me that it was your interrogation that made him remember he saw Abner at the Smithfield Market a while ago. Like I said, you might want to consider police work."

Had Ian told Sam about our moment of romance? I looked at him and he, ever so slightly, shook his head. He hadn't, which pleased me. I liked the idea of keeping my personal life personal. Besides, who likes a guy who kisses and tells?

"I'll keep that in mind," I said. "Sam, how about you and I go help Allison? Ian, we'll see you later?"

"Yes, you will."

Sam and I made our way down the aisle. I didn't keep my arm through his because my hip was working better but, in execution of our plan, we walked close enough that we hopefully gave the impression we were *together.* I wondered if any of this "show" was necessary. I doubted that anyone would recognize Sam as an officer who had been on the scene the day of the murder. He didn't look a thing like the uptight cop who didn't sweat. He might have been able to show up at the dinner without using me as a date/excuse. He smiled, and we chatted easily about unimportant matters. Everyone probably thought they were seeing me with my soon-to-be third ex-husband.

And no one really looked at us, anyway. Most of the vendors were either busy with customers, packing up their stalls, or visiting with family members who had shown up early for the dinner.

"I don't think we're making much of an impression," Sam said.

"Did I tell you I've been married twice?"

"No."

"Yes, they were both named Scott. Scott number one was an intellectual and part of my wild youthful days. Scott the second was a good ol' country boy who didn't know how to either get or hang on to a job. I'm not sure anyone takes my dates all that seriously. I hadn't thought of that problem."

"Hmm. Well, that could work to our advantage. The

better I can blend into the background, the better I can eavesdrop. Plus, my name's not Scott."

"True." I laughed. "And even with that shirt, I think you're blending just fine."

Sam laughed, too.

"Becca." Stella waved us over from her booth. She'd packed up her bakery items, but there was still a scent of fresh bread hovering in the air. Her two teenagers, Jacquelyn and Richard, sat at the back of her stall and were engrossed in some sort of heated card game.

"Hi, Stella, how are you? Ricky, Jackie, hi."

The kids waved and went back to their game.

"Great, but I haven't seen you in a while. Where've you been?" Stella said.

"Busy with some other stuff. You know, business stuff."

She smiled at me with a one-sided dimple.

"Uh-huh," she said as she wagged her eyebrows at Sam. "Or is it that you have a new boyfriend?" Stella wasn't shy.

"Oh, well, this is Sam. Sam, there isn't a person in the universe who can bake better bread than Stella."

"Nice to meet you," Sam said, extending his hand again.

"You, too." She was trying to figure out how she knew him, but she didn't say anything. "Becca, I'm so glad Allison kept the dinner scheduled. It'll be good for all of us."

"I think so, too."

"So, have you heard from Abner?" she asked, too forcefully. I realized that was why she'd called us over in the first place. She hadn't been interested in Sam at all. She knew how close Abner and I were—everyone did. I thought about Barry's questions in the parking lot a couple of days ago. No one knew what I'd been up to, but they noticed I'd been gone. And Abner had been gone. Did they wonder if Abner and I were both up to no good—perhaps together?

"No, not even once," I lied.

"I wish we knew what was going on."

"I'm sure the police have everything well in hand," I said.

"Becca, Allison might need our help," Sam said.

"Sure. Of course. Stella, we'll see you at the dinner."

We said our good-byes and continued down the aisle. We extended casual greetings to others and casual greetings were sent our way. When I really looked at Sam, I saw his serious eyes were in constant movement, but the rest of him kept up the appearance of a guy on a date. He really was a great cop.

The Fall Equinox Dinner was always held at the end of one of the aisles in a space that was mostly used for storage. A few tent walls were placed here and there, and no one saw the hidden display tables, product racks, and white boards. Allison had been hosting the dinner for ten years. It was always successful, and each year the storage items had to be pushed closer and closer together to make space for all attendees, the number of whom had grown considerably over time.

We greeted Allison as we entered the back area. She wore jeans and an old T-shirt, and her long, dark ponytail swung behind her as she carried a box of something to the front buffet table. She had three or four teenagers helping her. I was sure they were all the offspring or relatives of vendors, but I didn't recognize any of them.

"Becca, Sam, hi!"

"Hey, Sis." I hugged her.

"Allison, nice to see you again," Sam said. "What can I do to help set up?"

"Oh, you could you help Sander with the platform. I've got a small band coming, and we need a better place for them than by the bar. Becca, I'd rather you just sat still."

"No. I can help, too. Don't start that with me. I'm fine, just a little stiff. Actually, the movement will be good for me."

Allison looked at me a long moment. "Okay, help me unfold some chairs."

"That's better." Allison and I went to get the chairs as Sam went to find the teenager named Sander.

"Becca," she whispered to me as we were unfolding, "I really hope this isn't in bad taste. Despite what everyone said the other day, I almost canceled it. I don't want to appear disrespectful to the memory of Mr. Simonsen."

"Allison, I think that canceling it would have been a bad idea. The vendors and their families look forward to it so much. It'll help us all move forward."

"It won't be as much fun as it has been. I did cancel everything I'd originally planned and just got a small three-piece country-western group. I'm not doing any games or awards or anything. Just dinner, dessert, and a little music."

"It'll be perfect."

"We'll see. And I invited Pauline and Jessop Simonsen."

"What did they say?" I wished I'd told Allison about Pauline's total history of men, but it was too late now. If I mentioned anything about making sure the Simonsens didn't sit by Barry's family, she'd get more stressed than she already was. I'd have to try to intervene if necessary.

"I called and told them that we'll offer a moment of silence in honor of Matt. I wanted them to know that it was something that was planned far in advance and . . . well, I just . . ."

"It's all good, Sis," I said. There were few moments in our thirty-five years when I was the soothing one. I had some terrific friends, but as my bad choices in husbands illustrated, my insight into people was sometimes nearsighted. Allison was usually the voice of reason. So, though I hadn't had much practice, I hoped I did a decent job of soothing her concerns.

"I hope so. Hey, how's it going with Officer Brion?" We both glanced to where Sam and Sander were setting up a microphone.

"Fine. He's not so bad for a fake date."

"I wonder how fake he thinks it is. Did you get a chance to talk to Ian?"

"Responding to those backwards, yes, I talked to Ian. No big deal. And what do you mean, 'how fake he thinks it is'?"

"Becca, you're brilliant. You graduated at the top of your class from a respected university, but somewhere along the way, you totally missed out on understanding men."

"Guess I can't argue with you there."

"Allison, someone's asking for you out front," one of the teenagers said.

"Go on. I get what we're supposed to do here. Sam and I can figure it out," I said.

The party was definitely going to be mellower than it had ever been. In years past, there had been distinct themes—Carnivale, Hawaiian, Broadway. This year was originally was going to be Monte Carlo, but there were no gambling tables anywhere. Instead, everything was simple, white-tent-walled, and understated. The band arrived before Allison returned, and with the hope that I wasn't stepping on her toes, I asked the three men dressed in checkered shirts, straw hats, and overalls if they knew any square dance stuff. Fortunately, they did, so under my guidance, Sam and the teenagers rearranged the tables just enough to leave a space for those interested in dancing. If no one wanted to dance, fine, but it was something.

"This looks nice," Sam said once we'd spread the last white tablecloth.

"Almost, but I have one more idea. I need to find Linda. I'll be right back," I said.

"Uh, you want me to go with you?" Sam asked.

"How about you help the band with their instruments?" I said as one of the musicians lugged a big bass to the platform/stage area.

"Becca, what're you up to?" Sam asked.

"I'm just asking Linda for some napkins, that's all. Honest." I crossed my heart.

"If you're not back in fifteen minutes, I'm coming to look for you."

"It'll take me ten." I smiled and waved as I left. Really, I wanted to find the checkerboard napkins I'd seen in Linda's stall. However, I also wanted to talk to Barry. I wanted to forewarn him about the possibility of Mrs. Simonsen and Jessop showing up. I didn't want Barry's wife to feel uncomfortable.

I hurried first to Linda's stall, where she had already packed up whatever was left over of her inventory. She was out of her pioneer garb and in jeans and a light sweater instead. Her blond curls that were normally hidden by a bonnet sprang up around her head in a halo. She was a very pretty woman even if the bonnet hid it sometimes. But there was something else that lit her up this late afternoon.

She was talking to a man I'd never seen before. He was the epitome of tall, dark, and handsome. At first glance, I had the urge to inspect his chest for a big red S.

"Linda," I said, pulling her attention away from Mr. Gorgeous.

"Oh, hi, Becca. How are you, darlin'?"

"Great. Hi," I said to the man I hoped was her date. She'd have some good stories for me if he was.

"Hi." He walked as though he'd practiced in front of a camera, and his teeth sparkled with a smile.

"Becca, this is Drew Forsyth. Drew, my very good friend Becca."

"Nice to meet you, Becca," he said in a perfect voice.

"You, too. You joining Linda for the dinner?" I asked.

"Yes, she was kind enough to invite me," he said as he turned his glance to her. He really liked her; it was either that or he just smiled fondly in everyone's direction.

"Great. We'll have to sit together," I said to Linda.

"I'll plan on it. What's up?" Linda said.

"You know those checkered napkins? You still have some?"

"I have a bunch."

"Can I buy them off you?"

"No, but I'll give you some. You want a whole box?"

"Yes, please. I'll bring you some jam."

Linda gathered the box of napkins from behind her back tent wall as Drew and I made small talk. There was no way he was as wonderful as he seemed to be. It wasn't possible. I'd have to ask deep, probing questions at dinner.

The box of napkins secure under one arm, I headed toward Barry's stall. Though most of the shoppers were now gone for the day, the aisles were becoming more crowded with vendors' families, so when I first caught a glimpse of Barry, the view wasn't clear. He was looking up as he spoke to someone. I craned my neck to see who it was, but between my short stature and the movement of the small but mobile crowd, I couldn't tell exactly.

Finally, I got a quick look at the back of the person facing Barry. He was tall, very tall, and wore a hat on his head. He also wore a long trench coat with the collar turned up. I snaked my way through people and toward Barry and the person I presumed was Carl, though his disguise was awful. How would anyone not know that it was him? There were very few people in Monson with that tall, skinny build.

Barry happened to look in my direction just as I made my way around someone's kids. His face flashed panic, and he pushed on the other person's arm as he said something vehemently to him. He turned to look in my direction, but someone walked in front of me right at the moment when I would have seen the mystery person's face. And then, much to my anger and disappointment, the tall person turned and ran in the other direction.

You've got to be kidding me, I said to myself. What was going on? Why had Barry sent him away? I was perturbed at myself for having wanted to do him the favor of letting him know about the Simonsens. Whose side was he on?

"Barry, who was that?" I said as I reached his stall.

He shrugged and said, "Didn't see anyone."

I slammed the box of napkins down on an empty display table.

"Tell me who that was, or I'm going to have the police arrest you right this minute."

"On what charges, Becca?"

"Murder."

Barry's face went red and pinched. That pose lasted for a good thirty seconds before he calmed down.

"Becca, do what you have to do, but I can't tell you who that was," he said.

"Was it Carl Monroe?"

"Who? No," he said almost believably.

"Dammit, Barry, why won't you tell me?"

He shrugged. "It's not important right now. If it becomes important, I'll tell the appropriate people."

"I hate that answer."

"There's nothing I can do about that."

I didn't chase after the tall man. He could probably move faster than me anyway, and I'd told Sam I wouldn't be gone much longer. Plus, if it was Carl, I'd already been there, done that. I wanted to choke Barry, but considering that my date was a police officer, that might have been a bad idea.

"Barry, please?"

"Becca, you need to just stop whatever it is you're doing. You don't need to worry yourself about this stuff."

"Don't worry my pretty little head, huh?" I said as I went from simmer to boil.

"Something like that, yes." Barry turned and walked out the back of his stall.

I took ten deep breaths to calm my anger, then had to add two more. What the hell was going on? I grabbed the napkins and maneuvered my way back to the party, telling myself that I needed to put on the face of calm and collected, or Sam might put the place on lockdown.

"Becca," Ian said from behind me.

"Ian, hi."

"Oh, hey, you okay?"

Anger had probably made my face so red that the makeup had burned right off. I thought about telling Ian about my moment with Barry, but I didn't have the time and I still needed to cool down enough to speak calmly.

"Fine," I said, almost convincingly. He didn't buy it, but he didn't push it, either.

"Let me carry that?" He nodded at the box of napkins.

"I got it, but thanks. You heading to the party?"

"Thought I'd see what I could do to help."

"Great. I'm going back, too," I said as I turned.

"Becca," Ian said as he reached for my arm. "I need to talk to you for just a minute."

"Sure," I said, pushing back my anger and confusion some more.

"The other night, on the phone, it didn't seem appropriate to talk about it, but I hope you know that I'd like to spend some more time with you. I have a sudden urge to tell you this, so if Officer Brion sweeps you off your feet tonight, you'll know . . ."

There were too many people around; people I knew, people who knew me, people who would see me with Sam when they got to the party. But I didn't care in the least. My anger was gone, erased with that magic that Ian seemed to have over me—had he touched me with his poisonous spit again? I stepped forward, stood on my tiptoes, and whispered in his ear, "I'd like to spend more time with you, too."

And I'm certain we were *that* close to another kiss, a real one this time. But from my vantage point, I could see Carl Monroe walking toward us. He held the hand of a little boy I didn't know. Carl saw me, blanched slightly, and then smiled stiffly before looking away and returning to minding his own business.

I gasped and stepped to Ian's side so I could watch Carl. As I moved, I clumsily dropped the box of napkins right on my potential new boyfriend's toes.

"Oh, I'm so sorry, Ian," I said as I reached for the napkins. "Did I hurt you badly?" The box, obeying some physics principle I wasn't familiar with, fell corner first. So, though the box itself wasn't heavy, the corner was sharp enough to cause damage.

"I'm okay." Ian smiled at the higher tone of his voice as he tested putting weight on his damaged foot.

"That had to hurt. Should I get you some ice? Should you sit down?"

"I'm fine, Becca. I think I can walk it off. You have lousy timing, though."

I actually blushed. "Well, I owe you one." The moment for kissing had passed right on by, probably with Carl Monroe, who was nowhere to be seen now.

"I'll keep that in mind. Come on, let's get to the party." Ian picked up the box of napkins.

We made our way to the party area, both of us trying not

to limp. Whatever hadn't been put in order before, Sam had taken care of. All the tables were covered with tablecloths and arranged nicely, the band's instruments were set up, and the caterers had put the food on the buffet tables. As we entered, Sam was standing in the middle of the room, surveying the layout.

"We brought the napkins," I said.

He looked over, his face becoming stern when he noticed Ian.

"One of the helpers told me that Allison would be right back," he said as he took the box from Ian. "People have been stopping by, but I keep telling them we're not quite ready. I thought Allison should be here first."

"Good idea."

We placed the napkins on the tables. It wasn't much, but it added a little needed color and they fit with Allison's last-minute theme switch to hoedown, or whatever.

As the last napkin was put in place, Allison swooped in. She'd changed into a silk blouse and nice slacks. She'd rebrushed her ponytail and it shone, even under the unflattering fluorescent tent lighting. She was so gorgeous. I sensed that even the two men I stood next to took a moment to appreciate her beauty. And I took a moment to be proud of her.

"Oh, Becca, I love the napkins. Perfect," she said. Tears came to her eyes for a moment, and she hugged me tightly. She'd been under so much stress. I wished I could have helped her more.

"You're welcome." I hugged her back just as tightly.

"Sam, Ian, thanks," Allison said.

"I did nothing but supply a soft place for the napkins to land," Ian said. "Sam and Becca did all the work."

Sam waved off the gratitude. "I think people are getting

anxious, Allison. I know you'll be sitting at the table in the front, right?"

"Yes."

"Becca, I'd like us to sit at a table close to where everyone will be coming and going. Ian, would you like to join us?"

"Sure," he said with a smile, probably just to see what Sam would do. Sam kept his face steely. "But, sadly, I offered to sit with Barry. His family can't make it, so I agreed to be a poor substitute."

"All right, then. I'm sure we'll talk to you later."

So Barry's family wouldn't even be there? I was doubly angry at myself for my earlier concern about his feelings.

There was no abrupt beginning to the party, but pretty much everyone filed in in an orderly fashion and found places to sit. The mood was easy and cheery. I didn't know Mrs. Simonsen, but I didn't see Jessop anywhere, so I assumed that neither of them was in attendance.

Carl Monroe was there with the little boy I'd seen earlier. Carl looked at me, smiled politely, and then looked away. The person who'd been talking to Barry knew I'd seen him, and Carl wasn't acting like he'd been caught doing anything wrong. I'd talk to him before the evening was over; hopefully without making a scene or having to chase him down. He did, I noted to myself, sit with Barry and Ian.

Sam and I sat at a table by the entrance to the party area. We could see the entire space from our vantage point, which was Sam's goal. Linda and her gorgeous man Drew sat with us, as did Stella and her kids, Richard and Jacquelyn, who, in sync with our farmers' market lives, entertained us with tales of killer tomatoes, lethal corn, and possessed pastries.

Allison began the dinner with a welcome and the moment of silence for Matt Simonsen. It was somber and respectful, and it felt right. I realized that everyone needed to pay their respects even though most of them hadn't known Matt Simonsen—the moment of silence achieved what was needed. This annual dinner was a part of our tradition. The murder of Matt Simonsen was the most horrible thing possible, but we would be able to move forward from here and still honor his memory.

And no one had mentioned the events from my time with Abner in the woods, so hopefully the dinner would proceed smoothly, and maybe even reveal who the murderer was.

"Sam, what do you do?" Linda asked. She'd lasered me with raised eyebrows when she saw I was with someone.

"I'm in law enforcement," he said honestly. I was surprised that he wasn't acting undercover or anything.

"You're a police officer?"

"Yes, ma'am."

Linda's forehead crinkled. "Oh, wait, are you the same officer who was here the . . . the other day?"

"Yes."

"Really?" Linda was about as subtle as I was capable of being, so I was intrigued at what she might say next. "And that's where you and Becca met?"

"Yes. I'm not fully convinced of her innocence, so here I am."

Sam's tone was serious and confident. I wasn't sure what to do or say, so I sat still and waited.

A moment later, the corner of his mouth twitched. This break in his armor cued everyone that they might laugh now.

"Well, I'm always curious about Becca's innocence," Linda said.

When it was our turn at the buffet table, Sam and I held back from the rest of our group.

"That worked out pretty well," I said.

"What do you mean?"

"Allison said that if you were here with me, everyone would relax around you. That's exactly what happened."

"Your sister is probably smarter than you give her credit for."

"Oh, I give her plenty of credit, but I think we're at the wrong table," I said. "See that one over there?" Sam casually looked to where I'd head-pointed. "Barry, Ian, and Carl Monroe are sitting together."

"Okay."

Now that we could talk, I told him about what I'd seen when I'd gone out for the napkins. Of course, I left out the part that I was going to warn Barry about the Simonsen family. I hadn't done as much, so it didn't matter anyway.

"You think it was Carl who was talking to Barry?" he asked.

"I do."

"Why would he need to disguise himself? He's here and they're sitting together. If Carl wanted to talk to him, why didn't they just talk?" Sam asked.

"I have no idea."

"Hmm."

"Yeah, I agree—hmm."

"Okay, we'll go talk to them later. Let me observe from afar for a bit."

Plan in place, we sat back at our original table and enjoyed the good food and even better company.

Linda's date, Drew, was awesome. Stella's teenagers behaved in ways that teenagers weren't always capable of, and I enjoyed their sibling banter and their wild imaginations. And Stella made us all laugh as she told us stories of her husband, Frank, and his adventures as a restaurant owner. He hadn't been able to join us for the party because he had to work, but he was there in spirit as we heard hilarious stories about his employees and their assortment of excuses for skipping their shifts. My personal favorite was the kid who called in and said he'd bumped his head on something and the required hairnet wouldn't fit over the lump.

"Frank said that they'd find him a larger hairnet. And the kid told him that, sadly, that wouldn't work because the doctor had told him hairnets of any size would be out of the question for the next few days," Stella said.

"What did Frank do?" I asked as I laughed.

"Asked the kid for his doctor's phone number so he could guarantee him that he had only low-pressure hairnets. Of course, the kid had an excuse for not having the phone number with him." Stella sighed. "He never showed up to work again."

"Lots of turnover in the restaurant business?" Sam asked.

"Constant," Stella said.

As dinner led to dessert, the band came out and started to play. They were unbelievable, and with only three instruments and lots of attitude, they were a perfect fit. No one was acting strange, and Sam's constant survey of the room didn't seem to turn up anything suspicious.

Just as I spooned a bite of cheesecake into my mouth, someone familiar walked through the entryway. The woman was tall and beautiful, though dressed differently than the last time I'd seen her—*coming out of Carl Monroe's house.*

"Mamma," I mumbled.

"What's that?" Sam asked quietly, not wanting to interrupt the rest of the table conversation.

"That's Mamma Maria," I said. "She works at the Smithfield Market. She makes amazing pies. What's she doing here?" *And why was she at Carl Monroe's yesterday?*

We watched her scan the crowd. Her face broke into a smile and she stepped forward confidently and wove her way through the tables right to Carl Monroe; well, more specifically, to the little boy first. She kissed his cheek and then sat down in the empty chair next to him. She and Carl reached their hands together and squeezed them briefly as they smiled at each other. Barry smiled at her as it seemed they were introduced, and Ian got out of his chair to greet her with a hug. She'd told me she knew Ian, so that didn't seem so strange.

"Why didn't she tell me she knew Carl?" I said.

"What do you mean?" Sam asked.

"I went to Smithfield and told her I worked at Bailey's. Why didn't she tell me she knew Carl? And, Sam, that was the day I chased him."

Sam wiped a napkin over his mouth and said, "Maybe it's time to go over and talk to them."

"Yeah."

We excused ourselves and made our way to the other table. Ian saw us coming first, and his expression went from surprise to mischief. I tried to ignore it.

"Hi, everyone," I said. Barry and Carl looked away from my eyes, but Ian smiled happily.

"Becca," he said, "this is Mamma Maria. She works at the Smithfield Market."

"We've met. Hi, Mamma." I extended my hand. "The pie was simply amazing."

She blinked in thought, but recognition soon lit her eyes.

"Of course. Preserves, right? Becca?"

"Good to see you again," I said. "This is Sam Brion." I introduced him to everyone around the table, and though I could tell Barry thought he knew Sam, he wasn't certain from where.

"And this is my son, Nick," Mamma said as she put her arm around the little boy. "Carl was kind enough to bring him early."

"Oh, are you and Carl dating?" I asked. The only person who wasn't surprised at my bluntness was Sam. I think he liked it.

"Well, um, I think we are. Kind of. We only recently started dating, I guess." Mamma's face was red, and Carl sat a little taller.

Suddenly, my thoughts were pulled into something I couldn't define. I looked at Carl's long frame and realized I was missing something important; something that most definitely had something to do with the murder. But, sadly, I couldn't put my finger on it—it had to do with Carl's height, but not because he might be the murderer. What was I missing?

"Becca?" Sam said, nudging me lightly in the side.

"Huh? Oh, sorry. So, may we sit with you awhile?" I asked. I couldn't leave these people yet. There was something here, and I needed to understand what it was.

"Well . . ." Barry began.

"Of course," Ian said. "Let me get you some chairs."

Ian and Sam gathered a couple of chairs, and we sat. I looked around the table and focused my thoughts toward each person.

Ian was the outsider in this small group; that was obvious. Carl and Barry had a connection that I didn't understand.

"So, Mamma, how are things at Smithfield?" I asked.

"Fine. Very good, actually. It's a great business to work in, isn't it?"

"Yes, it is. So, how did you and Carl meet? Did you two already know each other when I visited with you that day?"

Mamma's face changed from friendly to confused. "Well . . ." she began as Sam laughed lightly to ease the moment, but he didn't retract my question. "Yes, I think we knew each other, met shortly before the day you were at Smithfield, if I'm remembering events correctly. Why do you ask?"

"Just curious. Where did you meet?"

"At Smithfield." She looked around the table for some help.

"Becca, what do you want to know?" Carl said, his tone impatient.

"Well, Carl, I want to know how well you knew Matt Simonsen. Did you and Mamma meet when you were at Smithfield, perhaps visiting Matt Simonsen?"

Carl looked at Sam and then back at me. I suspected that he knew exactly who Sam was.

"Of course I knew Matt, Becca. We're both in the peach business. But I wasn't visiting Matt when I met Mamma. I was at Smithfield for another reason when we met."

"What was the reason?" Sam asked.

"It was specifically to see Mamma Maria," he said, his cheeks reddening. "I'd heard about her, so I went there to meet her. I was visiting her the day I saw Becca. It was that simple."

"Why did you run from me?" I asked, not deterred by embarrassing a man I recently thought was one of the nicest I'd ever known.

"I didn't mean to be so dramatic," he said. "I saw you

talking to Mamma, and I guess I just didn't want . . . my personal life is personal, Becca."

I nodded stiffly. I got that, but still, something on the edge of my memory tapped at my consciousness. But I wasn't letting it in yet.

"Were you talking to Barry before the party? Were you dressed in a trench coat and a hat and talking to him at his stall?"

"What? No."

There must have been a lot of chatter in the room, because the sudden silence was alarming. At first I thought it was because of my bold questioning, but then I realized it was something happening behind me. I turned and craned my neck to look at the entrance.

Allison was escorting someone into the room. That someone was really tall and wore a trench coat that looked eerily similar to the one I had just been talking about, but no hat.

"Who's that?" I mumbled.

Barry, who was next to me, leaned toward my ear. "That, my dear Becca, is Pauline Simonsen."

"Pauline Simonsen is tall?" I said the first thing that popped into my head.

"Very," Sam said.

He was right. She was probably more than six feet. Matt had been tall, Barry was tall, but Abner was short. I remembered Barry telling me that everyone thought it odd that Abner and Pauline got together because they didn't fit together well—was the height difference what he meant?

I silently chastised myself for not stepping out of stereotypes. Why couldn't Abner and Pauline have dated?

"Damn," I said. I turned to Barry. "Is that who you were talking to in your stall?"

"No."

"Barry?"

"Excuse me," Barry said as he maneuvered himself out of the chair. "I'm going to give my condolences to the widow." To the best of his body's ability, he made his way toward Pauline, who was at the entrance and talking to Allison.

The noticeable silence was slowly ending. It was clear that Allison wasn't going to make any sort of announcement about our special guest, so everyone went back to their own business. The band was in the middle of a break, which I was grateful for.

Not only was Pauline Simonsen tall, but she was still striking. I thought of the picture that had been in Abner's house of him and the blond woman. Pauline wasn't blond—she had reddish hair—but her face, though older, seemed to be close to what I remembered. Her features were sharp and dainty, and somehow combined nicely on her tall but thin frame. It must have been the same woman, though the earlier version had bleached hair. This version's hair reminded me of her son, Jessop. I looked around to see if he'd joined her, but I didn't see him.

Was Pauline the person Barry had been talking to? The only answer I could come up with was maybe, maybe not. I turned to Sam. We spoke at the same time.

"I think we should go talk to her."

Barry was now standing with Allison and Pauline. He held Pauline's hand as the two of them shared a moment of conversation. Allison didn't budge, and I was proud of her. Manners were always high on her priority list, but at the moment she focused on the two people in front of her. She wanted the murder solved, too, and she wasn't going to miss an opportunity to maybe learn something pertinent.

Out of the corner of his eye, Barry saw us approach. He turned a nasty look our direction and said good-bye to Pauline.

"Ms. Simonsen, this is my sister, Becca, and our friend Sam," Allison said as we approached.

Pauline extended her long-fingered hand. "Pleasure to meet you," she greeted each of us.

"So sorry for your loss," I said as I shook her hand gently.

"We've met," Sam said. It probably would have been wrong not to remind her that he was a police officer, but I wished he hadn't.

"Ah, yes, Officer Brion, I believe? Well, it's nice to see you out of your police mode."

"I hope you're well, Mrs. Simonsen."

"I'm . . . all right, thank you." She turned her attention to Allison. "You've been extremely kind. Matty only worked at Bailey's a short time and . . . well, all of your efforts have been appreciated. I wanted to be here earlier for the moment of silence, but was held up at home." She paused, which automatically made me think she was lying. "I just, well, I just want everyone at Bailey's to know that I don't hold anyone here tonight responsible for the . . . what happened. I know Abner Justen is a suspect and I heard he's been arrested, so I . . . gosh, well, I wanted to say thank you and tell you that I think all of this horribleness is behind us now."

"Abner was arrested? I hadn't heard," I lied.

We all looked at Sam, Pauline included. He didn't bat an eye or say a word, and he did it without looking uncomfortable or uncertain.

"Well, I don't know anything for certain," Pauline continued when it was obvious that Sam wasn't going to confirm or deny anything, "but I got a phone call from a friend who works downtown, near the jail. She thought she saw him being taken in."

"I see. Well, that's a relief. That must ease your mind," I said.

"Quite a bit, actually. From the beginning, I thought he killed my Matty." She looked purposefully at Sam.

"Really? Why?" I asked.

"There's a history there that I won't go into, but it wasn't pretty." Her eyes teared, and I felt a twinge of pity for her. I told the twinge to go away.

"When was the last time you and Abner spoke?" I asked.

"Oh, a long time ago." She smiled through watery eyes. "Barry"—she nodded in the direction he had gone—"and Abner have lived close to me and Matty for years. We've all known each other since we were very young."

I tried not to let it show, but I wanted to shake my head like cartoon characters did after they'd been hit by an anvil. I knew Barry's address, but the one address I hadn't thought to explore was the Simonsens'. I assumed they lived in Smithfield. Had I been wrong? I looked at Sam, who read my confusion. He wasn't confused at all—he knew where everyone lived. I hadn't asked enough questions.

"I know where Abner lives, Ms. Simonsen, but where do you live? And I thought Barry lived across town from Abner." I literally scratched my head.

Her eyes opened wide. "Oh. Sorry, yes. Barry sold his farm some time ago—oh, my gracious, a long, long time ago—to Carl Monroe; I don't know him all that well, but he's a nice man. I think I've been reminiscing so much lately that I still think about Barry living next door. Anyway, it's probably been decades."

Barry used to live in Carl's monster house? He'd told

me that he'd gotten out of the peach business. So Carl's orchard used to be Barry's?

Pauline Simonsen had the full attention of her audience of three. I didn't think she was as confused as she seemed—I thought she was putting on an act, but I couldn't figure out if it was for the benefit of Allison, me, or Sam. And even though she said she was sure Abner was the murderer, it seemed that she'd found a way to throw Barry into the suspicion pile, too. Apparently, she wanted us to know they had all lived near one another at one time.

"Decades? When was this, exactly? What was the precise date that Barry moved?" I asked. I wasn't sure of the relevance of such information, but it seemed like the right question to ask.

Pauline's eyes dried and then flashed. Her pretty face suddenly wasn't as soft as it had been. It was as though that question had made her angry. "I . . . I can't remember right now. Why?"

"Just curious."

"No, I don't really know," Pauline said as she sniffed and looked at me. Apparently, she had tired of my questions. "I suppose I should go, but I really did want to thank you." She turned to Allison.

"Thank you for coming by," Allison said soothingly. "We're all so very sorry for your loss. Please let us know if you need anything at all."

Pauline Simonsen turned and left the party tent with sure, almost defiant, steps.

"I didn't mean to offend her," I said. "I just couldn't quite figure her out."

"It's okay," Allison said. "No disrespect to the dead or the grieving, but there's something about that woman that rubs me the wrong way. I hoped you'd get to the bottom of it."

"Really?" I looked at her and then at Sam. "Did I mess anything up?"

"Not at all. I was hoping the same thing as Allison. It was odd, the way she almost acted as though she wanted to answer my questions until she suddenly didn't. I talked to her and her son after the murder. They were both genuinely shocked at what had happened, but you're right, Allison, there was something . . . almost fake about her tonight, like she'd scripted her words. And the way she mentioned Barry . . ." Sam looked toward the table Barry had been sitting at. He wasn't there.

"Do you think she really heard about Abner's arrest?" I said.

"I suppose it's possible, but I think more people at the party would be talking about it if someone had seen him being taken in."

"Well, I'll tell you this, I want to know what's up with her. It's rare that I feel something so wonky from someone. Excuse me. I need to see to the band." Allison took off.

I watched her walk away. "You know, she knows people better than anyone. There must be something up with Pauline if she says there is."

"I don't disagree, but 'wonky' doesn't hold up well in a court of law."

"Right. Who should we question next?" I asked, excited at the idea.

"I don't know. We'll keep our options open. Tomorrow I'll look into some things that have come to light tonight, but for now, we dance."

"Really?" I said, both horrified at the idea and curious that Sam even had "dance" in his vocabulary.

"Really. Come on." He took my hand, and though neither of us knew how to square dance (Carl and Mamma Maria were pros, by the way), and though Ian had a difficult time remaining amused by the idea of my fake date with Sam Brion, and though Barry was nowhere to be seen, we still managed to have a great time.

Twenty-two

Sam took me home right after the party. We had no more revelations regarding the murder, but we did have fun.

I actually danced some, though it was ugly and brief. At the late hour of 10:30 P.M. my recovering body was exhausted. I fell into bed with Hobbit and slept until eight o'clock; the late hour was unheard of. I woke up, jolted at the time that showed on my clock, and made the decision that I'd take it easy one more day. It was the Monday after one of Bailey's biggest weekends. It wouldn't be very busy. Plus, I still needed to work on building up my inventory. And finally, Hobbit deserved to have me at her disposal for at least the entire morning.

First on the list was a long walk around the property—for Hobbit, and to stretch my tightening muscles. I brought a pencil and my light green note cards, but my dog didn't care just as long as we kept walking as I read through my notes.

Barry's was the first card on my pile. To my already suspicious notes, I added his strange behavior at the party. Why wouldn't he tell me who was in the trench coat? Where did he disappear to? Why had Pauline seemed to make it a point that we knew he lived on what was now Carl's property at one time? None of what he'd done since the murder seemed to jibe or make sense.

But really, was Barry a killer?

The secrets he kept to himself had *something* to do with the murder, I was sure, but I didn't know what or how. His past with Pauline Simonsen might have been incentive enough, because love always is the perfect motive. But Barry had moved on, he'd even left the area where Pauline lived and he'd gotten married. I knew his family, and they were a good group of people. So, despite his secrets and his conversation with a mystery trench-coat-clad person, my gut told me he wasn't the one who swung the axe.

"But he either suspects or knows who the murderer is," I said to Hobbit. "I'm sure of it." I pulled out my cell phone and tried to reach him. It was no surprise that he didn't answer.

Last night Sam had said that he'd have another conversation with Barry, but it would be to no avail. Barry wasn't telling anyone anything. There had to be something else that would steer us in the right direction.

I looked at Carl Monroe's card next. Of everyone, I thought I'd probably been the most wrong about Carl. Talk about being in all the wrong place at the wrong time! Did I believe that he had been at Smithfield to see Mamma Maria and that he had run from me because he didn't want me to know about his personal life? It seemed likely. Carl had always been quiet, and he and Mamma acted as though they liked each other a lot. The Fall Equinox Dinner was a perfect spot to bring a new girlfriend. I still wondered why she had been at his house, but for all I knew, it was to drop off a toothbrush. Did I still think Carl was the person who'd knocked on Allison's door when I'd been snooping? I had no idea, so I added three question marks. And even if he had been, so what? He had a right to talk to Allison whenever he wanted. But again, my gut kicked in—there was something strange about that visitor.

"I just don't know, Hobbit. I guess it's possible, but I don't know."

Hobbit nudged my knee enough to let me know she was listening but wasn't all that interested in the conversation. We'd walked to the low crest above the pumpkin patch. The temperature was cool but not cold, and the sky was dotted with puffy white clouds. I took a moment to breathe in the fresh air. Not enough people on the planet get to do what my dog and I were doing; I understood her choosing the interests of the out-of-doors over the murder investigation.

"But like Barry, Carl knows something," I muttered to myself. "Abner had been at his house, and his house had once been Barry's. Somehow Carl has become involved, but it has been against his will, I bet."

Ian's card was next. My curiosity about him had only increased, and my thoughts that he might be involved in the murder had all but gone away. That might not be a good sign. Maybe he was involved and just a pro at diverting attention. At this point, I had to hope he wasn't involved. Plans for him were forming in my mind. Once the murder was solved, I'd get back on my normal schedule and maybe throw in a date or two. Ian seemed to be interested in the same idea.

I sighed. Hobbit looked at me and rolled her eyes.

The last card in my stack was Abner's. And, sadly, he seemed the most likely person to have committed the murder. He'd loved Pauline and she'd chosen Matt Simonsen; he'd stayed close—geographically—to them; he was the one who "found" Matt's body; the bloody axe had been discovered in his greenhouse—an axe had been used on the tree with his and Pauline's names.

But what about the shooting? Was Sam right? Had Abner planned for someone to shoot at the cabin to plant the idea of another suspect? Who? It had been frightening, but the gun ended up being harmless enough. I still wanted to ask Abner some questions.

I flipped open my phone and dialed.

"Becca? Everything all right?" Sam answered on the first ring.

"Fine. Hey, I have a question for you. It's not standard operating procedure, I'm sure, but can I come talk to Abner?"

Sam was silent for a beat. "Well, prisoners are sometimes allowed visitors—*very briefly*—but I can't give you any sort of official questioning authority. Besides, you aren't going to investigate murders anymore, right?"

"Sure, I get it. I'll be a good *visitor.* When can I come see him?"

"Today about one o'clock will work."

"I'll be there. Thanks."

"You're welcome. See you then."

"Sam . . ."

"Yes?"

"Thanks for escorting me to the dinner last night. It was fun."

"Yes, it was," he said, his officialness shaken by my friendly tone.

I laughed. "See you later."

"Yes, ma'am."

I closed the phone.

"Sorry, Hobbit. I only have the rest of the morning. You run, I'll walk carefully."

I couldn't remember the last time I ventured into town twice in one week. Normally, once per week, maybe only twice per month, was typical. And my favorite bookstore, coffee shop, and new friend Ian's apartment were on the other side of Monson. The other side of town was only a short five-minute drive, but I wanted to stick to my plan and get back to Hobbit as quickly as I could.

Monson's downtown was two streets long. There was still an old drugstore with a soda fountain on Main Street, along with a bar, a pool hall, two banks, and other small retail stores. First Street held an old one-auditorium movie theater, the town library, a store that still called itself the Five and Dime (though the items for sale were now ninety-nine cents), a couple of appliance stores, and the county courthouse/jail/sheriff's office. I'd always thought the red-brick jail building was the prettiest building in town, but I'd never seen the inside of it. Until today.

As I went through the front double doors, I was reminded of the smells of a school building—some combination of linoleum floor cleaner, dust that would never be cleaned out of corners, and the greasy scent of a real cafeteria. At first sniff, I liked everything about it.

There was a buzz of activity all around. Everyone was working; everyone seemed to be moving at a pace that didn't fit with living on a farm and being surrounded by crops instead of coworkers, but it wasn't terrible.

"Can I help you?" a girl at the information desk asked as she timed noisy chews on her bubble gum in between words.

"I'm here to see Officer Brion," I said.

"Back that way. He's in the second office on the left. Sign in." She pushed a clipboard forward, shot me an obligatory smile, and turned back to whatever she had been looking at on her computer screen.

I did as she instructed and then made my way to Sam's office, the door of which had one word painted on it: Police.

I didn't know if I should knock, so I didn't.

The area reminded me of a 1970s cop show, the name of which I couldn't remember. There were six desks filling the front open space and three glass-walled offices at the back of the room. Sam sat at one of the front desks, a phone propped at his ear and on his shoulder as he wrote notes. I noticed that he wrote with his left hand and he used a yellow number 2 pencil. All trace of the fun Sam, the one who wore colorful printed shirts, was gone.

I couldn't hear his exact words through the hum of activity, but his face wasn't pinched in concern.

"Ms. Robins," Officer Norton said as she walked toward me. "Sam said you'd be by. Come on in and have a seat over there. Sam will be with you in a minute. Coffee?"

"Sure. Thanks." I sat in a duct-taped-together vinyl chair that was next to a burping copier. A second later, Officer Norton was back with the coffee. I watched her biceps flex as she handed me the paper cup. Just to know what it felt like to be burly, the thought of attempting weight lifting ran through my mind. And then directly out of it.

"Thanks," I said again.

"You're welcome. You need anything else?"

"No, this is great." I saluted her with the cup.

"Let me know if you do. I'll be right over there. I've got some calls to make."

I took a sip of the coffee as Officer Norton went back to her desk. It was the worst coffee I'd ever tasted, and I hoped no one saw my eyes tear up and my mouth turn downward at the bitterness. Conveniently, there was a small garbage can next to the copier.

There were four officers at their desks, each of them in a state of "busy." There was only one person in the glass-walled offices. He was dressed in civilian clothes, and I'd never seen him before.

Who knew that Monson had enough crime to have so many officers? I was impressed.

Sam hung up his phone, looked at me, stood up, and walked my direction—all without one smile or one hair falling out of place. He was definitely in work mode.

"Becca," he said as we shook hands.

"Sa . . . I mean Officer Brion."

"The prisoner is in a back holding cell. I have clearance for you to visit him, but he'll remain in his cell. You'll have to sit outside of it. We have only one interview room, and we can't use it for visitors."

"I understand."

"I'll have to search you."

"What?"

Finally, the corner of his mouth twitched. "I wanted to see your reaction."

"My reaction is that I'm glad you broke form for a minute to make a joke, but if you tried to search me, I'd have to hurt you."

Sam smiled, fully. "This way."

He led us through a door I hadn't noticed before but

was next to one of the glass-walled offices. We went down a small hallway, passing what I thought was the interview room he had spoken about and some bathrooms.

"Did you talk to Barry or the Simonsens yet?" I asked.

"Not yet, but it's in the works, boss."

I laughed. "Thanks for the fake date, Sam. It was really fun."

He turned and looked at me. "I had a great time. You work with some terrific people."

"And potentially a murderer."

"There is that."

We went through another doorway and into a room that had three cagelike cells. Two of them were empty except for bare cots. Abner sat on the cot in the third one. He was hunched over, his head in his hands. He looked up as we entered and threw together a smile.

He wasn't able to hide his exhaustion or the years that he'd piled on over the last few days.

"Becca?" he said as he stood. "I'm so sorry about the other day."

I waved him away. "No harm done. How are you?" I walked to the cell and touched his fingers as he held on to the bars.

Sam cleared his throat. "You may not touch the prisoner, and you have only a few minutes."

I looked at him and he shrugged lightly. Rules were rules, I supposed.

"You may sit here." Sam put a chair in front of the cell, about five feet away from it.

"Will you be staying?" I asked him.

"Only if you want me to."

"I don't."

"There are no recording devices in here. Whatever you

say will remain between the two of you. But you won't have long. This isn't necessarily proper procedure."

I nodded. "Thanks, Sam."

"Okay, then. Let me know if you need anything at all." Sam looked at me and then sent a stern stare to Abner. Abner looked away and I felt sorry for him, and suddenly mad at Sam. I was glad when he left the room.

"So," I said.

"Yeah, so. Thanks for coming to visit me."

"How're they treating you?"

"Fine. Officer Brion makes sure I get real food. Don't know why, don't think he likes me, but maybe because he knows you and I are friends."

"Do you need me to get you anything? Cigarettes, a file?" I said.

Abner smiled. "Both would be great, except that I quit smoking in 1980 and a file might not get me very far."

"Just saying."

"Thanks, Becca. I don't want you to be angry with me, no matter what."

"I guess I'm not mad, really. You've infuriated me a few times over these last few days, but I could never really stay mad at you."

"Even if I was a murderer?"

"You're not, that much I know."

"Thank you, thank you for that."

We were both silent a second, each of us gathering surprise emotions. I hated seeing my friend behind bars.

"But Abner, you and I are the last two people to know that, and me knowing it 'just because' isn't going to help prove your innocence. Talk to me, tell me something," I finally said.

Abner let go of the bars, rubbed at his chin, and sat back on the cot. "There's nothing I can tell you, Becca. I can't."

"Even if it means going to jail? What is your loyalty to the murderer? Does he have something on you?" Abner's eyes flashed, but then he looked away again. "That's it, right? He's got something on you!" I stood. "But what?"

"Becca," he pleaded.

"He's threatening to expose whatever it is he has if you turn him in." I was on a roll.

Abner kept his eyes averted from me.

What could the murderer possibly have? Did Barry or Carl have something so damaging to Abner that he couldn't face it? They had all known one another for so long that I wondered what hadn't met the statute of limitations yet. I knew that murder never expired. Was there another murder that Abner was concerned about? Something in the past?

"But why not mention it at this point? You're already in trouble for murder. It couldn't hurt things any more if there was another one," I mumbled to myself.

"What's that?" Abner asked.

"Well, I was wondering what the murderer had on you that you couldn't face exposing him, and the only thing I can think of that's more awful than murder is another murder. Did you kill someone in the past?"

"No, Becca, I've never killed anyone. Not my style."

"What is it, then? Tell me, what does someone have on you? Don't tell me the who, just tell me the what."

"No one has anything on me."

I looked at him. Deep disappointment and frustration played around in my gut. Every time I thought I got close to something, I was thwarted. But he was telling the truth, that much I knew—it wasn't that someone had something on him.

Again I said, "Something, Abner, give me something."

"Becca, aren't there people in the world you'd take the

fall for? People you care about so much that their life is more important than your own?"

"My sister. My parents."

"See, when you care so deeply for someone, you're willing to give up your own freedom."

The only person I knew of that Abner had loved that deeply was Pauline Simonsen. Is that what he was telling me, that she was the murderer?

"And you loved Pauline Simonsen," I said.

"Yes, many years ago, but she's not the only person I've ever loved."

"Who else?"

"I adore my sister, Helen, but when my brother Jake was alive, I probably wouldn't have done squat for him."

"Helen is a murderer?"

"No."

"Pauline?"

"No."

I sighed. Was he being purposefully cryptic or just plain cryptic?

"What were you doing at my house the day after the murder?"

"I wasn't there. I told you that already."

"Then who put the flowers in my pumpkin patch?"

"It wasn't me, I swear." His forehead crinkled as though he was concerned, but he ironed it out quickly enough.

"What were you doing at Carl's the night before you met with me?" I'd kept this bit of knowledge to myself until that moment.

"Damn! You were spying?"

"Absolutely."

"Nothing, really, just trying to convince another old friend that I'm not a murderer," he said.

"I don't believe you."

"It's the truth."

"You and Carl and Barry are old friends? It doesn't always show."

"We *are* old friends. Well, Barry and I go way back—Carl has worked at Bailey's a long time. You know us old-timers, though. We don't spend a lot of effort showing affection or anything silly like that. We get to work early, stay until we're sold out, and then go back home and get ready for the next day. We're friends in our own ways."

"Yeah, I've always admired that about you guys. I try to be an 'old-timer,' but I don't always manage to be on time," I said absently. Abner had just said something that was ringing that bell in my mind. "Abner, say what you just said. Say it again."

He repeated his words and I still thought there was something to them, but again I couldn't figure out what it was.

"Hmm."

"What, Becca?"

"I don't know yet, but I think . . ." *What was it?*

"Becca," Sam said as he opened the door, "time's up. You need to go."

"Already?"

"Yeah, sorry. Strict rules."

"Yeah, okay," I said, but I didn't get up.

"Becca," Sam said.

I stood and went to Abner. "I'll come back. I'll have more questions."

"Becca, thanks for coming to visit. I really appreciate it," Abner said as though he thought he might not ever see me again.

"Becca," Sam said.

I turned away from Abner, surprised at the emotion that swelled in my chest. It wasn't easy to leave a friend in a prison cell. I tried not to let either Abner or Sam see any tears.

"Oh, wait, Abner." I turned around. "Has Pauline always loved hummingbirds?"

"Uh, well, yes . . ." Abner eyes flashed, and he closed his mouth with an audible snap. He knew I was on to something.

"Abner, you don't care for hummingbirds, do you? You made sure your sister told me as much. You want me to know, or at least you want me to figure it out," I said. "Or Helen does."

He looked away.

"He doesn't like hummingbirds, Sam," I said. He processed everything everyone around him did or said, so I was certain he was remembering all the feeders around Abner's greenhouse. The sorrow that I'd felt a moment ago was replaced with a hopeful zip in my step. "He doesn't like hummingbirds."

Twenty-three

"I'm not sure it's relevant," Sam said as we stood on the side-walk outside the police station/jail. His arms were crossed in front of his chest and his eyes, though focused on me, were probably still noticing everything all around.

"Sam, you saw the hummingbird feeders around his greenhouse. If he doesn't like the birds, why would he have the feeders?"

"I asked him about that."

"Oh. What did he say?"

"He said they'd been on his greenhouse for a long time and he never wanted to take the time to take them down. He hung them years ago when he thought he might enjoy them. He didn't, really, but he was too busy to do anything about them."

"But he continued to fill them? That would be more time-consuming than taking them down," I said as I thought back to the filled feeders and the nectar that had been spilled on Abner's porch. "Besides, you saw that greenhouse. Abner probably took the time to pick up microscopic grains of dirt from the floor. It was immaculate. Something doesn't fit."

Sam sighed and bit at his lip. "You might be right. I'll talk to him again. But when I asked him about it before, he made it seem like it was no big deal." But the wheels were turning behind Sam's observant eyes. Was it possible that he had missed something? I didn't really think so, but there was a first time for everything. And if he had, why was Abner not liking hummingbirds of any significance?

"Sam, when you talk to him about it again, ask him about Pauline liking hummingbirds. We need to know more about that."

"I will." He could have made those two words sound like he was giving me the brush-off, like he didn't want me to know that I might have pointed out something he'd missed. But they didn't sound that way at all. Instead, they held a grateful tone.

"Thanks, Sam. I'd love to hear what you find out," I said with a smile.

"Well, we'll see."

"Talk to you later." I turned and walked toward my car.

"Becca?" Sam said as he turned from the door he'd opened.

"Yeah?"

"Let me do the investigating this time. I promise I'll give you a call. Hey, I'll do one better. Let's go out to dinner tonight. I mean, well, you have insight into Abner, and probably everyone else, that I should know about—I noticed that last night. I'll share some details with you that I shouldn't share, and you can let me in on some of that insight. We'll go over what happened at the party and see if we might have missed something there."

"I show you yours and you'll show me mine?" I smiled.

"Something like that." Sam laughed.

"Deal," I said. "What time?"

"I can't get out of here any earlier than seven o'clock. Will that work?"

"See you then, but I'm not wearing a dress again."

"I couldn't take the shock two days in a row." Sam went back into the building.

I didn't think he was asking me out on a date, so to speak, but he might be under a slightly different impression. I'd have to clear up any misconceptions this evening, but as it was, I was looking forward to learning some things about the case—if that was what his intentions really were. And I was kind of looking forward to the company.

Hadn't I just told Ian that I wanted to get to know him better?

"Yikes, I need to get all these cards put on the table," I said aloud as I started my truck and headed back home to Hobbit.

Hobbit was happy to see me and then not so happy when, a couple of hours after I got home, I decided I needed to leave again. My dinner with Sam wasn't for a few more hours, and though I'd agreed to leave the investigating to him, I couldn't let go of the thoughts of hummingbirds. Specifically, I couldn't let go of wanting to know if Pauline Simonsen had a thing for them. I didn't yet understand why it might be relevant at all, but I wanted to know.

I'd just drive by the Simonsen property, see if there were

any hummingbird feeders on the grounds, and then drive back home. Either way, I'd have more information to give Sam.

I didn't know exactly how to get to Simonsen Orchards, but I still remembered how to get to both Abner's and Carl's. Knowing now that the three properties had some form of joint boundaries, I'd find my way.

I wasn't sure why I made the decision not to take Hobbit. Later, much later, I would realize it was because deep down I knew I wasn't going to just drive by. I knew I was going to take my curiosity and exploration further. Probably too far.

But I wasn't thinking of "later" as I once again approached Abner's property—a place I hadn't known a thing about until recently. And in just those few days, his little white house and enormous science-fiction-like greenhouse had gone from frightening to lonely. My heart hurt as I got out of my truck in front of the empty house. Even though I knew it innately, I was always surprised when I noticed the connection between humans and the places where they lived, the places where they played in their own dirt, either just because they liked to or because they made a living from the things they planted, grew, and harvested. Abner's property missed him; I could feel the earth sigh in disappointment when it noticed I wasn't him.

He wasn't a murderer. I just knew it. But how was I going to prove it?

I climbed the porch steps. The hummingbird nectar was gone, so I could walk undeterred. The screen door opened easily, but the inner door was locked tight. I wanted to go back inside the house, but I didn't have the pick-a-lock skill set, so I settled for a glance through the window at the top of the door. The coffee table had been righted and I couldn't tell if there were still pictures on the floor, but nothing else seemed different.

I walked to the greenhouse and looked at the partially filled hummingbird feeders that were still attached. I grabbed a cinder block that was beside the door, moved it under a feeder, and climbed up to inspect the plastic tube closely.

It wasn't dirty. None of them really were. If the feeders had been there a long time, they'd be dirtier, wouldn't they? Just being outside would make something grimy or at least rain-spotted. These were fairly new feeders and someone had put them up recently. Abner had lied to Sam about the timing. But why?

I ran back to my truck, put on a pair of work gloves, and ran back to the feeders. Though the gloves weren't dainty and could maybe erase a fingerprint or two, I did the best I could to pull a feeder from the building without destroying evidence. I'd give it to Sam and ask him to see if he could find any fingerprints—hopefully, other than Abner's.

I made another trip back to the truck to put the feeder and gloves on the front seat. Then I went back to the greenhouse. The door was unlocked, so I invited myself in. I flipped the switches, but the lights didn't turn on. It wasn't dark outside, so I could still see pretty well, but the only inside light was from the little white one. It must have been some sort of emergency feature—when the power was off, this light offered at least something. But what bothered me more was that the irrigation system had been turned off. The soil seemed dry, and some of the flowers were beginning to look rough around the edges. I didn't want to think about the fact that if Abner did spend the rest of his life in jail, the health of the flowers wouldn't matter. For now, though, it mattered.

There was nothing I could do—I had no idea how to manually turn on a system that required power to get it started. Plus, I thought, as I looked at the mechanics, I might not be able to figure it out anyway. Since there wasn't a hose attached to a faucet in sight, I couldn't see a way to help, but I'd talk to Sam later about my concerns.

I left the greenhouse and Abner's property, and drove around to Carl's. I figured that Simonsen Orchards had to be on the other side of Abner's land, and the only way I knew of to get to that spot was by passing Carl's.

Carl's mansion hadn't changed since my last visit. Even down to the small detail of Mamma Maria's truck being parked in the driveway. Did I think they were inside the house mulling over details of murderous plots? No, I didn't. In fact, I thought the last thing on their minds at the moment was murder. I wasn't the only one taking Monday off.

"Well, they seem to be getting along," I said as I drove by, choosing not to spy this time.

There was a road sign just past Carl's that helped significantly. It read Simonsen Orchards—This Way and had a large, bright yellow arrow.

Pleased at my crack investigative skills, I turned down the road. It was paved and groomed, and a canopy of perfect trees soon appeared overhead. The road veered to the left, which made me think I was now heading closer to Abner's property than Carl's. By the time I reached Simonsen Orchards, I estimated that the cabin where I'd met Abner was smack-dab at a point equidistant from all three properties, though the only driveable road to it was from Carl's.

Simonsen Orchards was impressive; big and beautiful. There was real farm equipment in the orchard, and a wrought-iron gate with a Welcome sign suspended from chains. The orchard went on forever; so far, it seemed, that I wondered why Abner's property wasn't lined in peach trees from the Simonsens' orchard. I wanted a better grasp of where I was in relation to the land I already knew about, but the large number of trees made that tricky.

This was a big-time operation, much bigger than anything I was accustomed to.

Just past the gate, a smooth driveway snaked toward a large, immaculate ranch-style house. The drive made a circle at the front of the house and then reconnected to the straightaway I was on. There wasn't one hummingbird feeder in sight, but there was something else.

A brown truck, similar to Carl Monroe's, was to the side of the house, in front of one of the four oversize garage doors. It could have been the mystery truck, but so could the hundreds of others I'd noticed lately. There certainly were a lot of brown trucks in and around Monson.

Without realizing it, I had driven to the front of the house and put my own truck in Park. I had no idea what I was going to say to Pauline or Jessop if they were inside the house, but I couldn't stop myself from walking to the front door and ringing the bell.

There was something here, I could feel it. I was angry at myself for not seeking out Simonsen Orchards' address in the first place. Sam, of course, had known all along where they lived, but I hadn't even thought to ask him. Matt and Jessop had worked at the Smithfield Market for a long time—they'd had to travel almost thirty miles there and back each day. Bailey's was much closer.

I'd been bothered by addresses this whole time, and this was probably the most important one. Now, in front of the Simonsen house, I sensed that I was only seconds away from maybe understanding my own foggy inkling about why where everyone lived was important.

I knocked. Shortly, footfalls came in my direction.

Pauline Simonsen opened the door. She was dressed in a blue denim, long-sleeved, button-down shirt and faded jeans. Without the trench coat I could see her thin, statuesque frame much better. Her hair was pulled back into a short ponytail and there was no makeup on her face. This was the look she was meant for. She wasn't young, but at the moment she didn't look her age. Her cheeks were pink and her blue eyes were bright. She was still stunning.

"May I help . . . oh, we met last night. Becca, right?" She was friendly.

"Yes. Becca Robins. I work at Bailey's."

"Yes?"

"Allison, the market manager, is my sister . . ."

"Of course. Well, what can I do for you?" Her eyes glazed, probably at remembering how annoyed at me she'd become.

"I was wondering if you had a few moments, Ms. Simonsen."

She looked at me as though she didn't have one extra minute of time, but the glaze in her eyes became more curious.

"Sure, come on in." She stepped back as I walked in. "Iced tea, coffee?"

"Iced tea would be perfect."

"Well, have a seat." She waved me toward a large leather-furniture-filled front room and then made her way back to the kitchen.

There were two big couches and more chairs than I wanted to take the time to count. I noticed a piano at the far end of the room that was covered in photographs. I suddenly wanted—no, *needed*—to see those pictures. I beelined my way to them.

As I suspected, there were pictures of Jessop, Pauline, and a man I assumed was Matt Simonsen. As a younger man, he had been handsome in the way of movie stars—tall, broad-chested, perfectly coifed dark hair. He had a sharp mouth and a sharp nose, but he was very lovely to look at.

And Pauline had been the female movie-star match for him. Though she was still attractive, when she was younger, she had been knockout gorgeous. I wondered if she'd spent any time as a model. There was not one picture of her with blond hair, but the face was most definitely the one I'd seen in the picture at Abner's. I didn't doubt that in the least now.

There were more pictures of Jessop than anyone else. As a baby, he'd been chubby, but as he grew through the pictures, he became tall and thin, just like his mother. He'd never had that movie-star quality, but instead was more gangly and looked as if he spent a lot of years trying to figure out what to do with his long arms and big feet. As an adult, he was handsome enough, but his looks didn't hold a candle to either of his parents' seemingly effortless glamour.

"Do you have a piano full of pictures, or perhaps a mantel?" Pauline said as she came into the room. She held two glasses of iced tea.

I moved back across the large room and joined her at one of the couches.

"I guess I have a shoe box," I said. I'd always loved looking at pictures, but I'd never managed to organize them.

Besides, when one has had two husbands, it's best not to keep the evidence out in the open.

"I see." She handed me a glass and waited for me to sit.

"Ms. Simonsen . . ."

"Pauline, please."

"Pauline, how are you?"

"Oh, I'm okay. I'm keeping busy. I try not to dwell on things too much. The paper this morning confirmed that they've arrested Abner. Things will be resolved soon, I think."

I took a drink of the tea. I'd forgotten all about checking the paper. Hopefully, my name wasn't mentioned in the story as well—*Local market vendor arms herself with a hammer and goes to visit a murder suspect.*

I couldn't worry about that now. How was I going to approach this? But I was beyond that concern, wasn't I? I needed some answers. I swallowed.

"Pauline, you and Abner were once a couple, right?"

Her eyes opened wide with surprise.

"Well, goodness, I, uh . . ."

I took another drink and waited for her to gather herself.

"Becca, that was a hundred years ago." Pauline laughed as her fingers flitted at her throat.

"Sure, but it was some kind of love, wasn't it?"

For an instant, Pauline's eyes fixed on something in the distance, most likely the distant past.

"I don't remember," she said as she pulled her eyes back to mine. "And he must not have, either. He killed Matty. Whatever love we had for each other was over a long time ago, and now . . . well, now . . ."

"What makes you so sure Abner killed your husband?"

"Doesn't the evidence point in that direction? At Bailey's, Abner threatened Matty's life a few days before he conveniently found Matty's body. And the axe—the police told Jessop that Abner's fingerprints were all over it. And I suppose there must be more, but I don't know exactly what it all is."

"Okay, but why? If the love you had for each other was over a long time ago, why would Abner kill Matt?"

"I wish I knew."

I thought about my original and incorrect assumption that the Simonsens lived near Smithfield.

"Why did Matt work at Smithfield, anyway? It's a long drive, and Bailey's is so much closer. And since he did work at Smithfield, why did he finally decide to come to Bailey's?"

"He started at Smithfield a long time ago. You might have noticed that we're a pretty big operation. Matty didn't just have the market business, but a wholesale business, too. He did lots of different things."

"I still don't get it. Why Smithfield over Bailey's?" I tried the question again.

She sighed. "Oh, I suppose it doesn't matter if I tell you, but it will only make Abner look guiltier."

"Tell me."

"Years ago Matty and Abner agreed that they'd work separately and Matty would take the longer drive."

"Why did your husband break the deal?"

"Oh, shoot, Matty and Jessop had a few of their own battles—nothing serious, but Matty thought they should take a break from each other for a while, and it had been so long that he thought he and Abner would be able to work through their problems."

"Really? What did your husband and son fight about?" I said.

"Nothing important. You know, Jessop's young, he has ideas on how the business should be run and Matty didn't agree, simple as that. They just needed a break is all." Abruptly, Pauline stood, the ice in her tea sloshing a drip of liquid over the side of the glass. "Ms. Robins, I'm tired now. Please excuse me, but I think it's time for you to leave."

"I'm sorry, Pauline." I remained seated. She was acting strangely again—unpredictable. But though her sudden move did surprise me, I wasn't ready to leave. "You know, really, it's because I'm such a romantic at heart." I paused, waiting for the lightning strike that might accompany such a lie, but it didn't come, so I continued. "But I'd love to hear the story of your youth; the time when they all loved you—Abner, Barry, and Matt. You know, it might help to tell me about it. I know this has been a difficult time for you. If you'd be willing to share, I'd really like to hear it."

Pauline glanced down at me with doubtful eyes. I was less than one second away from giving up when her face softened and she sat again.

"Really, that's what this is all about? You're a romantic?"

"Oh yes, and your life has been so full of romance." Still no lightning. Awesome.

"Well, it *is* a lovely story."

"I'm sure."

She sighed, and her eyes lit back to their happy state. "Well, this was mine first," she said possessively as she waved her hand through the air. "My daddy bought this property over fifty years ago. We moved to South Carolina when I was sixteen, and he bought all this land, hoping to work it himself. But Daddy had that special knack that some people have—whatever he touched turned to gold.

He bought the land as well as put some money into other things." She leaned toward me. "I was never certain, but I think his other investments included things that verged on illegal, but he never went to jail, so . . ."

I smiled.

"Anyway, he never needed to work this land, not even for one day. After only a few months in Monson, he declared to me that the land was mine, his only child's, and whoever I married. Though you might think my inheritance was a loving gesture, it wasn't so much that as it was a reason to doubt." She pinched her mouth and looked at the brown pattern on the rug at our feet.

Helen and Barry had both told me about Pauline's money, but neither of them had mentioned that she'd had land, which in our farming community was probably more valuable than any amount of money.

"You mean you began to doubt people's motives toward you? You thought that maybe boys liked you because of the property?"

"Yes. Monson is a small town. Everyone knew the arrangement. It was difficult."

"So who did you date?"

"Lots of boys. I was a looker, too. Anyway, Barry Drake was the first boy I loved."

"Tell me about him."

"Oh, he was just a farm boy who had a smile that always preceded trouble. When I was sixteen, I liked that."

"All sixteen-year-old girls like boys who promise trouble. It's part of growing up."

"I suppose."

"How long did you and Barry date?"

"Not long. Abner came into my life with the force of a perfect storm."

"Really? Little, old, bald Abner?"

Pauline laughed. "Everyone thought what you're thinking, Becca. We made an odd-looking couple, but he was the most wonderful boy ever. He loved me and I loved him more than we thought possible at the time—this, by the way, spoiled us because we both thought that was what love was supposed to be like. He was smart, kind, and generous."

"Wow, it sounds like he was perfect. Why didn't you stay together?"

Her face soured. "Pride and stupidity."

"Sorry?"

"He was too proud and I was too stupid."

"What do you mean?"

"Abner would never have lived on this land. He was too proud to take the land of someone he married. He wanted to make his own way—he had his own family land. I was stupid. This was my land, and if he didn't want it, I thought he didn't want me enough." She sighed. "Truth be told, his refusal to take this land meant he loved me all the more. I was so very stupid."

"And he was so very proud," I said. I got the principle of what Abner had felt, but seriously, there should have been some way to compromise. "He wouldn't budge?"

"No, not an inch. And then Matty got really sick with pneumonia. Even though I dated Abner, we were all friends, and Matty's mother had died years before. I offered to help take care of him. You have to understand, it was a different time. People still die from pneumonia, but back then . . . well, Matty and his father didn't have much of anything. Matty spent most of his time getting better at his house, not a hospital. When Abner, Barry, and I visited him, I was horrified at the condition of his home. I offered to help take care of him. Abner was fine with it even though our relationship had already become strained at that point." Her eyes went to that distant place again.

"You fell in love with Matty while you were taking care of him?" I prompted.

"Becca, we were very young. I thought I was feeling love for Matty but, well, it was . . ."

"That caregiver/patient thing that sometimes happens."

She nodded, and her eyes teared up. "And Matty had no problem coming to live with me on my land. He was a good, good man, and I'm so very happy we were married and had Jessop, but . . ."

"You were never really in love with him?"

"Not totally. But that's unfair, too. I loved him, but not like Abner."

"Abner probably didn't take any of that well at all."

"It was horrible."

"Uh-huh," I said.

"Matty was the best-looking boy I knew." She sniffed. "And how silly was it that that became what I held on to, what I kept in my mind as being thc reason I left the love of my life? I left Abner for someone better-looking."

In a way, my heart broke for them all. But in another way, I wished I could have been there to tell them how stupid they were being. I stamped down my sympathy—I still had to figure out who'd killed Matt.

"I don't understand something. How come this land was next to Abner's and Barry's?"

"Abner's land was in his family for a long time. Barry's land was actually ours—mine and Matty's—for some time. But shortly after we were married, Barry claimed that his family had had that property for years, too. It was an ugly scene, but Barry was able to prove that he was right. He got his property. But he was never happy there, so about twenty years ago, he sold it to Carl Monroe's family. Carl's been working the orchard for about ten years."

Suddenly, she seemed very lucid. This must have been the land dispute Barry spoke about. So, he hadn't been completely lying.

"Was Barry unhappy because of you and what you did to him? Is that why he moved away?"

"I don't know, never did know. Last night at the party was the first time I'd talked to him in a long time. That's why I seemed confused. I'm afraid I'm a big mess of emotions right now."

"Uh-huh," I said unsympathetically. "Why didn't Abner leave?"

"Pride again, I suppose. He built that greenhouse and made his land more successful than any of his family before him. He wasn't going to let me or my marriage to someone else force him out."

That sounded like the Abner I knew.

"Pauline, tell me about the three trees."

"What trees?"

"The three trees on the border of these three properties."

"How do you know about those trees?" Her face reddened so quickly, I thought her cheeks might feel hot to the touch.

I didn't answer but did my own shrug instead. I probably wasn't supposed to know about the pictures that we found in Abner's house. I didn't tell her I'd seen the trees live and in person as I spied on Carl.

"Ms. Robins, it really is time for you to leave now." Abruptly, her tone changed to unwelcoming again.

"Pauline," I began.

"Now."

She grabbed my glass from my hand as I stood. She marched us to the entry foyer and to the front door. She opened it with a violent pull.

"I'm sorry, Pauline, I didn't mean to upset you. I have just a couple more questions, though"—her eyes blazed at my gall—"when were you blond, and what do you love so much about hummingbirds?"

I thought she might slap me, so I braced myself. She was significantly older than me, but she was also lots bigger.

Instead of slapping, she slammed—the door practically exploded the frame. She looked at me with anger and something crazy.

I took a step backward and patted my pocket. I'd left my cell phone in my truck, sitting next to the gloves and the hummingbird feeder. I was going to have to run if her demeanor turned any more dangerous.

She reached behind an umbrella container I hadn't noticed before. The look on her face was now purely murderous. Did she have an axe hidden among the rain gear?

As she reached, I did what was sure to end my career as a criminal investigator.

I screamed like a little girl.

Twenty-four

Pauline's eyes widened and then got small. She wasn't reach-ing behind the umbrella stand, but into it. She rummaged around and then pulled out a frame; it was short and wide—wide enough for about three pictures.

"Why did you scream?" she asked as she held the frame.

I'd misunderstood her completely. She wasn't murderous at all. I think she was sad, instead.

"I . . . I thought . . . I don't know." I was horrified, relieved that she hadn't pulled out an axe, and amused at my own silliness. "You had a frame in your umbrella stand?"

"It was in the back of my closet for years, but I found it here last week. The pictures were gone. I just left it here because I wasn't sure what else to do with it. The police confronted me with the pictures, but I lied and told them the woman wasn't me." She sounded lost.

"Okay."

"This"—she held the empty frame for me to see—"held

the only evidence of me having blond hair, Becca. Somehow you've seen the picture that was in the middle of this frame. How? Unless you searched the back of my closet, you saw it somewhere else. Where? Did the police show it to you?"

"Were there pictures of trees there, too?"

"Yes, the three trees . . . and then . . . and one tree. Where did you see these pictures? Where did the police get them? They wouldn't tell me."

I stepped toward her and took the frame from her shaky hands. The glass was still intact, but the places where the pictures were supposed to be were void of anything but off-center paper backings.

"This was in your closet?"

"Yes, until the day before Matty was killed."

"The man with you was Abner, right?"

"Yes."

"Why were you blond in the picture?"

She sniffed. "I was in disguise."

"Why?"

"I'll tell you if you tell me where you found the pictures."

"The day of the murder—that night, I went to Abner's house to see if he was okay. He wasn't there, but the door was unlocked so I went in anyway. The pictures were on the floor, next to his overturned coffee table." The truth flowed but felt somewhat foreign.

"Abner broke into my house and took the pictures?"

"I don't know. But why were you blond?"

She sighed heavily.

"It was the disguise I used to wear when I went to meet Abner. After Matty and I were married. Do you understand what I'm saying?"

"After you married Matt, you continued to see Abner?"

"Yes." She hung her head in shame. "We met when we could at the cabin. But that picture was from a trip we took to Florida. The wig wasn't necessary, but I still wore it. I don't know. It made me feel less . . . less deceitful, I guess. Stupid and silly. It's possible that Matty found the pictures and confronted Abner."

"That sounds like a reasonable scenario. I can see your husband snooping around in your closet. How long were the pictures there?"

"Decades."

"And he just discovered them, right before he went to work at Bailey's? Is that really why he went to work at Bailey's? Did he want to keep an eye on Abner or torment him?"

"I don't think so."

The loud roar of a truck interrupted the questioning. We were still standing in the front entryway of the house. Pauline opened the door and I peeked around her as another brown truck sped to a quick stop right beside my bright orange one.

Jessop Simonsen swung his long body out of his truck and then walked over to look inside mine. He could easily see the gloves, the feeder, and my cell phone. Him knowing what was on my front seat made me strangely uncomfortable.

Pauline closed the door. "Don't tell Jessop we've been talking about this. Let's go back into the front room and sit down. I don't want him upset. He's had such a hard time with everything."

We did as she instructed. As I sat, I whispered, "Pauline, I need to know about the hummingbirds before he comes in the house."

"I loved hummingbirds when I was younger. It was the nickname Abner used for me." She spoke quickly, then calmed her face just as Jessop walked through the door.

So what? was what ran though my mind. If Abner killed Matt, did he put up the hummingbird feeders to honor his old love? Who would do something like that? Maybe a psychopathic murderer, but the act didn't seem worth the effort.

"Mom?" Jessop said with scrunched eyes and a tight mouth.

"Hello, dear. This is Becca Robins." Pauline stood.

"I know who she is. She came by Smithfield one day."

"Oh?"

"Yeah. What's she doing here?"

"Just paying her respects, Jessop."

They both looked at me as though it was my turn to contribute something to the conversation, but I didn't. Instead, my eyes were fixed on Jessop's face and the familiar look it had just held.

And when I looked more closely, I realized that Jessop not only could twist his facial features in a familiar manner, but his entire face was familiar.

No. Way.

"Paying her respects, huh?" Jessop said, filling the silent air.

"Jess, come help me with something in the kitchen for a minute. I'll be right back, Ms. Robins," Pauline said.

They walked away, Pauline practically dragging her son with her. Had she seen something on my face that made her realize what my brain was putting together?

I stood and went back to the piano. I found a picture of

a twenty-something Jessop and put my fingers over the full hair. The face was younger, but still one I knew.

Jessop had Abner's face. He was tall like his mother, but Jessop was Abner's son. I would have put every dime I had on that fact.

It suddenly seemed very obvious. How could anyone look at the three people involved—Abner, Matt, and Pauline—and not know that Jessop belonged to Abner more than he belonged to Matt? Abner might have been short, but Jessop clearly got his build from his tall mother. And he most definitely got his face from his father.

How did this help me know who the murderer was? I switched my thinking into overdrive. Though it was now obvious to me, Pauline, Abner, and perhaps Matt probably knew all along. How did this get Matt killed? Did Abner finally want to be a father to his son and Matt felt threatened? Did Matt just figure it out and confront Abner, and Abner killed him?

Still, while all of that seemed possible, none of it quite fit. Abner kept claiming that he didn't commit the murder, but he wouldn't say who had. If that was true, it meant he was protecting someone; someone he loved. That could be his sister, Helen, Pauline, me . . . or his son. I knew it wasn't me and I also knew I was in a house with the two strongest suspects. I had to get out of there, or at least get to my cell phone and call Sam for help.

I turned back from the piano and stepped quickly toward the front door. With each step, something else became perfectly clear. When I'd visited Abner earlier that day, he'd said something that rang a bell. I suddenly realized what it was—it was about old-timers. Barry had kept bringing up old-timers, too. Old-timers were the market vendors who got to work early every day. *Early to rise, early to sell.*

That was it! That was what had been nudging at me this whole time.

I knew exactly who the murderer was, and I was most definitely in the house with that person.

I turned my quick steps into a run, made it out the front door, and was halfway to my truck when the familiar boom of a shotgun made me instinctively hit the ground and cover my head.

"Where are you going, Ms. Robins?" Jessop said as he stood on the front stoop, the butt of his gun resting on his thigh.

With my ears ringing from the explosion, I lifted my face out of the dirt and looked at the tall, young, crazy version of my friend Abner. There was nothing friendly about this man, there was nothing right about him. He was the one having the breakdown. He was the one who'd discovered the pictures, perhaps the trees, and whatever else it must have taken for him to recently learn that Abner Justen was his biological father. And Matt Simonsen wasn't. Jessop was the killer.

"I was just going to get my cell phone. I'm expecting a call," I said. "You scared me to death, Jessop. Was that really necessary?" I was surprised at how calm my voice was. My insides were mimicking circus mice on crack, but I knew that I was dealing with someone who was missing some marbles. It was best that I remain calm and not make any accusations.

"You're not getting your cell phone, Becca Robins. You're coming back into the house, right this minute."

"I'll just be a second," I said as I stood and started walking toward the truck once more.

The gun boomed again, and I froze in place. He was still shooting into the air, but I knew where he'd aim next—right at me. I turned slowly and made my way to the maniac with the shotgun.

I didn't have any idea how I was going to get myself out of this mess.

Twenty-five

If I'd been able to really think about what was happening, I'd have been so freaked-out that I couldn't have managed to put one foot in front of the other. As it was, I felt like I was outside of myself, in a way, as I stepped toward Jessop and his shotgun. He'd shoot me if I ran, I knew that. I didn't want to go back into the house with him, but my frenzied mind couldn't put together another plan. A plan—Allison always had a plan. What would she do?

I had no idea.

Fortunately, I had a little help. In a flash of denim, Pauline rushed at her son and hit him on the head with a huge frying pan. He dropped the gun and bent over from the blow.

"Run, Becca!" Pauline yelled.

I was going to run to my truck, but Jessop was recovering too quickly. If I got to the truck and managed to get inside it, Jessop would have plenty of opportunity to shoot me. I needed to run fast and far away. Ignoring any leftover pain from my earlier injuries, I sprinted toward the cover of the woods.

I felt like I was going both fast and slow; my feet were flying and pulling taffy at the same time.

I hadn't gone far when another shotgun blast rattled the leaves on the trees around me. I stopped cold and turned toward the house I'd been running from.

The shot didn't sound as though Jessop had made it to the woods yet. Had he just shot his mother? The thought took me to my knees.

She'd hit him so I could run away, and now he'd killed her? His own mother? Of course, he'd killed his father, biological though he might not have been. What would have driven him so over the edge as to kill his entire family? Until these last few days, I hadn't known anything about the Simonsen family. I hadn't really known much about my friend Abner. And now my entire world had changed because of the craziness that had been going on without my knowledge and right under my nose. I was angry and devastated.

But now, I had to get up and get out of there.

I stood and looked around.

I had no cell phone and I was out in the middle of the woods. I knew someone was at Carl's, so that was the direction I needed to go, but I couldn't figure out which way it was, exactly, unless I got to the cabin first. I thought I could find the cabin, so I set off in that direction.

With the instinct for survival pushing all other thoughts away, I ran. I hoped I was going the right way, but there wasn't time to ponder anything, so I put my energy into moving my legs.

As if to punctuate my thought process, the shotgun blasted again; this time it was closer, but it wasn't right behind me. I focused on that sound and tried to guess how far away it was.

I had a head start, but not by much. And Jessop wouldn't keep firing the gun. He was shooting on purpose, at something. When he wanted to sneak up on me, he'd be quiet.

I was more hell-bent on the destination than on being careful, and I tripped over a tree root that bumped up through the surface of the ground. I went down with a sliding thud, scraping the skin on the front of my right leg.

I felt no pain, but there were small, sharp pebbles embedded in the skin and enough blood mixed with the dirt that I acknowledged it would probably hurt at some point. For now, I had to get moving again.

When I thought I might almost be at the cabin, I slowed and hid behind a big, round tree. Darkness was coming on, and I wanted to look behind me while I still could. It had been eon-minutes since I'd heard the gun. It was worse not knowing where Jessop was. Had he not followed me at all?

Was the second shot I heard . . . had he killed himself?

"No . . ." I said aloud at the amplifying tragedy. Another wave of desperate devastation washed over me, but I couldn't let anything cloud my need to get safe. It would have been crazy to go back to Simonsen Orchards. The best thing to do was to keep going.

I left the tree and hurried along, finding the cabin in only a few moments. I'd been running in the right direction! I was almost to Abner's, and I knew exactly which way to go. Relief that this might all be over soon made me stop and catch my breath.

As you might guess, that was stupid.

The door of the cabin burst open. Jessop Simonsen, alive and in one piece but unarmed, came toward me and grabbed my arm before I could lift one foot from the ground or let out the scream that jumped to my throat.

"I took the shortcut," he spat in my ear.

I twisted and turned, trying to get free from his grip.

"Let go," I said, wasting important energy on words he wouldn't listen to.

"Right. I don't think so." He yanked and pulled. He was much bigger and stronger than me.

I knew that if I went into that cabin, just as if I'd gone into his house, he'd kill me. Probably instantly. But I couldn't break from his grip. He threw me inside the door, and I landed on the floor next to the bed, adding more scrapes to my leg.

I did a quick survey: the gun was in a back corner, but other than that addition, the cabin didn't look much different from the last time I'd been in it. Was he going to shoot me? He didn't reach for the gun, but instead stood tall above me with his hands on his hips.

"Who are you?" he asked.

"Becca Robins," I answered stupidly.

"Yeah, we met. But why do you care about any of this?"

"There was a murder committed at my place of work. My good friend is in jail for it. He's not a murderer. I wanted to figure it out." I kept my eyes on his.

"Ha!" Jessop said. "That'll teach you."

I wanted to stand, but he probably wouldn't have let me. I supposed there were worse ways to die than being shot. The space was small and close, and he was a maniac who was so much bigger than me that he could probably just stomp down and that'd be it. Death by bullet seemed better than that. I scooted back and pulled myself up onto the bed. It wasn't much better, but it wasn't the floor.

"Why did you kill your father? Why would you do that?" I asked. I didn't think he'd answer.

He took a step backward and rubbed at his chin. "My father? I didn't kill my father."

"No? Who did?"

"My father's still alive. I *framed* my father for the death of the man who posed as my father."

"Okay, why did you kill Matt Simonsen? And why would you frame your father for murder?"

Jessop put a chair in front of me and straddled it. He had an enthusiastic bounce to his movements, as though he wasn't going to talk about murder but about what he'd done last weekend. I swallowed the sickening fear bubbling in my chest—he was so far from sane.

"It's like this, see," he began. "I found the picture of my mother and Abner in her closet. I found the letters where he called her his 'little hummingbird.' And I found the stupid trees; the one with Abner's name was the only one that didn't have the name crossed out. I'm a much better investigator than you." He smirked. I didn't react. "Anyway, apparently my mother was the queen of all whores in her day. While she was married to my father, she was screwing that short piece of crap who . . ."

"Who what, Jessop?"

"Who I might have only seen twice in my entire life. Can you imagine that?! He lived pissing distance away, he knew he was my father, and he never came to the house once. And get this, he came to the Smithfield Market a month or so ago as a 'friend' of my mother's. Dad—Matt—was out of town, so she came to the market to help me. And she invited Abner to stop by. She introduced him as a friend of the family, but I knew . . . I knew something was strange between the two of them. Even after all those years . . . that's when I started snooping around, looking for something—what, I didn't really know, but I knew there must be something, somewhere."

Was that the day Ian had seen Abner at Smithfield?

"But what if your mother wasn't a whore? What if she really loved Abner? What if Abner stayed away because he, your mom, and your father—yes, Matt was your real father, Jessop. It takes more than sperm donation to be a father—what if they all thought it was in your best interests for him to stay away? Abner didn't move, he was close by all the time. It was probably torture for him. Your mother might have invited him to Smithfield because she thought he might want to see you."

"When you're married, you don't sleep with other people. You don't fall in love with other people. You don't . . ." He slammed his fist on his leg. "You don't forget to tell your son that his biological father isn't the man he thought he was."

"Jessop, they didn't tell you because they wanted to protect you. That's all. Abner is still protecting you. He knows what you did, but he won't tell the police. What these people did are things that people do when they care about someone, not when they just want to keep secrets."

"Right, whatever," he said. But I thought I might have made him think twice.

He had no idea what he'd done. He'd just done it. When it soaked in, he was going to fall apart even further. And I didn't want to be around when that happened.

"I'm sorry, Jessop," I said. "I'm sure you're in a lot of pain."

His eyes, so much like Abner's and so much *not* like Abner's, glistened with anger.

"How did you figure it out? And why did you come to the house alone?"

I flinched at my own stupidity. "I didn't figure it out until you got home. When you pulled your truck next to mine and looked inside it—that's when I figured it out."

"I don't understand."

"It was right in front of us all the whole time. It was the Monday before the fall equinox, a day that lots of vendors take off work. But not you, you were trained to be an old-timer. But you didn't go to work the day your . . . the day Matt was killed."

"So?"

"Like I said, you're an old-timer, Jessop—even if you're not old, you learned the market business from your father. You're never late for work. If you'd gone to Smithfield, you wouldn't have heard about your father's death until about the time I did. That was about 7:00 A.M. You'd have already been at work like any good old-timer would be. Someone would have contacted you there, and then you'd have gone home, or to . . ." I was going to say "the morgue," but that sounded too gruesome. "Anyway, when you got home today, I thought about your long hours and the fact that you'd probably been at Smithfield since early this morning, like any old-timer. Someone at the Smithfield Market told me you hadn't come to work the day Matt was killed, and that they didn't remember you ever missing a day. If you weren't already there by 6:00 A.M, there was something wrong—or you were committing murder."

Jessop glared at me. "If you didn't put it together beforehand, why were you at my house?"

"I wanted to ask your mom about hummingbirds. I saw a bunch of feeders on Abner's greenhouse. I wondered if she knew where they came from. Did you kill your mom, Jessop?"

Jessop huffed and ignored the question. "That was a nice touch, wasn't it? I hung those feeders and spilled nectar on the porch—I wanted it to look like blood. I tipped the table and planted the pictures just for fun, and the axe—that was Abner's, anyway. It had his fingerprints all over it. I wore gloves when . . ." His eyes went funny again.

"Were you at my house, on my porch, waiting for me?"

"Yeah, that was me."

"What did you want from me?" He'd been at my house the day after the murder. How did he even know who I was?

"I was with Abner the night before. He found me out in the woods, at his cabin. He tried to talk me into going to the police. Wasn't going to happen, but I wanted to show him what I'd done to his house, so we were going there when we saw the truck pull into the property. Together we spied on you and your long-haired friend. Abner didn't want to, but he told me who you were. And when he did, he spoke about you like . . . like you were his daughter. He loves you more than he loves me. I wanted to talk to you, see how you'd managed to do something I'd never had the chance to do."

"Abner and I are just friends."

"Right, whatever you say. The good news was that you drove away. When you pulled into the driveway, I realized that coming to talk to you was a bad idea, even if I'd brought you flowers. I ducked, thinking you hadn't seen me. I was going to run away. You'd have been suspicious if we'd met then—I realized that."

I looked at this crazy man. He wouldn't have run away.

He would have killed me. I knew that. His jealousy was something he wasn't capable of handling.

"You left the flowers in my pumpkin patch?"

"Yep. Another nice touch, I thought. The police were bound to think it had been Abner."

"Did you come see my sister that day I met you at Smithfield?"

"Oh, yeah. I wanted to know what you were up to, stopping by my stall. I wanted to see if you and she knew something. I got lucky there, too. It was good she didn't answer—I probably wouldn't have handled that well, and she'd have become suspicious. How did you know I was there?"

My turn to ignore a question. "At the time I knew nothing."

"Well, you know something now, don't ya?" Jessop stood abruptly, propelling the chair right into my bloody leg.

That time I felt the pain. I don't know if I cried out or screamed, but I bent over with the tidal wave of agony.

"And I'm gonna have to take care of that loose end, aren't I?"

In that warped moment, when I was in pain and scared to death, I had only one choice, maybe one chance. It was definitely a cheap shot, and it was neither a good idea nor a smart one, but it was all I had. He grabbed my arm and hoisted me up.

I've often despised my short stature, especially when compared to someone tall, and in Jessop's case, extraordinarily tall.

But today, I figured it might work to my advantage.

As I was being yanked, I pulled back the arm that wasn't in his grip, formed a fist (remembering an odd fact—that you keep your thumb on the outside of the fist that will be used for punching), and thrust that fist forward with the one and only spurt of adrenaline-filled fear I had left.

And somehow, I hit the target. Jessop let go of my arm and went down into the fetal position that men favor when they've been damaged in just the right spot.

If we'd been in a movie, I'd have had some clever words to spew. But we weren't in a movie, and though it would be more than a couple of seconds, Jessop would come back to life, this time probably more murderous than before.

I stepped toward the gun, but he was in the way and grabbed for my ankle. I kicked his hand away and realized—I just had to get out of there.

I left the cabin and started running again.

To get to Carl's, I'd have to run up the open road. My panicked mind thought that it wouldn't be worth the risk, even though I knew someone was there—or had been when I'd driven by earlier. I chose the cover of the woods and the direction toward Abner's house. I knew the electricity was off, but I remembered seeing a phone plugged into the wall. It was the old-fashioned kind that didn't need electricity to work.

I ran.

I just ran.

And ran.

And didn't look back.

Another few minutes or so of infinity and into the darkness, I made it to Abner's property.

One light provided illumination—it was attached to the outside of the greenhouse and cast a stark line toward the small house. I hadn't noticed it earlier, but realized it must be another emergency light of sorts—one that didn't run off the main electricity. It was almost totally dark, and the light was an arrow, telling me to get into the house and to the phone.

I didn't waste a moment checking the doorknob—I knew it was locked. I used my elbow, which fortunately was covered with a sleeve, to break the glass on the door. I reached in, unlocked it, and barreled my way through.

I reached the tattered chair and the phone on the stand that I'd noticed all those days and hours ago.

I yanked the headset to my ear and . . . there was no dial tone.

"Hello!?" I begged, but no one answered. The phone wasn't in service. "No way." Just like they did in the movies, I pressed the white plugs, but nothing changed. It was an old-fashioned phone and was stuck into a wall outlet, but it wasn't in working order. The phone had been shut off, just like the electricity.

I threw the useless contraption at the wall before propelling myself to the front door. There was nothing careful about the way I stepped onto the porch, and the finger of light that had pointed me to the house was now crooked in the middle—right where Jessop Simonsen and his shotgun deflected it.

"You might as well quit running," Jessop said calmly. "You can't get away." He raised the gun and aimed.

I turned and leapt back into the house, shutting the door behind me. I put my back against the wall leading into the hallway and tried to think—*What will he do next? Will he come to the front of the house or the back?*

I put my money on his coming to the front, so I made my way to the back. I didn't remember a back door, but Ian and I hadn't explored everything.

My frantic heart swelled in relief when I did indeed see

a back door. It was past a small bathroom and down a short hallway that was hidden from the front entrance.

I didn't know for sure where Jessop was, and I couldn't make my next move until I knew whether I was going to try to escape out the front or the back. I crouched down in the short hallway and listened. *This couldn't be happening, could it?*

Fortunately, Jessop wasn't being quiet. He was yelling—unfortunately, he had chosen to come to the back of the house. I swallowed a scream of frustration and stood up as I moved away from the back door and toward the middle of the main hallway. He might be trying to trick me—he might turn now and come in the front door instead.

The scream I'd stifled shot out of my throat as Jessop kicked in the back door.

"Becca, really, this is stupid. There's no place for you to go. I've recovered from your sassy-girl maneuver. I can run faster than you. And I have the gun."

I heard him, but I was in a cold run out the front door as he finished the threat. He was right, though. I couldn't get away—I wasn't familiar enough with the woods to think he wouldn't find me, and the main road was a huge distance from Abner's property. Jessop was right. He was bound to catch up to me.

But somehow, one more last-chance idea lit in my mind. I ran to the greenhouse, to the side of the line of light. Jessop would see me, but I didn't need to make it easy.

I went in and closed the door, knowing it wouldn't lock. The small white light was a gift—the greenhouse was dark except for this small white emergency bulb that didn't illuminate much of anything.

Perfect.

I grabbed the rope I'd noticed twice before and ran down

the middle of one of the aisles, my fingers guiding me by sliding along a table, to the spot next to where Ian and I had found the axe. I couldn't see much of anything, but I could feel. I groped at the plants on the table and immediately felt the sharp points of what I was looking for: the Carolina horse nettle, Abner's favorite plant, the plant that he could place in a bouquet with such skill that a thorn never touched customers' tender fingers. I needed this plant.

Since I didn't have much time, I was going to reach into the middle of it, to hell with my own skin. But I bent down and did a quick search of the floor under the table and next to the irrigation canal.

My luck was improving—the pockmarked oven mitts were there.

I slipped them on and yanked out as much of the plant as I could manage. I was still stuck in a number of places, but it didn't matter.

I hurried back along the table, about halfway.

"Becca?" Jessop yelled from outside. He was most definitely out of the house, but he still didn't know I was in the greenhouse. I'd caught a small break—he hadn't seen where I'd gone. He'd be here eventually, but I had the one extra moment I needed.

At the halfway point back along the table, I set the trap. This was truly my last chance. I knew the greenhouse didn't have a back door.

Just as I finished, Jessop came in the door.

"Beee . . . ca, oh, Beee . . . ca, I know you're in here," he said.

I scrambled to the back of the greenhouse again. When I spoke, he had to believe where I was. He had to know exactly where to come get me.

"Becca."

"Okay, Jessop," I said with a heavy breath. "I give up. I've hurt myself—twisted my ankle. I need your help. Do you have a flashlight?"

"No, and the electricity's off."

"Go find a flashlight, and you can help me."

"Right. I'm not leaving until I've taken care of what I need to do."

That was what I wanted to hear.

"Okay, well, promise you won't hurt me? Come help me, please?" I sounded pathetic. But he didn't know me well, so maybe he'd buy it.

"Uh-huh, keep talking and I'll be right there."

"I'm down the middle aisle. Just come straight down. Thank you. I'm really hurting."

I heard him step tentatively at first, then with heavier, quicker steps. I was seeing things better, but he had just entered the darkness, so he still wouldn't be able to see well. Hopefully, he'd come forward with the confidence of someone carrying a weapon.

A cacophony of noises that soon followed told me the trap had been tripped—Jessop bellowed, the shotgun crashed to the ground with a metallic thump, the long plant tables rumbled from Jessop's clumsy maneuver. And then he broke out in terrible, hair-raising screams.

I darted up and then ran down the next aisle. I could now see the tables fairly distinctly, but I still used my hand to guide the way. I knew I was almost to the door when the shotgun blasted once again, the sound reverberating and shaking the walls.

I screamed and covered my head, and kept running.

The greenhouse door flew open, and the glare from a large flashlight bulb blinded me to a frozen stillness.

"Now I can see you just fine," Jessop said.

I turned, and saw the shotgun aimed in my direction. My trap hadn't been perfect, but it had hurt him and slowed him down. He was covered in drips of blood from the jabs and cuts of the persistent thorns of the plant I'd strewn on the floor. It was an old-fashioned trap, one made with sharp things and a rope to trip up the bad guy. As a drip of red slid down the side of his face, Jessop became every horror movie image I'd ever seen, minus the hockey goalie's mask.

And I was about to die.

But another gunshot shook the room, and I watched Jessop fall instead of me, his shotgun going one direction, his body going the other.

I didn't know what had happened, but I looked toward the large light. This time it went something like this:

"Becca, you okay?" It was Sam's voice attached to some person who was hidden in the shadows.

"Uh . . ." was all I could say for some time.

"She wasn't home. We had a date, and she wasn't home. Things she'd said earlier made me think she went to Simonsen Orchards, and then Barry called and told me his suspicions regarding Jessop. I found Pauline at Simonsen Orchards, tied up but otherwise unharmed. She told me what had happened. I just followed her leads."

"Thank you, Barry, Sam," Allison said as she put her hand on Sam's knee. Mathis was intrigued by this maneuver, and he reached out and touched Sam on the knee, too.

We all laughed, and it felt good.

We sat around in chairs and benches on my back patio. Allison, her husband, Tom, and Mathis were there; so were Abner, Carl Monroe, Mamma Maria, Sam, and Barry and his wife, Cloris. Ian, self-anointed Master of Hamburgers, was in charge of the grill, and he was doing a fine job.

At Sam's mention of the word "date," Ian sent me a

quick and private raising of the eyebrows. I smiled, and he smiled back.

"You saved my life. 'Thank you' seems weak, but it's all I've got," I said to Barry and Sam. I'd said it a million times already, but I didn't impose a limit on how many more times I'd say it.

Barry waved away my words.

"No, it's not all you've got," Sam said.

Silence fell over the patio. Was he being flirtatious? I avoided Ian's glance.

"No, you've got, well, you *will* have pumpkin preserves very soon. I'll take some of those, please." Relief washed over the party.

"You can have as many as you want," I offered.

"Pukins, pukins. I want a pukin," Mathis said.

"Well, come with me, little man. We'll find you one right now." I stood and took my nephew's hand, and we moved away from the crowd and into my pumpkin patch.

I walked like I was injured but would be fine. I was very grateful to have escaped any permanent damage. My emotions were still too close to the surface, though, and I hoped that the tears and choked voice would stay at bay for the evening.

As Mathis led the way, I was once again convinced that there might be no better place in the world than the middle of a pumpkin patch. It was currently a delightful array of green and orange. Fall, perfect fall. The sunlight had just the right amount of yellow and the air had just the right amount of clean coolness. It was good to still be around to enjoy another fall and be among my plants.

Mathis was easily entertained, and wanted to thoroughly inspect every gourd. I sat and watched him and the people on my patio.

My sister and her husband were sitting very close together, as though the events of late made them not want to be far from each other for very long. I approved.

Barry had surprised me by being more emotional than anyone else. He had grabbed me and pulled me into a close hug. He didn't let go for a long time, and he was still intermittently dabbing at his eyes.

He'd known all along who'd killed Matt Simonsen—or at least he'd suspected. Though he had moved away, both physically and emotionally, from his past, he had observed his old friends over the years. They'd all known who Jessop's biological father was—Barry included. He'd told them that it was a bad idea to keep secrets from Jessop, but no one had agreed.

Barry had sought out Jessop the day after the murder and confronted him. Jessop denied everything, but Barry knew better—he just couldn't figure out how to prove it. Jessop had been his mystery trench-coat-clad visitor the night of the party, there to tell Barry that Abner had been arrested. He'd known this because he was the one who shot at Abner and me when we were in the cabin. He drove away, but returned and hid as he watched the rest of the events unfold.

Barry knew Jessop wasn't stable, and that was why he'd wanted me to quit "worrying my pretty little head" over the matter.

Barry'd wanted to protect me, and I'd just gotten angry at him. Fortunately, he finally called Sam and told him as much of the story as he could. Sam took it from there.

I'd invited Carl and Mamma for two reasons. I wanted to apologize for being so weird around them and suspecting Carl of anything. And I knew Mamma would volunteer to bring some dessert. She did—Mamma Maria's Mmmm-Amazing Lemon Meringue. Yum!

And Carl had come with his own apology. He had seen Jessop chop at the tree. He'd gone out and stopped him from going further. I had observed Abner begging Carl not to go to the police with the information. Carl might never forgive himself that he hadn't told Sam sooner.

We'd all forgiven him, though.

Officer Sam Brion had saved my life and had become a friend. I didn't know what our friendship would evolve into, but I was pleased to have him in my life.

Jessop Simonsen was still alive. Sam's shot hadn't killed the killer, but injured his shoulder enough that Jessop would be in the hospital awhile before he went to jail, probably for the rest of his life. Jessop's madness had come on suddenly and had stayed long enough to do some terrible damage, but along with help for his physical wounds, he was getting emotional help, too. But there were terrible times ahead for him. He'd realize what he'd done and would probably never be able to forgive himself.

Pauline Simonsen had been totally in the dark about what had happened. She really thought Abner had killed Matt. I couldn't imagine what she would have to overcome to live the rest of her life in some sort of peace. She'd saved me from her son, though, and for that I was very grateful.

Abner was free from jail, even if he never would be free from the ghosts of his past.

A few days before Matt started at Bailey's, Jessop had started snooping around the house for evidence of his mother's past. What he'd observed between Pauline and Abner at the Smithfield Market had been eating at him, and he finally decided to see what he could find.

It didn't take long for him to discover the truth of his birth—he found a letter from Abner to his mother and the pictures in his mother's closet. Then Jessop, for all practical purposes, fired his father from Smithfield. Thinking time had healed most wounds, Matt took it upon himself to set up a space at Bailey's. He was wrong, and Abner and he couldn't find a way to get along, but it hadn't been Abner who killed Matt. It had been Jessop, who though he'd gotten Matt out of his work environment, couldn't forgive the lies that had been told for more than forty years. He killed Matt, hoping to frame Abner and expose his mother's past, hopefully embarrassing and hurting her more deeply than he thought she could stand.

Abner would eventually be fine, but his decades-earlier affair with Pauline would haunt him for the rest of his life—sometimes the truth doesn't set you completely free. He would have taken the fall for Jessop, but he knew Jessop's breakdown wasn't over. In fact, Abner knew that Jessop wanted to harm me because of my snooping. When Abner asked me to the cabin, it had been his goal to make me stop my investigation. He was going to turn himself in that day, anyway—the drama of what happened in the woods made him wish he'd done it earlier. He thought that if he really did go to jail, Jessop would leave me and everyone else alone.

That might have been correct, but *I* wasn't capable of leaving anything alone. I couldn't let my friend go to jail for something he hadn't done. My curiosity had almost done me in, but not quite.

I had been irritated at Abner for not sharing his address with anyone, but over the course of the last week, I had found that I'd been almost as guilty of such negligence. I hadn't known where some of my closest coworkers lived, and I'd never invited them over for much of anything except maybe to help with the pumpkins. But I knew where they lived now, and this barbecue was the first step of what I hoped was a new phase of friendship in all our lives.

It really wasn't that I'd made a lot of new friends as the result of a terrible tragedy, but that we all had become closer. And one of the new friends I had made and most looked forward to getting to know better was flipping hamburgers with a hand marked by a sun tattoo and was the owner of potentially magic spit.

I smiled at the memory of our kiss and at the fact that because I hadn't been gunned down in the greenhouse, there might be more kissing ahead.

"Did you find the one you want, Mathis?" I stood slowly, favoring my sore hip, road-rashed leg, and stiff shoulder. It wasn't pretty.

"Yes." He pointed at the biggest pumpkin in the patch.

"Good choice. Let's grab it and go have some dinner."

"I don't want a m'burger, Aunt Becca. I want peanut butter and some of your strawberry jam."

"That sounds good. Come on, I'll see if the cook will help me in the kitchen. He and I will find you some peanut butter and jam."

I smiled at the thought and, hand in hand, we walked toward family, friends, and hopefully a fruitful future.

Recipes

Becca's Jam, Jellies, and Preserves Canning Tips

Start with good fruit at its peak, not overripe. Canning doesn't improve the quality of the ingredients you use.

Don't add any butter or other fat to a recipe. These don't store well and could increase the rate of spoilage, as well as slow the rate of heat transfer, which could result in an unsafe product.

Always "heat process" your products by water bath or pressure canning (I use water bath process). Ignore any recipe that tells you to invert the jars as the final step.

To sterilize them, boil small jars for at least five minutes, large jars for at least eight. Higher altitudes might require more time. Always check recipes.

To prevent darkening of your cut fruits:

Use a commercial product made to prevent the darkening.

Put the cut fruit in a solution of 1 teaspoon ascorbic acid (vitamin C, available in a powdered form from the drug store) and 1 gallon water. Drain before canning.

Or

Put the cut fruit into a lemon juice solution (¾ cup lemon juice to 1 gallon water). Drain fruit before canning.

Use standard mason / Ball / Kerr (etc.) jars for home canning. Commercial food jars, such as mayonnaise jars, are not heat tempered and often break easily.

Do not use jars larger than specified. Quart jars are the largest size you should ever use.

To remove scale or hard-water films on jars, soak the jars for several hours in a solution of 1 cup vinegar per gallon of water. Keep the jars warm until ready to fill them—this will help reduce breakage from thermal shock.

Prepare the two-piece metal canning lids by washing them in water and following the manufacturer's instructions for heating the lids.

Check the jar seals twelve to twenty-four hours after processing for leaks and broken seals. Press down on the lid. If it is sealed, it will be sucked down tight. If it did not seal, it will flex and make a popping sound when pressed.

If it didn't seal, refrigerate the product and eat it as soon as possible. If one of my seals is broken, I don't take the jar to market, but just use the product myself instead.

Most important tip: enjoy every minute of your time within your crops and in your kitchens. There's not much else that is as satisfying as growing something, preparing it, and then seeing someone enjoy the "fruits" of your labor.

BECCA

Becca's Strawberry Preserves

4 pints strawberries to yield 4 cups crushed berries
7 cups sugar
3 oz. liquid fruit pectin
Strawberry Hullers (if you don't have a huller, you can use a small knife, or some people even use a paper clip)
8-fluid-oz. canning jars
Baking sheets
Canning lids
Colander
Food processor
Big saucepan
Boiling-water canner (some people use a pressure canner, but I prefer the boiling-water method)
Tongs

Boil jars (at least five minutes). My dishwasher has a fancy-schmancy sterilize mode, but that feature is still rare.

Remove the jars with tongs and place them on a cookie sheet to dry and cool.

Prepare lids by placing them in a saucepan of gently boiling water. I don't ever use the dishwasher for the lids.

Prepare the strawberries by dipping them in a sink of cold water and immediately putting them into a colander to drain.

Hull strawberries, using a sharp paring knife or a strawberry huller or even a paper clip. Place half the strawberries at a time into a food processor and process for 5 to 10 seconds; they should still be slightly chunky. This step becomes intuitive over time. Some people like larger chunks of fruit in their preserves, but I prefer uniformly sized pieces that make an even "spread." (Hint—the chunks of fruit are what make the preserves. Jams are made with totally crushed fruit and, typically, less sugar.)

Place the strawberries into a 6- or 8-quart pot. Stir the sugar into the fruit and mix them well. Bring the fruit to a full, rolling boil over high heat, stirring constantly.

Add fruit pectin and return the mixture to a full, rolling boil. Boil hard for 1 minute, stirring constantly to prevent scorching.

Remove the preserves from the heat and skim off and discard any foam, using a metal spoon. Ladle the preserves into a liquid measuring cup and fill the jars immediately to within 1/8 inch of the tops.

Wipe jar rims and threads with a clean, damp cloth.

Place the lids on the jars and screw them on tightly.

Fill the canner half full with water; then cover it and heat the water to boiling.

Using a jar lifter, place the jars filled with food on the rack in the canner. If necessary, add boiling water to bring water 1 to 2 inches over the tops of the jars. Do not pour boiling water directly on the jars. Cover them and boil for at least five minutes. Longer for higher altitudes (check the recipe on the package of pectin).

As soon as the processing time is up, use a jar lifter to remove jars from the canner. If liquid boiled out of the jars during processing, do not open them to add more. Do not retighten screw bands, even if they are noticeably loose.

Check the seals after one hour to make sure the lids are curving down. If seals are not tight, refrigerate and use the product as soon as possible.

Becca's Pumpkin Preserves

The preparation and preserving methods used for the strawberry preserves are the same for the pumpkin preserves. The ingredients and recipe are different and are as follows:

4 lb. pumpkin. Wash the pumpkin and peel off the rind. Use the inside "meat" but don't use the seeds.
2 lbs. sugar
2 to 3 lemons
2 to 3 oranges
½ teaspoon salt
1 dozen or so whole cloves

Cube the meat of the pumpkin. Layer the pumpkin, sugar, salt, and orange and lemon slices in a roasting pan. Allow them to sit overnight, refrigerated. Transfer to another pot.

Place the roasting pan over medium heat, add the cloves.

Cook until pumpkin is transparent, stirring frequently—this will take a couple of hours.

WATER-PRESSURE PROCESS:

The texture of this preserve is very similar to a marmalade.

This is amazing on toast, biscuits, and ice cream. This is one of Becca's co-vendors' favorite holiday gifts.

Mamma Maria's Mmmm-Amazing Lemon Meringue Pie

Makes one ten-inch pie

PIE TIPS:

1. Make the pie on a sunny, nonhumid day so meringue doesn't fall.
2. Use ultrafine white sugar, anything else won't make good filling or meringue.
3. Eggs shouldn't be fresh; the best meringue is made with eggs around a week old.
4. When separating egg whites from yolks—NO yolk can get into the whites or the meringue won't set. If yolk does get into the whites, DON'T use your finger to remove it; only use egg shell or meringue won't set.
5. Freshly squeezed lemons make the filling just tart enough to offset the meringue's sweetness.

6. A glass pie pan works best for all pies because it does a better job of evenly distributing heat.
7. Mix meringue in a bowl that has not been used to make anything with oil or grease, or meringue won't set.

Bake pie shell in a glass pie pan at 400 degrees for 10 minutes. If you're using ready-made pie crust, follow package directions.

FILLING

5 egg yolks, slightly beaten
2½ cups and 1 tablespoon ultrafine white sugar
½ cup corn starch plus an additional 1 ⅔ tablespoons
2 ½ cups water
1 cup freshly squeezed lemon juice
3 teaspoons grated lemon peel

For filling, stir together sugar and corn starch in medium saucepan. Blend egg yolks and water in a separate bowl; once they are blended, stir them into the sugar mixture in the saucepan. Cook over medium heat, stirring constantly, until the filling mixture is thick and begins to boil. Let it boil for 1 minute—remove from the heat, stir in the lemon juice and lemon peel, and pour the mixture into the baked pie shell.

MERINGUE

5 egg whites (NO YOLK!)
¾ teaspoon cream of tartar
1 cup ultrafine white sugar
⅓ teaspoon vanilla

For meringue, beat egg whites until stiff, adding cream of tartar as egg whites are beaten (hand mixer or electric mixer works best). Once the cream of tartar is added and the egg whites are stiff, begin adding the sugar, one tablespoon at a time, continuously beating the meringue mixture. Continue mixing until soft peaks form (they should look like soft mountains), add vanilla, and mix for a few seconds more so vanilla is completely mixed into the meringue.

Heap meringue onto pie with a rubber spatula, taking care to seal the edges where the meringue and pie crust meet. Make peaks on top of the meringue with the spatula and bake the pie at 400 degrees for 10 minutes or until meringue peaks are golden brown.

Let pie completely cool prior to serving.

HUGE MERINGUE

10 egg whites (NO YOLK!)
1½ teaspoons cream of tartar
2 cups ultrafine white sugar
⅔ teaspoon vanilla

For meringue, beat egg whites until stiff, adding the cream of tartar as the egg whites are beaten (hand mixer or electric mixer works best). Once the cream of tartar is added and the egg whites are stiff, begin adding the sugar, one tablespoon at a time, continuously beating the meringue mixture. Continue mixing until soft peaks form (they should look like soft mountains), add the vanilla, and mix for a few seconds more so the vanilla is completely mixed into the meringue.

Heap the meringue onto the pie with a rubber spatula,

taking care to seal the edges where the meringue and pie crust meet. Make peaks on top of the meringue with a spatula and bake the pie at 400 degrees for 10 minutes or until meringue peaks are golden brown.

Let pie completely cool prior to serving.

Mamma Maria acquired this mmmm-amazing recipe from Amy Snyder Hackbart and Patricia Snyder. Many thanks!

Linda's In-a-Hurry Easy and Amazing Razzleberry Pie

2 ready-made pie crusts. These usually come two per package.
2 cups or 16 ounces raspberries
2 cups or 16 ounces blackberries
1/3 cup sugar
2 1/2 tablespoons flour
pie tin
cooking spray or butter

Preheat oven to 400 degrees

Thaw fruit if it is frozen, and pour it in a colander to strain the juice.

In large bowl, mix fruit, sugar, and flour together. Line bottom of pie tin (sprayed with cooking spray or lightly buttered) with crust. Fill with fruit mixture.

Before adding the top layer, cut some vents into it. Lay it over the top of the fruit, moisten the edges with water to "glue" the two crusts together. With the back side of a fork pinch edges together, or pinch them with fingers.

Lightly brush the top crust with water.

Sprinkle sugar over the top.

Cover edges with a 1 ½-inch strip of foil.

Bake for 30 minutes at 400 degrees. Remove the foil and bake the pie for an additional 10 minutes until the crust is golden brown.

Most of the time Linda makes her crusts from scratch, but either way this pie is mouthwateringly delicious.

Mathis' Favorite Grilled Peanut Butter and Preserve Sandwich

This is for one sandwich. You can increase or decrease the amount of the ingredients per your tastes or to accommodate more sandwiches.

2 teaspoons or so butter
2 slices bread (Mathis prefers white bread)
2 tablespoons or so peanut butter
2 tablespoons or so Becca's strawberry preserves

Heat griddle or skillet to 350 degrees.

Spread butter on one side of each slice of bread. Spread peanut butter on unbuttered side of one slice of bread, and the preserves on the other. Place one slice, buttered side down, on the griddle. Top with other slice, so that peanut butter and preserves are in the middle. Cook for 4 minutes on each side, or until golden brown, and heated through.

Mathis can't get enough of his aunt Becca's strawberry preserves, especially when they're mixed with peanut butter!